JO ANN BROWN

Promise of a Family

D0124666

W9-BQT-030

◆H HARLEQUIN® LOVE INSPIRED® HISTORICAL

LOVE INSPIRED BOOKS

Recycling programs
for this product may
not exist in your area.

ISBN-13: 978-0-373-28324-8

Promise of a Family

Copyright © 2015 by Jo Ann Ferguson

www.Harlequin.com

Printed in U.S.A.

"One day the children will appreciate that your family has provided for them. Not every abandoned child is so blessed."

"What happened to you, Drake?"

"The neighbors took me in with their brood, which was large enough that they never seemed to notice one more."

"So they became your family?"

"No. They were never cruel to me, but I was always an outsider. I was never allowed to call them mother and father."

"Oh, how horrible! You must have been so alone and so lonely, even in such a crowded house."

"No one else has ever said that." He quickly looked away.

"If I have pried too much…"

"No, it feels good to have someone understand." He shook his head with a grin.

Before she could ask another question, the twins called to her. As he stood, she went to swing the girls out of the sleeping hammocks. He could sense that Susanna was just as anxious to leave the solitude belowdecks. As for himself, he would be glad to return to where they would not be able to talk about the past and what he planned to do in the future.

A future when the rolling waves of the sea would come between him and Susanna.

No, he definitely did not want to think of that. Not until he had to.

Jo Ann Brown has always loved stories with happy-ever-after endings. A former military officer, she is thrilled to have the chance to write stories about people falling in love. She is also a photographer, and travels with her husband of more than thirty years to places where she can snap pictures. They live in Nevada with three children and a spoiled cat. Drop her a note at joannbrownbooks.com.

Books by Jo Ann Brown

Love Inspired Historical

Matchmaking Babies

Promise of a Family

Sanctuary Bay

The Dutiful Daughter
A Hero for Christmas
A Bride for the Baron

And Jesus called a little child unto him, and set him in the midst of them, and said, Verily I say unto you, Except ye be converted, and become as little children, ye shall not enter into the kingdom of heaven.
—*Matthew* 18:2–3

For Jo Piraneo
Who has an amazing gift for making my
jumbled comments into something beautiful

Chapter One

Porthlowen, Cornwall
1812

"There! It is leaking right there!"

At the shout, Drake Nesbitt looked down into his ship where his first mate and crew were struggling to fix the damage *The Kestrel* had suffered after crossing the path of a French privateer. Sunlight sparkled on water in the depths of the ship. Hurrying to join his crew, he muttered under his breath as he pulled off his new boots. He had thought the last of the holes in *The Kestrel* had been plugged yesterday.

He set the boots where the water would not reach them, then joined his crew. They stepped aside to let him examine where water washed into the ship with the rising tide. He pushed away a lantern. Even though it would have helped him see the damage to the hull, he did not want his crew to view his frustration. They must have enough of their own.

For a fortnight *The Kestrel* had been moored in Porthlowen, a cove beneath the hills rising like broken steps to the Cornish moorland. The mouth of the cove narrowed to a curved strait between high cliffs, providing a sheltered mooring for his ship and a fast current on the tides that would take them back to open water once his ship was seaworthy again.

His ship. He enjoyed saying those words. He had worked hard for years to be able to invest in the ship and finally buy her outright. Now he worked even harder to save enough to purchase another, with his eye on building a fleet of trading ships along the southern coast of England.

He had known it would take time to make repairs, but he ached to be back upon the sea, to know the freedom of moving with the waves, to escape the memories that still gnawed on him whenever he set foot on land. When he steered his ship from one port to another, he could avoid risking his heart as he did once. Then, he had ended up looking like a fool.

Never again.

That pledge had echoed through his head every day and every night, anytime when he was alone and his thoughts caught up to him. He had believed Ruby was as precious as the gem whose name she shared, so he'd offered her his heart, despite the difference in their social standing. He had dared to believe that the daughter of a baronet and the captain of a trading ship could ignore the canons of Society and marry and live happily for the rest of their lives.

It had not been Society that destroyed his hopes. Ruby had betrayed him when, within hours of his setting sail after they had pledged their unending love to each other, she was seen in the arms of another man.

Never again.

Standing up as much as he could in the cramped space, he said, "Close it up, lads."

Drake climbed to the main deck, knowing that the crew would work better without the captain watching over their shoulders. He sat on the stairs to the quarterdeck and tugged his boots back on. The soft leather was as comfortable as he had hoped when he saw it hanging in the cobbler's shop. The boots were stylish, too, but he did not care what was de rigueur in Society. Treating himself to a new pair of boots had been a spur-of-the-moment decision, the kind he made with skill. The proof of that was the profit from *The Kestrel*'s recent voyages where he had followed his instincts with cargoes and routes.

However, he had bought his new boots in Penzance days before *The Kestrel* was ambushed by French privateers and half their cargo of barley and wheat was ruined during the battle. The other half had been unloaded in Porthlowen. He had sold it for far less than it was worth because the damp grain would have gone bad before he reached the merchants waiting for it in Dublin. Now he had to reimburse the English traders who hired him to deliver their goods. In addition, he had bills to pay for the supplies needed to repair the ship.

Gazing at the masts where the sails were tightly furled, he sighed. Two wasted weeks. How much longer before they could leave Porthlowen and be on their way again? He had never expected it would take longer to handle the repairs than to make arrangements to hand over their French prisoners to the local authorities.

A fierce smile pulled at his lips. *The Kestrel* had been damaged, but the French ship now sat on the bottom of the sea and the French privateers who had survived were in cells more than fifty miles away in Dartmoor Prison. There, they would stay until the English defeated the French. He had no pity for them in spite of tales of how appalling the conditions were in prison. He was glad there were fewer privateers to hound honest men trying to earn a living in the waters around Britain.

For now, fixing *The Kestrel*, which had been riddled with shot, forced Drake and his ship to remain in the harbor. He glanced toward the village that followed the crescent cove. Living in a small cottage and staring at the same scenery day after day would be a slow death for a man like him, especially when the siren song of the waves lapped upon the rocks and the sand. He raised his gaze toward the fine house situated where the moor met the cliffs that hid the cove's entrance. He had been told an earl resided there, but even such a luxurious life offered no appeal to him.

There were times when he imagined coming home to a woman and children who awaited his return eagerly. Sparkling eyes, warm lips, and arms that welcomed him—and only him—into them.

Never again.

Familiar footsteps behind him, echoing hollowly on the deck, broke into Drake's thoughts. Grateful to escape the memories of his greatest humiliation, he turned. "Benton, what happened below?"

His first mate, a gangly young man who never seemed to gain an ounce, raked his hand back through his sweaty hair, leaving red spikes across his head. "We missed one, Captain."

"We?"

"I meant *I* missed one." Benton shook his head, a glum expression lengthening his usually cheerful face. "I thought I checked every inch of her, but I didn't see that small hole. We will start at the bow and go back to the stern on both sides all over again."

"Good." He allowed himself a smile as his first mate

met his eyes. He trusted Benton with both his ship and his life. The crew called them Lightning and Thunder because they had learned that when there was trouble, Drake would be there in a flash, with Benton following quickly behind him.

"It should not take long to fix that one small hole, Captain, or to examine the complete hull."

"Take the time you need, because I don't want to get under way and find the ship is taking on water again."

"Aye."

Drake paused as he was about to answer. A strange sound, like a faint cry or mew, wafted over the water.

"What was that?" he asked, tilting his head to try to capture the noise.

Benton shrugged. "A gull probably."

The thin sound came again. Louder this time.

"That doesn't sound like a gull." Curiosity urged Drake forward. He reached the starboard railing in a pair of steps. Gripping it, he shadowed his eyes with his other hand. "Look."

It was a jolly boat, a small boat used to transport men and cargo from a ship to the shore. It was close to the rocks. Dangerously close. Even as he watched, the bow bumped hard against the wall of stone.

Something moved inside it. Was that what had made the whimpering sound? Had someone been so cruel as to toss kittens into a boat and push them out to sea? If he got his hands on—

The rest of the thought vanished as tiny fingers rose over the side of the boat and waved in his direction.

Benton gasped. "A child?"

Drake did not answer. He ran toward the plank down to the wide stone pier where *The Kestrel* was moored. He reached the quay in a pair of long steps and raced along the shore toward where the jolly boat slammed against the rocks over and over. It would not survive long, for the wood was already dried with salt stains and pocked with holes.

He sped past seaweed that had dried in thick clumps on the rocks. Clambering up one of the giant boulders, he jumped into the water on the other side. The water was cool, but he paid it no mind as he flung himself forward, wading toward the boat. Hearing shouts, he looked back to see several of his crew on the pier. They motioned wildly with their hands. He glanced forward and groaned. A small child was trying to stand up in the boat. If he did, he was sure to tip the boat over and end up in the water.

Drake reached the boat and grasped its bow to steady it. Only then did he look inside. His eyes widened as he counted six children, the youngest not much more than a newborn. It was swaddled, a piece of blanket covering its eyes so the sun did not burn into them. In addition, there were three older boys, possibly as old as three or four, and two girls who must be twins, because they were almost identical. One of the older boys, the one who had been struggling to stand, said something. It was baby gibberish, and he guessed that boy was closer to two years old.

"Sit down," Drake said, forcing a smile.

The boy hesitated, a stubborn scowl furrowing his brow beneath his wispy, brown hair.

"Sit down, and we'll go for a ride up onto the sand. Doesn't that sound like fun?" He needed the children's cooperation or they could set the small boat awash before he got them around the rocks and to safety. He doubted any of them could swim, and he did not want to have to choose which one to save.

The children began to giggle as he splashed through the water, keeping himself between the boat and the rocks. He grimaced when the waves lifted the boat and struck him so hard that he stumbled against stone. He fought to regain his footing. The sand slipped away beneath his boots.

He snarled wordless frustration under his breath. His new boots! Why hadn't he paused the short second it would have taken to yank them off?

His self-recrimination was interrupted by a sharp cry. An older boy sobbed loudly as a blond boy pinched his arm again.

"Stop that!" Drake snapped.

That set the blond boy to crying, too.

Benton waded through the waves and seized the other side of the jolly boat. "What is wrong with them?"

The younger boy began weeping, as well.

Drake motioned for his first mate to help him steer the small boat to shore. With two of them to balance the boat that wanted to skip and dance on each wave, they made short work of climbing out of the water and dragging the boat onto the sand.

All the children, including the baby, were howling now. Drake fired orders to his crew. Food and something to drink for the older children. The baby must be fed, too. Telling Benton to see to the children's needs, he turned on his heel.

"Captain?" called his first mate.

"What?" He did not keep his barely restrained rage out of his voice.

"Where are you going?"

Fury whipped through his words. "To find the rotters who put these children in a boat and left them to die."

"But how will you know who did this?"

"There is always one person in any village who can be counted on to know everyone in that village. He would know who is capable of putting these children in a boat and setting them adrift. In addition, he will be willing to help."

"Who is that?"

"The parson." He scowled as water squeezed between his toes in his ruined boots. "And when, with his help, I find those curs who were so cruel, I will make sure they are sorry they ever set eyes on these children. I promise you that." He strode toward the village.

Closing the book, Susanna Trelawney leaned back in her chair. The household accounts had balanced. At last. She needed to speak to both Mrs. Hitchens, the housekeeper, and Baricoat, the butler, about checking their reports more closely, because she had found too many mistakes. She was thankful for Mrs. Ford. As always, the cook's records were exact to the last ha'penny.

Just as Susanna liked. With a sense of order in the great house, chaos could be kept at bay. Her family could go about their lives without having to worry about something unanticipated upsetting them.

As it had that horrific week when grief had held the house and her family in its serrated claws, shredding their hearts. Her own heart had not had a chance to heal from being broken by the one man she had ever loved. Franklin Chenowith had run off to marry another woman on the very day that the banns were first read for Susanna's wedding to him. Susanna had considered that woman, Norah Yelland, her bosom bow. She had surrendered her sense of control when she fell in love, and she had paid the cost, losing both of her best friends in one instant.

The cost had been too high, and instead of vowing to love Franklin till death did them part, she had tried to forgive them. She had struggled with it, and she promised herself that she would never allow herself to be so foolish again. She would remain in control of her emotions and her life.

No matter what.

No! It did no one any good to dwell on the past. Instead, she should work to keep everything in proper order so serenity could reign in the house.

Susanna patted the accounts book and sighed. She loved working in this quiet room with its burgundy walls and coffered ceiling, even though the hearth was too narrow to heat the room much above freezing on the coldest winter days. She gazed out the window toward the moor. The undulating ground offered perfect grazing for both cattle and sheep. Like most of the windows in the great house Cothaire, it offered no view of the sea. A beautiful vista would be lovely, but cold winds blasted the seaside of the house, pitting any window glass and chilling rooms. Any room in Cothaire that faced the sea had thick exterior shutters that could be closed and locked from the outside in advance of a strong storm.

The sea was an integral part of their lives. Many of the villagers provided for their families by fishing and trading upon its waters. Her sister Caroline's husband had been one of them until he was killed far out at sea less than a week after Mama's sudden death. It had been a terrible time, and if she could have spared her sister—or her two brothers and her father—a moment of that sorrow, she gladly would have.

"Lady Susanna?" came a familiar voice from the doorway.

"What is it, Venton?"

The footman, wearing the family's simple gray livery, dipped his head in her direction. She and Venton had grown up together at Cothaire because his mother had been the nursery maid when Susanna was the last one living within the two-story nursery. Knowing Susanna was lonesome because she was more than a decade younger than her brother Raymond, Mrs. Venton had brought her son to the nursery with her until Susanna was almost six.

Since then, their lives had gone on separate but parallel paths. Venton had worked hard to rise to the rank of footman, and Susanna had learned to handle a household and be a proper wife to the man chosen for her by her father, the Earl of Launceston. Then her future had changed when her mother died five years ago and Susanna took over the management of her father's house while her older brother Arthur, who was the heir, assisted in running the estate.

"Lady Susanna, his lordship requests your presence," Venton answered, and she again pushed aside uncomfortable thoughts about the past. Lingering on them was silly.

"Of course. Where is he?"

"The smoking room."

Her brows shot skyward before she could compose herself. As she stood, she affixed a calm expression on her face, though curiosity roiled inside her. The smoking room was the domain of her father, her brothers and their male guests. She could not remember the last time she—or any other female—had been invited into it.

What a surprise! And she had hated surprises ever since she got such a public one when Franklin failed to appear for the first reading of their wedding banns.

As if she had given voice to her astonishment, Venton said quietly, "His lordship has been reading there all afternoon, and he had planned to take his tea there."

"Thank you, Venton," she replied as she walked past him. She understood what he had not said. Papa's gout must be plaguing him again. The painful condition was the primary reason that he had turned over so many of the duties of Cothaire to her and her brother Arthur as well as her sister, Caroline, the oldest sibling, who acted as Papa's hostess.

The smoking room lay beyond the main dining room. Like the drawing room, where the ladies could withdraw from the table, the smoking room allowed the men to converse more easily and blow a cloud of tobacco smoke if they pleased.

That strong odor greeted Susanna when she knocked on the door and her father called for her to enter. Chairs were arranged for the ease of conversation in front of a huge hearth. On every wall hung either swords and pistols or pictures of foxhounds and horses. Some of the portraits of horses were life-size and dominated the room.

"Ah, my dear," said her father with a wide smile. "Do come in."

Harold Trelawney, the Earl of Launceston, still had the tautly sculptured face that he had passed on to his sons. His hair, once as ebony as his children's, was laced with silver that matched the color of his eyes. Only Susanna had inherited his silver-gray eyes; her siblings' eyes were crystal blue like their late mother's.

Papa did not rise. She did not expect him to when he suffered from another acute episode of gout.

However, another man stood from a chair that had its back to the door. Her eyes followed, astonished by the height of the dark-haired stranger. Strong muscles moved lithely beneath his navy blue coat, and her heart-beat faltered, then raced like a runaway horse. As he turned to face her, she found herself captured by the brownest eyes she had ever seen, and breathing suddenly seemed a chore. A deep tan told her that he was a man accustomed to working outside.

As his gaze swept over her, she forced herself to breathe normally so he would not guess the unsettling effect he had on her. She could not chide him because she had been staring at him boldly. She lowered her eyes demurely and continued to appraise him from beneath her lashes.

The lines at the corners of his eyes suggested that he smiled often and easily. Perhaps so, but he was not smiling now. His mouth was drawn into a straight line, and his ebony brows lowered in a scowl. By his sides, his hands opened and closed with what looked like impatience. Was he in a hurry to be done with whatever business had brought him to Cothaire? Or was some emotion stronger than restlessness gripping him?

Into the silence that had settled on the room, Papa said, "This is my youngest, Lady Susanna. My dear, may I introduce you to Drake Nesbitt?"

"How do you do, Mr. Nesbitt?" She noticed the line of dried salt on the knees of his pale brown breeches and sodden black boots. Had he been wading in the harbor without taking off his boots?

"Captain Nesbitt," he corrected so coolly that the temperature in the room seemed to drop a dozen degrees.

Captain Drake Nesbitt? That explained, at least, why his clothing was stained with salt. But why was he here? Ships often sailed into Porthlowen Harbor without their captains coming to Cothaire.

Fighting to keep her voice even, she asked, "Papa, what do you wish of me?"

"I want you to…" He shifted, and a groan slipped past his tight lips. He motioned her to remain where she was when she started to step forward.

Susanna complied because his left leg was already wrapped in wool cloths. She knew they had been soaked in boiled goutweed in the hope of easing his pain. There was nothing more she could do.

"My lord," Captain Nesbitt said, "time is of the essence."

She frowned at his lack of compassion.

Before she could say anything, her father replied, "That is true. Please listen closely, Susanna, while I explain what has brought Captain Nesbitt here." He quickly outlined an astounding tale of a small boat drifting into Porthlowen Harbor carrying a cargo of six small children.

More than once, she swallowed a question as she glanced from Captain Nesbitt to her father and back. Captain Nesbitt nodded each time to confirm what Papa said. Not that she did not believe her father, but the tale was unbelievable.

"Where are the children now?" she asked when her father paused.

"Still on the shore," Captain Nesbitt answered. "I thought to obtain some guidance before I did anything further."

"But those poor children must be hungry!" She frowned at Captain Nesbitt. "And frightened and filthy."

"That is why I ordered my crew to find something for them to eat. My greatest concern is for the youngest child. It cannot be more than a few months old, and it needs a mother's milk."

Before she could answer, Papa said, "Susanna, I am certain that putting this problem in your competent hands is the best solution. I trust you and Captain Nesbitt are capable of handling it."

She opened her mouth to protest. To say she was the wrong one to see to the children. Her reaction had nothing to do with the many tasks she managed in the house. It had everything to do with Captain Nesbitt. She did not like how her heart seemed to beat a bit faster when he looked in her direction. Until she knew she could control that rebellious organ, which had led her to betrayal once, she preferred not to spend a single moment in his company.

But her wishes were unimportant when her father could hardly move. She would do as Papa requested and see to the needs of those abandoned children. She reached for the bell on a table by her father's chair and rang it. Hard.

Baricoat appeared instantly. The butler had a knack for knowing the family would be ringing for him even before they picked up the bell.

She gave quick orders. A footman was dispatched to have a carriage brought. Another ran to the kitchen with a request for a hearty tea to be ready for the children upon their arrival. A third headed for the village to see if one of the young mothers who had recently given birth would share her milk with a foundling. In the meantime, she had no doubts Mrs. Ford could devise something to feed the baby.

When a maid arrived with a straw bonnet, a pair of kid gloves and a light shawl, Susanna donned them. She walked out of the room, still giving orders to check the nursery that had been closed up since she left it herself years ago. Baricoat offered to prepare a list of what needed to be done to make the nursery suitable for the children.

"Thank you, Baricoat," she said. Looking over her shoulder, she added, "Captain Nesbitt, aren't you coming?"

His mouth straightened again, but he spoke a gracious farewell to her father before following her to the entry hall. When the door was opened, a small carriage waited by the front steps.

The coachman handed her into the carriage, then stepped aside to allow Captain Nesbitt to enter. For a moment, the captain hesitated, glancing at the seat where the coachman was settling himself and picking up the reins. Then he climbed in and sat beside her, leaving as much space between them as possible.

She was tempted to tell him that she was no more in favor of the arrangement than he was. Instead, she called to the coachee to get them under way. The sooner she reached the village and collected the children, the sooner she could be rid of Captain Nesbitt. And the sooner she could regain her composure that was jeopardized each time Captain Nesbitt's dark eyes caught her gaze.

It could not be fast enough.

Chapter Two

The earl's carriage rattled over rough cobbles as it entered the village, which was a collection of stone buildings. A few hardy plants grew in the lee of them. Drake did not see any trees rising more than ten feet and guessed that storms off the sea were dangerous to anything higher. The village had a smithy, where the smith watched them drive past while his assistant worked over the forge and never looked up. There were a few small shops, including one belonging to a cobbler. Drake resisted looking down at his ruined boots.

During the short ride from Cothaire, Lady Susanna had acted like a constable interrogating Drake for a hideous crime. She fired question after question at him.

"How old are the children?" she asked.

"I am not sure."

"Girls and boys?"

"Yes."

Her scowl warned him that she was not in the mood for jests. He was tempted to remind her that *he* had not asked her to tend to the children from the jolly boat. Her father had.

"Three boys and two girls," he said. "I don't know what the baby is, but I am sure it is either a boy or girl."

"What are their names?" she asked and glanced away as if she found the sight of him intolerable.

"I did not wait to be introduced," he retorted, vexed at her cool dismissal. Didn't she realize he was going out of his way to help? He hardly needed the problem of six small children when he should be supervising the work to make *The Kestrel* seaworthy once more.

"Captain Nesbitt, I am trying to determine how to help the children." Her voice was far calmer than his had been. "Why are you acting as if this is a game?"

Drake relented. Dealing with the children had upset his plans. No doubt, Lady Susanna had other things to do, as well, though he had no idea what important tasks a fine lady might have.

"Help me understand one thing," he said.

Lady Susanna had been staring at the square tower on the parish church, and he was unsure if she would give him the courtesy of looking in his direction. When she turned toward him, he was as staggered as he had been in the earl's smoking room by the unusual color of her eyes. With the strong emotions she was struggling quite unsuccessfully to keep hidden, they gleamed like burnished steel. Everything about her shone from her ebony hair to her pink lips. He could not keep from wondering what she would look like when she smiled. She was a dainty miss, the top of her head not quite reaching his shoulder, but he already had seen she was no fragile flower. Her spine seemed to have been fashioned of stronger stuff than the tin pulled out of the local mines.

"Of course, Captain Nesbitt," she replied in a tone

that suggested saying his name left a bad taste in her mouth.

He shoved his foolish thoughts aside. She did not like him. Well, that was fine. He had no interest in her other than making sure the children were taken care of and the person who put them in the boat paid for that cruelty. It was better, in the long run, for her to dislike him and for him to dislike her. That made it easier not to make the same mistake he had before when he had been beguiled by a pair of pretty eyes.

Never again.

"What do you need to understand?" she asked when he remained silent.

"After we brought the children's boat up on the sand, I went first to the parson of the Porthlowen church." His brows lowered. "His surname, if I recall rightly, is Trelawney, just like your family's. Is that a coincidence?"

"No, it is no coincidence. Raymond Trelawney is my brother." A hint of a smile added a new light to her eyes, and he guessed her full grin would be scintillating. "The living at the Porthlowen church has always been given to a younger son in the family, and Raymond is well suited for the position. His faith is strong, and he has a compassionate heart."

"Maybe so, but he was quick to pass the matter of the children from his hands to the earl's."

Her smile vanished. "As he should have. My father, Lord Launceston, needs to know when something as astounding as a boatload of babies washing ashore occurs. Everyone knows that, so whoever you had chosen to speak to in Porthlowen would have done the same."

"If you say so."

"I do." She folded her hands primly, her gloves white against the green-sprigged fabric of her gown. "If you are still in Porthlowen on Sunday, Captain, you and your crew are welcome to attend services at our church."

"Some of my men already have." He wished he could take back those words when her eyes narrowed.

"But you have not?"

"Not yet. Someone needs to oversee the work my ship needs, and that is the captain." He did not intend to add more. He believed in God, but his relationship with Him was lackadaisical. He figured if God needed to get his attention, He would. So far, that had not happened.

"I suppose."

Drake changed the subject that was making them both even more uncomfortable. "I asked Parson Trelawney if anyone had reported any missing children, and he said no."

Lady Susanna waved in response to a greeting called out to her by a young auburn-haired woman who stood in the doorway of the village's main shop. The earl's daughter called for the carriage to stop.

The redhead hurried over. "You have heard about the children?"

"Yes. Captain Nesbitt came to the house to explain how he found them floating in a jolly boat." She paused, then introduced Drake to the other woman.

Elisabeth Rowse was almost as tall as he was. Her face was plain, but her bright green eyes glowed with intelligence and kindness. When she smiled as she greeted him, her whole face transformed. The mouth that had looked too wide now was an amazing grin.

"I hardly believed what I heard when a lad came to the shop looking to buy milk," Miss Rowse said. "Six children abandoned in a boat. Have you ever heard of its like, Susanna?"

Drake was astonished how casually Miss Rowse ad-

dressed an earl's daughter, but said nothing until Lady
Susanna bade the redhead a good day and ordered the
driver to continue toward the strand. His amazement
must have been visible, however.

"Elisabeth is betrothed to my brother Raymond,"
Lady Susanna said. "They plan to be married soon."
Without a pause for a breath, she continued, "Do you
think the children were stolen?"

"It is a possibility." He would have to be on his toes,
because Lady Susanna had a quick, tireless mind. "Overlooking any possibility would be unwise."

"A horrifying possibility, I must say."

He nodded as the carriage came around the last building on the street. In front of them, *The Kestrel* tilted at a
steeper angle than earlier. The figurehead on the front,
a hawk raising its wings to catch the air, leaned so low
that its feathers almost touched the water. Instead of
his men plugging the leak, they must have come out to
watch him and Benton tug the jolly boat out of the water.
He scanned the beach, but there were so many people
gathered there that he could not see his men.

"That ship by the quay looks ready to be torn apart
and sold for scrap," she said with a shake of her head.
"Why would anyone leave a ship in that condition in
our harbor?"

"Because it is being repaired. Before you ask how I
know, I will tell you that is *my* ship."

"Oh."

He had startled her, because she did not have a retort.

"It was damaged in battle with a French privateer,"
he added when a flattering blush climbed her cheeks.
Not being on the defensive with her was a change. "It is
nearly repaired, but we discovered another leak today.

By the morrow, if all goes well, she will be proudly afloat once more."

"Was anybody killed?" she asked in a strained voice.

"Not among my men, but a couple of the French pirates did not survive."

"Papa laments that if the war continues much longer, Napoleon will have the chance to build many more vessels to harry our ships." She looked back at him, her face troubled.

He wondered if that was the first honest emotion she had shown other than her distaste for him. "Britain and our allies are winning more often than not in the Peninsular campaign."

"But Boney is a wily adversary with dreams of ruling the world. If he cannot have Spain, he will look elsewhere for lands to make his own. Mark my words."

Drake smiled in spite of his determination to keep distance between them. Her logic was undeniable, especially as he had argued much the same himself when he and members of his crew sat around the table in the wardroom.

"Everyone in Porthlowen must be on the beach, save for the few we saw along the street," Lady Susanna said, drawing his attention to the throng on the strand.

"Curiosity is compelling."

"Especially when this may be the most exciting thing to happen here." Again she gave him a half smile. "Perhaps ever."

He nodded. The villagers were accustomed to ships coming and going in every possible condition, and no one in the village had blinked when *The Kestrel* barely made it to the quay. Even marching the French prisoners of war through the village to where they could be handed off to the local militia to be taken to Dartmoor Prison had caused little more than a slight stir.

A jolly boat filled with children was something else entirely.

"Is that why you are asking all these questions, my lady? Because you are curious?"

Her frown returned. "I am asking because I want to be prepared for what needs to be done to help the children. I prefer not to be surprised."

The carriage stopped, saving Drake from having to answer. He got out and held up his hand to Lady Susanna before the coachman could. When she placed her slender hand on his much broader one, it was as light as a spring breeze. She stepped out, the fringe on her shawl brushing his arm. A flowery scent teased him, so faint that he had not noticed it until now when she stood beside him, closer than when they had been seated in the carriage.

She withdrew her hand and edged away, looking everywhere but at him. "Captain Nesbitt, if you will lead the way, please."

He considered offering his arm but told himself not to be addlepated. She was lovely, but he had been betrayed once by a beautiful woman. Not that it mattered. Lady Susanna Trelawney made it clear with every word and action that she considered him a bothersome disruption to her day. Maybe he should be grateful that she was more honest than Ruby had been.

Never again.

"This way," he said gruffly, vexed at how he had to remind himself of what that big mistake had cost his heart. Simply because a woman smelled delightful was no reason to do more than appreciate the moment.

Drake did not look back as he walked toward the

crowd. At first, he thought he might have to elbow past people who failed to move when he said, "Pardon me."

Then Lady Susanna spoke the same words, and the villagers stepped aside as if they were the Red Sea being parted by Moses. She thanked them prettily, and Drake noticed the men touching their forelocks and the women giving a quick curtsy. The Trelawney family was well respected and perhaps even well loved in Porthlowen. When she assured the onlookers that the children would be taken to the earl's house, the people thanked her before heading to the village and returning to what they had been doing before word of the jolly boat raced along the street. They obviously thought the matter resolved now that it was in the earl's daughter's hands. Maybe there was more to Lady Susanna than he had guessed.

Drake followed in Lady Susanna's wake through the dispersing crowd and saw most of his crew surrounding the small boat. The children sat on a piece of canvas beside it. Two women who were old enough to be the babies' grandmothers loitered nearby, handing pieces of cake to them. Another woman of the same age sniffed at the sight before pushing past Drake and Lady Susanna with a mutter about spoiling children.

"Pay Charity Thorburn no mind," Lady Susanna said under her breath. "From what I have heard, she and the Winwood sisters have not once seen eye to eye in the past fifty years. If one of the sisters said the sea is wet, Mrs. Thorburn would argue it was dry."

When Lady Susanna turned to greet the Winwood sisters, Drake could not help smiling. Splatters on the children's shirts and in their hair must have come from the soup Obadiah always had ready in the galley. The elderly cook was on his knees, holding the baby. An absorbent cloth was wrapped around his finger. He dipped it into a bowl by his side; then he placed it in the baby's mouth to let the infant suckle.

Lady Susanna bent to touch the baby's head. She smiled warmly at Obadiah, who gave her a toothless grin in return and flushed like a new cabin boy who had stayed too long in the sun.

"'Tis milk and water and a wee bit of honey," Obadiah replied to a question Drake had not heard. "'Twill fill the mite's belly for now. My da used the same mixture for lambs when the ewes wouldna let them nurse."

Thanking him, she turned to where the children regarded her with wide, red-rimmed eyes. They must have been crying the whole time he spoke with the parson and the earl and while he brought Lady Susanna to the beach. He was grateful the older women had come with fresh cake. He thanked them as Lady Susanna sank to her knees beside the boat and put her hand on it as she greeted the children.

"Who is *she*?" asked Benton quietly as he appeared at Drake's elbow. "Are there more like her in the village?"

Drake scowled his first mate to silence, then said, "She is Lady Susanna Trelawney, the earl's daughter."

Arching his brows, Benton whistled softly.

He did not have a chance to reply because Lady Susanna motioned for him to join her. Aware of the eyes of his crew and the few remaining villagers on them, he pushed down his resentment that she crooked her finger at him as if he were a dog trained to obey.

He squatted beside her and saw one of the older boys pinch the other one again. The second boy let out a shriek that was more anger than pain. He scooped up the two boys and carried them to Benton.

"Keep them apart," he ordered as he set them at his first mate's feet.

In an instant, the two boys were taunting each other and poking each other and ready to come to blows.

"How?" asked Benton, trying to pull them away from one another.

Drake shrugged. "You can handle a whole crew of cantankerous sailors. Two small boys should not be too great a task for you."

When he turned to go back to where Lady Susanna was talking in a hushed voice to the remaining children, he wondered if Benton realized that Drake had given him the easier chore. At least his first mate did not have to work alongside a woman who made no secret that she longed to be rid of him.

He wished he could say the feeling was mutual, but she intrigued him. Her hand gently cupped a tear-streaked face as she leaned toward the children. Behind her cool exterior, she had a gentle heart. So why was she revealing that to everyone but him?

Captain Nesbitt was definitely correct about one thing, Susanna decided. The two toddler girls, who looked to be around two and a half years old, were identical. They must be twins. With their fine black hair and dark green eyes, they would catch every man's attention once they were grown. Now they were frightened children surrounded by strangers.

Pointing to herself, she said, "I am Susanna."

The twins looked at each other and at a younger boy who was struggling to stay awake. Before he could tip over, Susanna picked him up and set him on her lap. She touched his forehead, but no hint of fever suggested he might be ill. She must check each child for signs of sickness, though if one was ill, they all probably would soon be. She wondered how long the youngsters had been in the boat. Their faces were red from the sun but not blistered. Either they were accustomed to the sun off the sea or they had been drifted quickly into Porthlowen Harbor after being set afloat.

"I am Susanna," she repeated to the twins. "Who are you?"

"Wufry," one of the little girls said.

"Ruthie?" asked Captain Nesbitt as he came to kneel beside Susanna. He held out his hands for the little boy.

Susanna shook her head because he had fallen asleep, and she did not want to disturb him until she must.

"Wufry." The little girl scowled at Captain Nesbitt. "Wufry!"

In a hushed voice, he said, "The females around here must learn that facial expression early."

"What?" She looked at him and found he was so close to her that she could not see anything beyond his broad shoulders. As she raised her gaze to his, everyone else on the shore seemed to fade into the distance. Could one disappear into the brown depths of another's eyes?

Then he grinned. "Her irked frown is just like yours."

Susanna gasped, knowing she should chide him for his rudeness, but she had been sent to help the children, not to teach Captain Nesbitt proper manners. Heat raced up her face when she recalled how many were watching and might have overheard his whisper. The best course of action would be to collect the children and return to Cothaire posthaste.

"Wufry!" insisted the little girl again.

Lord, Susanna prayed, *open my understanding as well as my heart to these children You have brought forth out of the sea.* She shuddered when she thought of how easily they could have died before reaching Porth-lowen. *Let me help them now and please guide me in tending them as carefully as You guided them to safety.*

Listening closely to the little girl, she repeated the child's word over and over in her mind. She smiled and asked to give herself more time to decipher the name, "So your name isn't Georgie?"

"No." The child smiled, and the little girl beside her looked at Susanna for the first time. "Wufry."

"And I guess your name isn't Aloysius, either."

Both twins giggled.

When Captain Nesbitt started to speak, Susanna waved him to silence with a curt motion. He scowled but nodded. Good. He could be reasonable.

"Wufry!" said the little girl again.

Hoping her first real guess would be right, Susanna took a deep breath and said, "So your name must be Lucy."

The little girl grinned, showing gaps in her baby teeth. She flung her arms around Susanna's neck, tugging her toward the boat. The edge cut painfully into her ribs because she protected the sleeping boy from the splintered wooden side.

"Me Wufry." The toddler pointed to her sister. "She Mowie."

"So you are Mollie," Susanna said after repeating the word in her mind. She smiled at the other twin, who seemed shier than her sister. "Lucy and Mollie. Two very pretty names. Captain, will you assist Miss Lucy and Miss Mollie to the carriage?"

He reached for Lucy. His nose wrinkled as he took her hand and then reached for her sister's. Both were in need of a change of clean clothes and fresh napkins because the ones they wore were soaked.

Susanna stood, balancing the little boy against her. He stank, too, but she had smelled worse.

Her gaze met Captain Nesbitt's over the children's heads. A smile quirked at his lips, and she found herself returning it. Something lit in his eyes, something powerful. She should look away. She could not. She was held by his gaze as surely as if he held her in his arms. A shiver ran through her at that thought. Not an icy shiver, but a heated one.

A small hand tugged at her bodice, and, grateful that she could break the connection between her and Captain Nesbitt, Susanna looked down to see the little boy was awake.

"Gil." The smallest boy jabbed a finger at his chest.

"You are Gil?" she asked.

He nodded and ordered, "Down!"

"As you wish." She set him on the ground. When she straightened, she saw the playful twinkle in Captain Nesbitt's eyes. No doubt he recognized Gil's tone because it sounded much like his arrogant one.

Why was she letting the ship's captain slip into her thoughts so often? Her focus should be on the children and discovering why they had been floating in a jolly boat in Porthlowen Harbor.

As if she had made that last thought a request, Gil took off running faster than she could imagine such short legs could move. She gave chase, but slowed when the little boy stopped beside the man who was feeding the swaddled baby.

Gil tapped the blanket and said with pride, "My baby."

Susanna glanced back at Captain Nesbitt. She was not surprised that he was watching intently. He had been honest when he said, because he had saved them, he considered these children his duty.

When he motioned for her to take the lead, probably because he had trouble understanding the childish talk, she asked, "Does your baby have a name, Gil?"

"*My* baby. My—"

A shriek silenced everyone, and she saw the two older boys swinging at each other. The man trying to keep them apart was not succeeding, because one boy ran in and slapped the other before the man could halt him.

"Captain…" she began.

He pushed past her, shoving the twins' hands into hers. Scooping up the blond boy, he draped him over one shoulder. Then he grabbed the dark-haired boy and balanced him on his opposite hip. They wriggled but halted when he barked a sharp order.

Susanna laughed. She could not stop herself. The two boys were frozen in shock, and Captain Nesbitt looked a bit green about the gills with one of the boys' rear ends close to his nose.

"My baby!" Gil cried, patting the baby's swaddling.

The baby screamed again.

He pulled back in horror. "My baby!"

Susanna gave him a swift smile. Babies cried, but not usually with such intensity. At least not when she held one during church services.

Looking past Gil to the old man holding the baby, she asked, "Is the milk fresh?"

"Aye." He motioned to a lanky boy standing beside him. "Tell m'lady where ye got the milk, lad."

He stared at his feet. "At the shop. The lady there said it was delivered this morning. Her assistant poured it out while I was watching, and it smelled as fresh as if it had just come out of the cow."

"What do you know of milking, boy?" demanded the old man.

"Grew up with cows, I did," asserted the boy.

To halt the argument before it went further, Susanna said, "If Miss Rowse told you that, it is the truth." She released the twins' hands and held out her arms. "May I?"

"Aye," the old man said gratefully. He settled the baby in her arms, then stood with the help of the lad who had gotten the milk.

As she went toward a row of low boulders, a young woman followed her and asked, "Do you need more milk for the little one, my lady?"

Susanna smiled at the young woman. The hem of her dress and apron were covered with wet sand like Susanna's. Wisely she had bare feet, so she did not have to deal with shoes caked with heavy sand.

"Are you Peggy who is helping Miss Rowse at the shop?"

She nodded. "Peggy Smith, my lady." She dipped in a quick curtsy but kept staring at her toes. No doubt, the dark-haired girl wondered what Susanna had heard about her, knowing that news spread quickly in the small town. A newcomer like Peggy would be the talk of Porthlowen until something else caught the gossips' fancies.

"Thank you for bringing milk for the baby. He or she seems full for now."

The girl started to say something, then hurried away. Sand sprayed behind her as she sped toward the village.

Behind Susanna, Captain Nesbitt barked an order, but the little boys kept swinging their fists at each other. They managed only to hit him. He put them on the ground, trying to keep them apart.

Gil refused to be parted from the baby. He had trailed Susanna to where she sat on a stone. He watched intently as she placed the baby on her lap. She cooed nonsense words to the baby, but it kept crying with all its power. His lower lip began to tremble, warning he was ready to sob, too.

What is wrong? Lord, help me help this suffering child. Both of them.

With care, she began to undo the blanket that had been wrapped tightly around the baby, keeping it secure and warm. It stank like the other children. Each motion of the blanket seemed to pain the baby—a girl, she discovered—more. She slipped her hand under the long shirt so she could rub the baby's stomach. It was not hard with colic, but the baby screamed again.

"My baby!" cried Gil, tears oozing out of his eyes.

Her own widened when she raised the shirt and saw a tattered piece of paper attached to the garment with a straight pin. Pink spots on the baby's chest and stomach showed where the point jabbed her at the slightest motion.

"Oh, you poor dear," she murmured.

"What is that?" asked Captain Nesbitt.

She looked up, shocked, because she had not heard him approach. His dark coat was stained, and the seam on one shoulder had torn. "The other children?"

"Being watched closely by some of my crew while others shake sand out of the canvas and fit it into the carriage so the seats are not ruined."

"Thank you," she said, telling herself she should not be astonished. He had shown his compassion toward the children from the moment she was introduced to him.

"What do you have there?"

"I don't know." Careful not to prick the baby again,

she drew out the pin and wove it through a corner of her shawl.

He caught the slip of paper before it could fall into the sand. As he scanned it, he clenched his jaw. He handed it back to her.

She struggled with the bad spelling and splotched ink. She guessed it said:

> *Find loving homes for our children.*
> *Don't let them work and die in the mines.*

Whoever had pinned the note to the baby's shirt must have been desperate to have that message found.

Beside her, Captain Nesbitt growled something wordless, then said, "Their own families put them in the boat and set them adrift."

She wanted to deny his words. She could not. Looking from the sleepy baby on her lap and the little boy leaning against her knee back to Captain Nesbitt, she whispered, "How could anyone do that to these sweet children?"

His eyes burned with fervor as he said, "*That*, my lady, is what I intend to find out."

Chapter Three

"Good night, sweet one." Susanna tucked the blanket around Lucy, who shared a mattress with her twin sister. Both girls were lost in dreams and sucking their thumbs, Lucy her right one and Mollie her left.

The house had been in a hubbub by the time Susanna returned with the six children. She had been sure that Captain Nesbitt would send someone from his crew with her, but he escorted them himself, insisting that he must speak with her father. She was curious what they discussed, but Papa would let her know if he felt it was necessary.

She had turned her attention to tending to the children and trying to restore order in the house. Baricoat had brought her a long list of obvious deficiencies in the nursery, so she decided to keep the children in her rooms until the nursery was safe and comfortable. Busy with making those arrangements, she still had noticed when Captain Nesbitt left.

He had stridden out with purpose and waved aside the offer of the carriage. He glanced over his shoulder only once before he vanished down the long drive to the gate. She had shifted away from the window so he would not see her watching him. Scolding herself for caring what he thought, she hurried back to the myriad decisions she needed to make to ensure the children's arrival disrupted the household and her family as little as possible.

There was plenty of room in Cothaire for six small children, but somewhere hearts ached with worry. She did not want to imagine what had compelled anyone to put them in a boat and push it out into the waves. Even if the children had been born outside of marriage, every parish had ways of providing for them.

Help us find these children's families, she prayed over and over. *Ease their fears and point us in the right direction.*

Two mattresses had been brought into Susanna's dressing room while the children, except the baby, were offered tea and sandwiches and cake at a table in the kitchen. Mrs. Ford and her kitchen staff had served the youngsters whatever they wished and made sure they ate slowly so they would not sicken. All the children were thin. She wondered how long they had been adrift. Or had they been half starved before they were placed in the boat?

The past year had been difficult for Cornwall. The wheat and barley harvests had been poor and the pilchard season a disaster. The small fish, which the rest of England called sardines, usually provided a ready source of food along the coast. With her father's permission, Susanna had ordered the Cothaire pantries opened weekly to allow local families to take food. She was unsure if other great houses shared the practice. If not, starvation among the fisherfolk, the farmers and the miners' families was an ever-present threat.

Straightening, Susanna went to the next mattress,

where the three boys were supposed to be asleep, too. Little Gil was rolled up like a hedgehog at one end, but the two older boys, who called themselves Toby and Bertie, were tussling again.

"Enough," she said in a loud whisper that would not wake the other youngsters. "It is time to sleep."

Toby, the slight boy with darker hair, whined, "He is taking my spot."

"He is taking *mine*." Blond Bertie glared at the other boy.

She took Toby by the hand and brought him to his feet. Picking up his pillow, she led him to the other mattress, where the twins slept. "Here," she said.

"But—"

"Sleep here tonight. Soon you will have your own bed."

His eyes grew as wide as tea saucers. "My own bed?"

"Yes, but you have to share tonight." She waited until he curled up at the foot of the mattress and then pulled a blanket over him. "Go to sleep."

He mumbled something as he looked past her toward the other mattress. She eased to her right, blocking his view of the other boys. Giving him a stern look, she waited until he closed his eyes.

Susanna left one light burning low in the dressing room and went into her sitting room. The lamps were dim there, too, but moonlight came through the trio of tall windows that looked out, as most windows in the house did, over the gardens and the rolling fields beyond them. She could mark the seasons by the flowers that bloomed and faded in the garden.

She dropped heavily to the chaise longue. Leaning her head back, she stared up at the ceiling. The mural there was lost in the shadows, but she could re-create in her mind every bright color of the fields and the orchard as well as the people who had gathered to flirt and pick apples.

Ah, to be so carefree! She could not even recall what it felt like. The weight of her added responsibilities ground down on her. On the shore, while she had the assistance of Captain Nesbitt, taking care of the children had not seemed like such a huge undertaking. Now...

A knock came at the door, and Susanna pushed herself to her feet. That must be one of the maids with the baby. Mrs. Hitchens, the housekeeper, had already selected a wet nurse from among the volunteers in the village. The young woman, who was about to wean her own baby, was willing to come to Cothaire several times a day to feed the nameless baby.

"Caroline!" Susanna gasped when she opened the door. She had not expected to see her oldest sibling at this hour when the family should have been at the table.

Caroline Trelawney Dowling had a welcoming face. That was what their mother had always said, and Susanna believed it was true. Kindness and warmth glowed from her pale blue eyes, whether she met a friend or a stranger. She was a bit plumper than fashion demanded, but that had not mattered to her late husband. John Dowling had loved her exactly as she was, and she had loved him for that.

Loved him still, Susanna knew. Neither death nor the passage of five years had changed that. Often, Susanna wondered what it would be like to have a man love *her* like that, but common sense always quickly returned.

"May we come in?" Caroline asked.

Only then did Susanna notice her sister carried a tiny bundle in her arms. "You did not need to disrupt your evening meal to bring the baby here."

"There was no disruption." Caroline smiled down at the baby. "Papa is taking his supper in his rooms, and Arthur has not yet returned from his visit to the far tenant farms. You know he never arrives home until long after dark when he goes there."

Susanna stepped aside to let her sister enter. Pointing to the half-closed door that led to her dressing room, she put her fingers to her lips.

Caroline nodded.

"I have a drawer lined with blankets for this babe," Susanna whispered, holding out her hands.

"May I hold her awhile longer?"

"Of course." She should not be surprised. Her sister had longed for children of her own, but that dream had been dashed when John died. "Why don't you sit?"

When her sister chose the chaise longue, Susanna turned up a lamp before sitting on a nearby chair. She watched as Caroline snuggled the baby close, gazing down at her with obvious affection. Susanna bit her lower lip. If her sister became too attached to the baby, her heart was sure to break when the children's parents were found.

"Don't fret, little sister," Caroline said as if Susanna had spoken her thoughts aloud. "I know this darling sprite is here only for a short time, but that is no reason not to savor every moment while I can." She looked up and smiled. "Tell me. Who was that very good-looking man who came to the house with you?"

"Drake Nesbitt. He is the captain of that listing ship in the harbor."

"He seemed very solicitous of you."

"You are mistaken. His thoughts were focused solely on the children."

Caroline chuckled softly. "Then explain why he was watching *you* all the time."

"He was?" She clamped her lips closed when her sister's smile broadened, but she could not halt the quivers from deep in her center. Oh, bother! She had not intended to say anything so silly. Gathering her composure around her anew, she said, "Captain Nesbitt rescued the children, so he wished to make sure they were comfortable here. As I am the one arranging that, he had every reason to watch that I did as I promised."

"I agree."

"Good."

"He had *every* reason to watch you, but why did you watch him leave Cothaire?"

Susanna refused to let her vexation surface that someone had noted her by the window and carried the tale to her sister. "I happened to be by the window." That was the truth. "He is a sailor. I will never be so want-witted as to tangle my life up with one of them."

Her sister's face lost all color.

"Oh, Caroline! I am so sorry. I did not mean you were foolish to marry John."

"I know you didn't." Her older sister sighed.

"I am sorry to remind you about him."

Caroline drew her feet up beneath her and leaned back against the high end of the chaise longue, shifting the baby in her arms. "You did not remind me. I never forget. Not ever." She squared her shoulders. "Papa tells me that I need to put the mourning behind me as it has been more than five years since John left on that voyage. I don't know how."

Moving to sit by her sister's feet on the chaise longue, Susanna said, "You could ask Papa."

"I don't think he knows, because he still misses Mama more than he will admit."

"What about asking Raymond?"

Caroline shook her head. "Take advice on love from my younger brother who is not yet married? I don't think so."

"But he is our parson."

"I know, and I appreciate his concern and teachings for our congregation." A faint smile smoothed out the lines of grief in her face. "Still, I cannot imagine speaking to my baby brother about the state of my heart. Perhaps I should speak to you instead."

"Me about marriage?" Susanna gave a sharp laugh. "I am less of an expert than Raymond is."

"But losing the one you love has nothing to do with being married. It has to do with healing your heart."

Susanna opened her mouth but clamped it closed when a sharp cry came from the dressing room. She jumped to her feet. Racing across the sitting room, she pushed open the door just in time to see Toby and Bertie roll off the mattress and across the floor. Bertie got up. Toby chased him. Bertie screeched. The other children woke up and climbed off the mattresses, eager not to miss what was happening.

Susanna reached out and took each little boy by the back of his shirt. She pulled them as far apart as her arms could stretch. Bertie was cradling his arm, and, even in the low light, Susanna could see a bite mark near his elbow.

"He bited me," Bertie cried, thick tears rolling down his face.

"Did you bite him, Toby?" She wanted to be fair, but she had seen the dark-haired boy tormenting the smaller Bertie all evening.

"He take my pillow." Toby puffed up in righteous indignation. "He gots pillow. Me want my pillow."

"He pinched me."

"He stuck out his tongue."

"He—"

"Enough," Susanna said, wondering how she was going to keep the peace when the little boys detested each other.

"Are they hurt?" asked Caroline as she stepped through the doorway.

"My baby!" Gil flung himself against Caroline so hard that he knocked her back a half step. Her shoulder thudded on the door frame. Pain rippled across her face. Her grip tightened on the baby, and her eyes filled with fear that she would drop the little girl.

Torn, Susanna wanted to help her sister but knew the boys would begin fighting the second she released them. She hesitated only a moment, then rushed to her sister and plucked the baby from her arms. Behind her, Bertie let out another screech.

"Give me the baby," Caroline said over Gil's demands to see "my baby."

"But you are hurt."

"I hit my elbow, and my fingers went numb. I am fine now."

"If you are sure—"

Bertie screamed.

"I don't think we have any choice." Caroline took the baby and bent to let Gil look at the little girl, who, remarkably, still slept.

Susanna whirled to halt the boys again. This time, she did not get as good a grip on their shirts. They squirmed away. Toby picked up a pillow and swung it at Bertie. The other children squealed with excitement.

"Stop now!" she ordered.

Toby hit Bertie again with the pillow. The blond boy fell to the floor and started screaming as if he had been dropped off the roof.

She wondered how much he was pretending to be hurt and how much was true. No matter. She needed to regain control. Again she asked the boys to stop. Again they ignored her. She seized the backs of their shirts, getting a better hold this time. They fought her and each other to escape.

"May we help?"

Not daring to release either little boy, Susanna looked over her shoulder. Raymond and Elisabeth stood beside Caroline. Her brother wore his usual black coat, waistcoat and breeches. One end of his white cravat popped out as he took Toby's arm and drew him away from her and Bertie.

Elisabeth knelt in front of the angry child and tried to soothe him. He refused to be placated.

Raymond gave them a sympathetic smile. "Let me take…"

"Toby," Susanna supplied, keeping a tight hold on Bertie.

"Let me take Toby," Raymond said in his deep voice that was perfect for the pulpit. "He can stay with me at the parsonage tonight."

"You don't have room for a child there."

"Quite to the contrary. I have far more room than I need."

Elisabeth stood, still holding Toby's hand. "If the situation remains tense, I have some special sweets at the store that might help."

Both boys froze at her words.

"Sweets?" asked Toby and Bertie at the same time.

"Only if you behave nicely tonight," Elisabeth replied. "I will check with Parson Trelawney and Lady Susanna in the morning."

They both nodded hard.

"That is settled, then." Raymond glanced toward where Caroline was gently rocking the baby. "Separating these two should make it easier on you."

"It will." Susanna relaxed a bit. "I have no idea how they did not tip the jolly boat over with their antics."

"Because the good Lord had them in His hand, guiding them to this shore, where they would find a haven." He smiled at them. "Don't forget that the Book of Proverbs teaches: *'Hear, O my son, and receive my sayings; and the years of thy life shall be many. I have taught thee in the way of wisdom; I have led thee in right paths. When thou goest, thy steps shall not be straitened; and when thou runnest, thou shalt not stumble.'*"

"And the right path was here to Porthlowen." Caroline cradled the baby close. "I'll have another mattress and that drawer brought to my rooms. I don't think Gil will let his baby sister out of his sight again."

"It appears we have excellent solutions for the children," Raymond said. "Don't you agree, Susanna?"

"So our solution is divide and conquer?" asked Susanna, only half jesting.

Elisabeth drew Toby with her toward the door. "Let's give the children a chance to get to know us, and then we shall see how we can convince these two boys to get along better."

"Thank you," Susanna said. The two words could not convey the depth of her gratitude. She needed help to bring the house back to its usual serenity, and she was glad she did not have to ask Captain Nesbitt for it.

Where had *that* thought come from? There were

many servants as well as her other brother to assist her with the children. Not that her older brother Arthur would volunteer as Raymond had. As the heir, Arthur seldom concerned himself with household issues, leaving, as their father did, such matters to Susanna. Even so, she had plenty of hands to assist her.

So why had Captain Nesbitt popped into her mind? Had it been Caroline's comments about him watching her? Those comments had sent a round of warm shivers rippling along her exactly as when the captain smiled at her. No, it was more likely because her neatly ordered existence had collapsed, and he was part of the reason. The best way to banish thoughts of him from invading her head was to end the tumult in the house.

She would start now. Thanking her sister and brother again, she led the twins and Bertie back to the mattresses and tucked them in. One small step, but it was in the right direction.

"Captain?"

Drake shook himself like a dog coming out of the water. Benton's voice had the impatient sound of a man who was tired of being ignored. Looking toward where his first mate stood by the main hatch and wondering how many times Benton had called, he walked away from the railing. He had been watching the crew sealing the outside of yet another small hole…until his thoughts drifted ashore and up to the grand house.

He forgot about the children's plight and Lady Susanna's dazzling eyes when he saw Benton's grim expression. "What is the bad news? More holes?"

"We did discover a few more in the starboard hull. Captain, we would be done much sooner if you didn't keep sending men off to ask questions about the children."

"A few days will make no difference." He saw disbelief on Benton's face and was not surprised. Three days ago, before he had spotted the jolly boat, Drake had been as impatient as a wind-filled sail to get under way. "And they are keeping their ears open for anyone who needs cargo moved. We need to have something in the holds before we sail."

"We could go to Padstow or around Land's End to Penzance and Truro. We would find cargo there."

"As well as the men whose cargo was ruined by the attack. I would like to have enough money to pay them for the lost goods before I encounter them."

Benton chewed on that, then nodded. "I understand, Captain. Our reputation and *The Kestrel*'s are at stake."

Drake was pleased. Even a year ago, Benton would not have comprehended the tough decisions a captain had to make. The young first mate would soon be ready to take over his own ship. Drake would miss Benton's willingness to tackle any job and his good rapport with the men.

Clapping his mate on the back, he said, "Let's get to work."

"Aye, Captain." He hurried to the hatch and down to the lower decks.

Drake started to follow, but again his gaze focused on the grand house beyond the village. He looked away. There was nothing there for him, but he could not keep from wondering how Lady Susanna and the children fared now that a few days had passed.

Less than two hours later, his curiosity overmastered his good judgment. He was admitted to the great house as soon as he reached its door, and a footman offered to take him to where he could speak with Lady Susanna. The footman led the way up one grand staircase and then along a long hallway decorated with paintings of people who must be Lady Susanna's ancestors. He could not imagine being surrounded by so much history of generations past. After all, he had known neither his father nor his mother, for they had abandoned him in a neighbor's care soon after his birth. He had found his first true family when he signed on a trading ship as cabin boy.

"This way, Captain Nesbitt," said the footman in his light gray livery that did not have a single piece of lint on it. He began up a narrow stairwell.

Drake followed, uncertain where they were bound. He had been in great houses once or twice, but never beyond the public rooms, so he had no idea what to expect when they reached the top of the steps.

It was as if they had entered a different house. An odor of dampness and neglect filled each breath he took. No thick carpets covered the wide floorboards that needed to be restained. The walls were bare, though he could see the shadowed outlines where pictures had hung between doors. They were closely spaced, so the rooms beyond them must be not much bigger than his quarters on *The Kestrel*. A few tables were pushed against the walls. All were either scratched or chipped.

As they left the double row of doors behind and walked along a blank wall where paint peeled off in long strips, voices emerged from a doorway at the far end of the hallway.

A man said, "The first thing we need is a good nursery staff."

"No," replied a female voice. "I believe you are mistaken on this."

Even if Drake had not recognized the melodious tone, he could identify Lady Susanna by her poised, self-assured words.

"The first things we need," she went on, "are uncracked windows and fresh paint on the walls. I doubt if anyone has been up here since the nursery was closed."

"Making all those repairs will take time and money. I doubt we can get the windows replaced in less than a month or more. By that time, the children will be back with their families."

"I hope you are right." A hint of humor warmed her voice. "In that case, you can see it as early preparations for your heir, Arthur."

The footman stepped into the doorway and announced, "My lord, my lady, excuse my intrusion. Captain Nesbitt is here and wishes to speak with you, my lady."

"Tell him," Lady Susanna said, "that I will be with him shortly. Thank you, Venton. Arthur, I am sure we can complete the nursery quickly if we put our minds to it."

"My lady, Captain Nesbitt—"

"I heard you, Venton. That will be all."

The footman cleared his throat and said, "My lady, Captain Nesbitt is *here*."

Drake stepped forward. He scanned the room. It was in as bad repair as the corridor, but shelves still contained carefully packed boxes that might contain toys or clothing or even books. He struggled to imagine how anyone could leave books in a damp room. He owned one book, a well-read copy of *Robinson Crusoe*, and he kept it carefully wrapped in oilcloth in his quarters.

"So I see," said the man who had been conversing with Lady Susanna. He had her ebony hair and high cheekbones. He affixed Drake with an icy stare.

Drake met it steadily. He might not be the heir to

an earldom, but he had information of import for Lady Susanna.

His supposition was confirmed when she said, "Arthur, allow me to introduce you to Captain Nesbitt. Captain, this is my older brother, Lord Trelawney."

Even though he hated to be the first one to look away, Drake could not halt his gaze from shifting to Lady Susanna. He realized he had been avoiding looking in her direction. Rightly so, because a single glance at her stole his breath away.

She was dressed in a simple pale blue gown that was covered by a gray apron. Her hair was piled up carelessly on her head. A few strands had escaped to curve along her left cheek, and he had to clench his hands at his sides to keep from reaching out to brush those tresses back along her face. A streak of dust shadowed her right eye.

"My lord," he said, offering his hand.

Lord Trelawney seemed astonished, but shook Drake's hand. "I will leave you to make plans for the children."

"Arthur, we need to discuss further repairs to the nursery." Lady Susanna frowned.

"I will study the list in the morning. As for now, if you need anything, Venton will be here to assist you."

Drake understood Lord Trelawney's true message to his servant. The footman would make sure that nothing untoward happened. The urge to laugh tickled the back of Drake's throat. Lady Susanna hardly needed a chaperone. She could freeze a man in place with a single look.

As soon as Lord Trelawney took his leave, Venton moved to stand just inside the doorway. The spot gave him a clear view of the main room and a smaller one beyond it.

"I thought you had taken your leave of Porthlowen," Lady Susanna said.

"When I did not return?"

"Yes."

He shook his head. "Unfortunately, there is still more work to be done on *The Kestrel*. And, if you remember, I told you that as long as I am in Porthlowen, I would do what I could to help the children. How are they?"

Her shoulders eased from their rigid stance, and an honest smile brightened her face. "Better than I dared to hope. The twins and Bertie have become inseparable. They are fun and funny. My sister is caring for Gil and the baby she's named Joy, because she is such a happy child."

"And Toby? Are he and Bertie still quarreling with each other?"

"Toby lives with my brother at the parsonage. We thought giving the boys some time apart would be wise. From what Raymond tells us, Toby has charmed most of the older ladies in the parish, especially Hyacinth and Ivy Winwood, who have made plenty of excuses to call at the parsonage." She hesitated, kneading her fingers together, then asked, "Have you come because you have news about the search for the children's families?"

He nodded, and color washed from her face. Was she fearing that he had found the children's parents or that he had not? True affection had been laced through her words as she spoke of them.

The spot beneath her eye looked even darker, and he frowned as he caught her chin gently and tilted her face toward the light streaming in through the cracked window. He ignored the growled warning from Venton. He drew in a sharp breath of his own when he saw the puffiness beneath the darkness near her eye. It was not dirt. It was a bruise. She had been struck.

"Who darkened your daylight, my lady? Tell me the cur's name, and I will make him regret being so discourteous to you."

She drew away and laughed, wincing when her eyes crinkled in amusement. "I appreciate your chivalry, but Miss Mollie gave me this black eye."

"One of the twins? But how…?"

"We were playing, and she flung her head back. I did not move swiftly enough. You see the result."

"Maybe I should invite her to join my crew. She could come in handy if French privateers try to board us again." He glanced over his shoulder at Venton, who was listening with sudden interest. Hadn't the tale of *The Kestrel*'s battle been told and retold throughout Porthlowen? Apparently the footman had not heard of it before or wanted more details.

"What have you discovered about the children, Captain?" Lady Susanna asked.

"I sent men along the shore as far north as Trevana and as far south as Land's End. No one they spoke to had heard that six children were missing. Or at least nobody would admit they had."

She gave a terse laugh. "Captain, even if the children's parents refused to step forward and own up to what they have done, others would notice children had gone missing. A single child might be hidden from neighbors until it was placed in the boat, but not six."

"Then we will continue looking. I can send men across the moors to Penzance and Truro. Even as far as Looe, if necessary."

She walked toward the shelves, her skirts whirling dust behind her. Running her fingers along the shelves, she wrinkled her nose when she looked at the dust on them. She slapped her hands together to clean them. The sound echoed in the empty room as she faced him.

"Maybe we are looking in the wrong place," she said.

"It is unlikely they came from beyond Cornwall. Devon or Wales is a great distance for a jolly boat to travel."

"But not a ship."

He was puzzled. Usually his mind could keep up with any conversation. It might be that he was paying too much attention to the sway of her skirts as she walked toward him.

"A ship, Captain Nesbitt," she said. "A ship can easily sail from Devon or Wales or even much farther away, as you know."

"You need not instruct me about sailing, my lady, but I would appreciate if you could enlighten me about what exactly you are talking about."

Her cheeks went from pale to flushed in a heartbeat. Her voice became as glacial as her brother's. "Let me put it simply. French privateers attacked *The Kestrel.* You halted them, Captain, but maybe another ship was not so fortunate."

What she was trying to tell him shot like a ball through his brain. Why had he failed to see that possibility himself? He had told her, after all, that they could not discount any theory until they were certain it would not lead to the children's families.

"I will have my men make inquiries about missing ships as well as missing children," he said.

"Good." She started to walk away again, and he knew he had been dismissed.

He did not move. "My lady?"

"Yes?" She kept walking.

"I hope your idea is wrong."

She stopped but did not turn. "Why?"

"Because if it is correct…"

She spun to look at him with horrified eyes. "Please tell me that you are not about to suggest that their own parents put them in the boat."

"No, because that is not how privateers work. They want the cargo and the ship. Once they board, the ship's crew and passengers are doomed." He closed the distance between them until she had to tilt her head back to look up at him. Raising his hand, he slipped the loose hair back behind her ear. He heard her breath catch, and his heart quickened like a ship driven by a gale.

It took all his willpower to ignore both her reaction and his own. His life was already too enmeshed with the events and people of Porthlowen, and he would be gone soon. But he could not leave without warning her of a truth he doubted she could imagine.

Wiping a bit of fluffy dust from her cheek, he held her gaze as he whispered, "If you are right, no ship and no port, including Porthlowen, may be safe."

He was shocked when she pulled back with the calm smile that was beginning to annoy him. He knew that expression was aimed at covering up her true emotions because her fingers trembled. Because he had touched her or because of what he had told her?

As if she spoke of nothing more important than the color of the water in the cove, she said, "We have never been assured of safety in Porthlowen. Before the French, there were other pirates and raiders, as well as storms and droughts and sickness."

"Very well. It seems you understand. Therefore, I will bid you a good evening, Lady Susanna."

"Good evening, Captain." She relented from her icy

pose as she added, "I truly appreciate you bringing me the information your men have gathered. We are grateful for your continuing efforts."

"*I* helped rescue those children. I would be cold-hearted not to be concerned about their well-being."

She nodded, and he wondered if she ever lost control of her tight hold on herself. Even when she had gasped at his touch on her cheek, she'd quickly reverted to her cool exterior.

Drake got his answer when her name was shouted from the hallway, and a maid burst into the nursery. The young woman's eyes were wide with dismay as she cried, "My lady! It is Miss Lucy! She tumbled down the stairs and landed on her head. We cannot wake her."

Alarm wiped all other emotion from Lady Susanna's face as she pushed past him. He caught her arm, and she whipped around, fury now mixed with fear.

"Let me go!" she ordered.

"I will, but I am going with you so *you* don't fall down the steps in your haste to get to her."

She nodded. "Hurry! I need to be there when she regains her senses."

He steered her out of the room past the maid and the footman, who exchanged worried glances. He knew their thoughts as surely as if they were his own.

What if the tiny girl never woke?

Chapter Four

The bedchamber was lit by only a single lamp, leaving shadows across the ceiling and huddled in the corners. At both windows, the draperies were pulled closed, even though night had claimed Porthlowen. Silence hung over the room, too heavy to be broken. The only sound was breathing from the grand tester bed set at one end of the large room. With the bed curtains pulled aside, a single person was cushioned by the thick mattress and pillows that were almost as big as she was.

Susanna sat beside the bed on a hard chair. Baricoat, as well as Venton and two other footmen, had offered to bring her an upholstered chair from another room. She had thanked them but declined. As hours passed and dawn neared, she feared a more comfortable chair would tempt her to give in to the cloying caress of exhaustion. Her back ached from slanting forward to lean her elbows on the covers, but she did not take her gaze from Lucy's motionless body.

With her hands clasped, she had prayed the same wordless prayer since Captain Nesbitt had carried Lucy in and placed the little girl on the bed. Lucy had looked like a rag doll, limp and unresponsive. Surely God, who had watched over the children while in the jolly boat, would bring Lucy healing.

Through the night, while Susanna kept vigil by the bed, she had looked for any sign of returning consciousness. Lucy breathed slowly and shallowly as if asleep.

The doctor had been sent for immediately, and when Mr. Hockbridge came, Susanna watched him examine the little girl with gentle, capable hands. Mr. Hockbridge had taken over caring for the sick around Porthlowen the previous year. His father had been their longtime doctor, but a heart condition had forced him to step aside. The young man, whose white-blond hair was thinning, had studied in London. If there was anyone in Cornwall who could help Lucy, it would be Mr. Hockbridge.

He had left no powders other than willow bark to ease any pain Lucy felt when she awoke. His only instructions were to pray. Telling Susanna he would be back before midday and that she should send for him if the situation changed, he had bidden her a good night.

Caroline had stopped in several times. The first time, she mentioned how distraught Mollie was. Lucy's twin had seen her sister tumble down the stairs. It had been Mollie's cries that brought the servants running to discover what had happened.

Each time, Susanna had nothing new to tell her sister. Caroline promised to stop by again in a few hours and then went to offer what comfort she could to Mollie and the other children.

So the hours passed while Susanna sat by the bed and prayed for Lucy to open her eyes. She never shifted her gaze from the tiny form on the big bed.

When she heard soft footsteps in the gray light before dawn, Susanna paid them no mind. People had been coming in and out of the bedchamber during the night. They had cast worried glances at the bed before leaving without a word.

"Lady Susanna," came Mrs. Hitchens's low whisper, "forgive me for interrupting, but Captain Nesbitt wishes to know if there has been any change."

Astonished, she glanced over her shoulder. "He has come back?"

"He never left, my lady."

Unexpected tears filled her eyes. She had assumed that Captain Nesbitt had returned to his ship once he set Lucy on the bed as carefully as if she were made of glass. That he had remained touched her heart that was so fragile when she faced another tragedy. Maybe she had misjudged him, if he put aside his other duties to wait for news about a child he barely knew.

"May I give him a message, my lady?" Mrs. Hitchens prompted.

Susanna came to her feet, wincing as her back protested moving after being in one position for hours. "No, I will deliver it myself. Where is he?"

"In the drawing room."

"Thank you."

"My lady?" The housekeeper glanced toward the bed.

"No change." She smiled sadly at Mrs. Hitchens, whose kind heart must be aching, too.

"Poor lamb. I will sit with her until you return."

"If—"

"If there is any change at all, I will send for you immediately."

Thanking the housekeeper again, Susanna went downstairs. The drawing room was to the right of the entry foyer, set past the stairs so the windows offered a beautiful view of the gardens on the hillsides rising toward the moor.

The room was nearly as dark as the bedchamber. She saw no one inside. Had Captain Nesbitt taken his leave or perhaps fallen asleep? That made no sense, because Mrs. Hitchens would not have dawdled bringing his message. She stifled a yawn and knew it would take her only seconds to surrender to sleep.

Going back into the hallway, she picked up a lamp and returned to the drawing room. The light spread before her, restoring color in the Aubusson rug. The red lines edging a pattern of white roses seemed overly bright. Out of the darkness appeared two chairs upholstered in red-and-white silk, followed by a matching settee. The elegant white marble hearth glittered in the lamplight.

The room was deserted.

She was about to call Captain Nesbitt's name when she noticed the French window leading onto the terrace was ajar. Crossing the room, she set her lamp on a table. She opened the door wider and saw Captain Nesbitt leaning his hands on the back of a stone bench. There, he could see the village, the cliffs that curved toward each other in a giant C to protect the cove, and the sea.

"This is my favorite view," she said as she walked out onto the stone terrace.

"I can see why your ancestors built this house here." Slowly he faced her. "How is Lucy?"

"There is no change. If I did not know better, I would say she is sleeping. She looks so peaceful."

"What did the doctor say?"

She sighed. "He said the only things we can do now are wait and pray."

"Not the prescription I had hoped he would give."

"Prayer is always the best prescription, Captain."

He leaned against the bench and folded his arms over his chest. His strong jaw was covered in a low mat of black whiskers that only emphasized its stubborn lines. "I cannot disagree with that, but I have found the results are not always something you can count on."

"You don't believe in God?"

"Quite the opposite. I believe in Him. I simply don't know if He believes in me."

She stared at him. The night was receding as the sun rose over the eastern hills, but his eyes still were dark pools that she could not read. "I believe that He hears our prayers, especially the ones from our hearts, and I have been praying all night."

"If prayer is the answer, it should come soon with the number of people praying for her. I have heard murmured prayers from every direction while I paced through the house."

"And you, Captain? Have you been praying?" Again she wished she could read the expression hidden in his shadowed eyes.

"Yes, but I hope others have better luck than I in getting their prayers answered."

"All prayers are answered."

"You sound so sure."

"I am."

He turned his head to stare out at the sea. "I wish I could be."

"All you need to do is have faith."

"You make it sound so simple." His terse laugh was laced with regret. "I have not found it to be."

"Surely you have felt God's presence in your life. What about when you were attacked by those privateers?"

"I thought *The Kestrel* and all its crew were bound for the bottom of the sea." He smiled as she started to reply. "I know what you are going to say. That by the grace of God we survived, and you may be right, but in the middle of that battle, there was nothing but death and dying."

Susanna pressed her hands to her abruptly roiling stomach, wishing she had never brought up the privateers. She did not want to think of death. She wanted to concentrate on life and how they could bring one small child out of a coma to embrace it.

A sob burst out of her before she could halt it. Putting her hands over her face, she wept, too tired to hold back her tears any longer. Her fear of not knowing what else she could do to help little Lucy pressed down on her.

Wide, gentle hands drew her against a wool coat that smelled of salt and fresh air off the water. Beneath the wool, a strong chest held a heart that beat steadily as she gripped his coat and released her fear and frustration.

When her last tears were gone, Susanna drew back and wiped her hand against her face. Captain Nesbitt held out a handkerchief. She hesitated and then took it, as embarrassment overwhelmed her. She had lost control of her emotions in front of this handsome man. How could she ever look at him again without thinking of his muscular arms around her, offering her comfort?

"I am sorry," she whispered, staring at her feet. "I usually hold myself together better than that."

"You have nothing to be ashamed of."

"That is kind of you to say."

He lifted his handkerchief out of her hand and dabbed it against her cheeks to catch a pair of vagrant tears. Bending so his eyes were level with hers, he said nothing. Now the shadows had been banished, she could see the emotions within his dark brown eyes. Raw, un-abashed sorrow at the accident that had left Lucy sense-less. He must be able to see the same in her own eyes, she realized, and she lowered them, not wanting to share such a private part of herself with a man who was barely more than a stranger.

She was unsure when the light touch of the hand-kerchief collecting her tears altered to slow, feathery strokes along her face. Quivers flitted along her like seabirds darting at the waves. In spite of herself, she raised her eyes to his again. The potent emotions in them had only grown stronger, and she wondered how long anyone could look into his eyes without becom-ing lost in them.

"My lady! Lady Susanna!" called a bellow from the house.

Susanna stepped away from Captain Nesbitt, one unsteady step and then another, as if waking from a dream. Had she fallen asleep on her feet? She would rather think that than believe she had intentionally stood so close to him, allowing him to caress her face with his handkerchief.

He placed his handkerchief beneath his coat as her name was shouted again.

"You might want to answer," he said in an emotion-less tone.

She wished her voice could be as calm, but it was not when she called that she was on the terrace.

Venton peered past the French windows. His eyes narrowed slightly when he saw she was not alone, but he said, "My lady! Come! Right away!"

"Is it Lucy?"

"She is waking up."

Gathering up her skirts, she ran into the house. She

heard Captain Nesbitt's boots behind her. She did not look back as she ran up the stairs.

In the bedroom, the draperies had been thrown open. Sunlight washed across the bed. For a moment, when she saw Lucy lying in the pillows, Susanna feared the child had lost consciousness again.

She rushed to the bed at a soft cry, but Captain Nesbitt reached it before her. He stepped aside only far enough for her to slip between him and the covers. His breath brushed her nape. She ignored the pleasant shiver that rushed along her and gazed down at Lucy.

The little girl's eyes were closed, but she was moving her head from side to side as if caught in a nightmare.

Dearest God, help her to awaken. She is only a baby, and she has endured so much already. Help me to know what is best for her.

"Should we wake her?" asked Captain Nesbitt from behind her.

"Mr. Hockbridge said we must be patient and let her come to her senses on her own."

"Mama!" came an anguished cry from the bed as tears ran along the child's face.

"Oh, dear!" Susanna wished she could throw all Lucy's pain out the window. When Captain Nesbitt stretched an arm around her to offer his handkerchief again, she murmured her thanks. She wiped Lucy's tears away as she asked Mrs. Hitchens to wet another cloth. The housekeeper quickly complied.

Susanna dropped the handkerchief and took the damp cloth. She draped it across Lucy's forehead, including the large bump that was a deep black. The lines in her brow eased slightly, so the warmth must be comforting.

Lucy's eyelashes fluttered, then lifted off her pale

cheeks. Susanna smiled when Lucy looked up at her, confusion on her little face.

"How do you feel, Lucy?" Susanna asked.

"Head ouch," she croaked.

"I know, sweetheart." She looked up as Mrs. Hitchens came forward with a cup of warm water.

Slipping an arm under the child, Susanna held the cup to Lucy's lips. She was thrilled when Lucy gulped it eagerly. Not wanting to give her too much too quickly, she drew the cup away, but Lucy's tiny hands grasped the cup.

"Slowly," Susanna cautioned. "There is plenty."

Lucy nodded, then gave a soft cry.

Susanna asked Mrs. Hitchens to bring the pain powder the doctor had left. Since it was willow bark, a small dose would be safe even for a child as young as Lucy.

When another cup was held out to her, this one with the powder dissolved into the water, turning it cloudy, Susanna took it. The second her fingers closed around the cup and brushed against the hand offering it to her, a buzz like a swarm of bees swept through her.

She looked up. Captain Nesbitt's worry threaded his forehead. She whispered her thanks, not wanting to talk more loudly because she did not trust her voice. Or her fingers that yearned to smooth those lines from his face.

Lucy wrinkled her nose when she drank from the second cup, but finished it when Susanna assured her that it would make her feel better. Mrs. Hitchens took the cup, stepping back while Susanna settled the little girl down into the pillowed nest again.

The child looked from her to the housekeeper and then to Captain Nesbitt. Her eyes widened, and she mewed in pain.

"Why don't you close your eyes?" Susanna tucked

the covers in around her. "Resting will give the powder time to work."

"I think the sun is bothering her." Captain Nesbitt strode around the bed, grasped the draperies on the nearest window and yanked them closed. Fabric creaked a warning, but the stream of light disappeared from across the bed. Turning, he walked back to the far side of the bed and asked, "Is that better, Lucy?"

"Papa?"

Susanna pressed her hand over her mouth to keep from chuckling when Captain Nesbitt's expression suggested the little girl had accused him of a crime.

"No, Lucy," she said softly. When the little girl looked at her again, she added, "He is not your papa. He is Captain Nesbitt."

"Cap?"

"Yes," Captain Nesbitt said before Susanna could reply. "I am Cap."

Lucy stretched up a small hand, and he bent forward. When she patted his bewhiskered chin and smiled, Susanna's eyes were not the only moist ones in the room. The little girl's motions were easy and showed no sign of the trauma she had suffered.

Susanna looked away before the child could notice her tears. After her weeping on the terrace, she had not guessed she could cry more. Maybe she had used up her sad tears but still had happy ones.

Hearing Captain Nesbitt's low, rumbling laugh, a sound she had never heard before, she wanted to hear it again and again. It invited everyone to join in. She had thought his laugh would be as clipped as his words; then she wondered how she could make any assumptions when she knew so little about him. This was not like the time she had started noticing interesting aspects of Franklin, because she had known her erstwhile betrothed since they were Lucy's age.

Don't think of that, she chided herself. She would not let Franklin and his betrayal into her life again.

No matter what.

He will be in your heart, reminding you of the pain you suffered, until you forgive—really forgive—him and Norah. She clenched her hands by her sides. *I have tried.* Even her own silent protest sounded weak. She knew that trying was not enough.

Susanna looked at the bed, where Lucy held up Captain Nesbitt's handkerchief and waved it like a flag. When it fluttered against his mouth, he blew it away, making Lucy smile. He showed a patience with the little girl that Susanna had not expected.

Again she scolded herself. She knew nothing of Captain Nesbitt other than he had fought off the French and ended up with his ship and crew in Porthlowen Harbor. No, that was not quite true. She had seen he was a man of deep compassion and deep anger. He had a strong sense of duty and just as powerful a sense of honor. Yet, he did not mind being silly if it made an injured child feel better.

She needed to acknowledge that Captain Nesbitt might continue to be a surprise, but he and his ship would soon be gone from Porthlowen. Her life would settle back into its routine again.

A tiny hand patted her fingers on the covers as Lucy asked, "Mama?"

Now it was Susanna's turn to be shocked. Somehow she choked out, "No, my dear Lucy."

"Yes. Mama!" A surprisingly stubborn scowl settled on the child's face. The motion must have hurt because she whimpered.

Susanna realized the futility of arguing with her now.
What did it matter how Lucy addressed her? Once the
pain was gone, Lucy would be herself again.

"Captain Nesbitt," she said, "I am sure Lucy would
love to hear about how you fill your ship with all sorts
of things."

Now she had surprised him. He gave her a peculiar
look that was halfway between a frown and bafflement.
When she hooked her thumb toward the door, he nodded and began to spin a tale for the child that had more
to do with dolphins and mermaids than the grain his
ship carried when it limped into the cove.

Susanna hurried to the door with Mrs. Hitchens fol-
lowing. She asked the housekeeper to have a maid fetch
Mollie. As close as the twins were, she guessed Lucy
would be thrilled to see her sister. And, according to
Caroline, Mollie had been asking for her sister all night.
Reuniting the twins would be good for both of them.

Drake brought his absurd story to a close when a
maid holding Mollie's hand arrived at the bedchamber
door. He watched as Lucy turned her head to see what
was happening.

She looked back at him and said, "More fish. Cap,
more fish."

"No more fish tales right now," he said, smiling when
she began to pout. "There is someone here who wants
to see you."

"Mama!" she called and held out her arms to Lady
Susanna.

"Mama?" repeated Mollie, looking around eagerly.
Her curls bounced on her shoulders. "Where?"

"There." Lucy sat and pointed to Lady Susanna.

He was not sure who looked more stricken. Lady Susanna or Mollie. He fought the temptation to pull them both into his arms so he did not have to see the dismay on their faces. Hadn't he learned anything from the mistake he had made on the terrace? Seeing a woman cry undid him completely, no matter her age.

No one spoke until Lady Susanna lifted Mollie and brought her to the bed. In a falsely cheerful voice, she said, "Lucy, Mollie wants to see you now that you are awake. She has been very worried about you."

"Who?" asked Lucy. "Why?"

"She is worried about you because you fell down." He did not explain how horrifying it had been to discover her at the base of the long staircase. "Why don't you give Mollie a hug?"

Lucy gave him a puzzled frown. "Who?"

"Mollie." Lady Susanna's smile began to waver.

"Who?"

Drake cleared his throat, halting Susanna's answer. When she glanced at him, he said, "I think she wants to know who Mollie is."

"Don't be silly."

He looked at Lucy, then paused when Mrs. Hitchens came in with a steaming bowl of what smelled like chicken broth. He ignored how his stomach rumbled and that he had not had anything to eat in almost a full day. Instead, he came around the bed, and taking Lady Susanna's elbow, he drew her and Mollie aside so Mrs. Hitchens could spoon the broth into Lucy's mouth.

Before Lady Susanna could say anything, he steered her and Mollie out into the hallway. He called to a nearby maid, who was carrying an armful of clean bedding, to take Mollie back to wherever the other children were. He could see Lady Susanna was amazed that he would give orders in her father's house, but as he had with his growling stomach, he paid her astonishment no mind.

"What we need to discuss," he said without preamble, "is not for Mollie's ears."

Lady Susanna sighed. "That is true. She is even more upset now that her sister is so confused."

"She is not just confused. She has no idea what you are talking about."

"Don't be silly."

He frowned at her as if she were no older than the twins. "One thing you need to know about me. I am never silly, Lady Susanna. Most definitely, I am not being silly about this. One look at Lucy's face, and you can see that she truly has no idea that she has a twin sister."

"She did strike her head hard when she tumbled down the stairs. Do you think the fall damaged her brain?"

"She can move, and she can talk as she could before. It may only be her memory that is injured."

"But if she cannot remember her own sister—"

"And she believes you are her mother."

She shuddered, wrapped her arms around herself and glanced at the bedchamber. "She was very insistent about that. I wonder why."

"Because a child needs a mother." He bit back the rest of what he had almost said. Lady Susanna had been reared in a loving home, and she could not conceive of a childhood without a loving family.

"Especially when she does not feel well."

"But Lucy does not *need* a sibling to have the security of knowing someone is watching over her. It appears she has forgotten everything she knew before she fell down the stairs."

Her eyes and mouth grew round before she stuttered, "E-e-every-th-thing?"

"At least her family, which is just about everything a child that age knows." He put his hands on her shoulders and tightened his hold slightly when she would have pulled away. "I think it is better you do not disabuse her of her illusions."

"You want me to pretend to be her mother?"

"Haven't you been?"

She flinched beneath his palms, and he wondered why the simple question had bothered her. He admired how the Trelawneys had taken the castaways into their home and their hearts. They could have turned over responsibility of the children's care to their servants or even to the villagers. Instead, they had treated the children like long-lost family.

Not waiting for her reply, he said, "I am getting the doctor. Maybe he can tell us something."

"Something to help Lucy?"

"To help all of us."

Chapter Five

Stepping out of the Trelawney carriage in front of a simple stone cottage, Drake was about to open the gate in the low stone wall when he heard someone call his name. He was surprised to see a young woman running toward him, waving her hands wildly to get his attention. She looked to be barely more than sixteen. Her dark hair had been pushed haphazardly back under a cap, and her feet were bare.

"Captain Nesbitt!" she shouted again.

"Good morning." The words tasted like bilgewater on the lowest deck of *The Kestrel*. He should be thankful that Lucy had regained her senses—and he was—but her faulty memory was troubling.

The girl came to a stop beside him. "Is it true? Did one of the children fall at Cothaire and die?"

He gave her what he hoped was a calming smile. "Lucy fell, but she is going to be fine." He refused to let doubt slip into his voice, not wanting to upset the girl more.

"But you are here at Mr. Hockbridge's house. If Lucy is fine, then why are you here?"

Instead of answering, he asked a question of his own. "You are…?"

"I am Peggy Smith." She bounced in a quick curtsy.

"The lass who has worked for Miss Rowse in her shop?"

She nodded so hard he feared he would hear her teeth rattle. "Yes."

"Have you always lived in Porthlowen village, Miss Smith?"

At his respectful tone, she flushed, then dimpled. "No, Captain. I am from a fishing village west of here, but when I heard of the opportunity for a job, I came to see if Miss Rowse would hire me. Who would have guessed in my first month here that something would happen as exciting as a boatload of children washing ashore? Now—" Her voice broke and she raised her apron to cover her face.

He peeled the linen back enough so he could see her eyes. "Miss Smith, Lucy is awake, and I was sent to get Mr. Hockbridge to look her over."

"Thank you, Captain!" She whirled away, racing back in the direction of the village shop.

Drake watched her for a moment, then, shaking his head, opened the gate. His knock roused Hockbridge from bed, because the doctor had been up late last night when a fisherman sliced his hand while repairing nets. It had taken some time to get the bleeding under control. When Drake began to apologize for waking him, the doctor halted him with an ironic comment about how such hours were the lot of anyone foolish enough to practice medicine.

Drake liked the doctor immediately, especially because Hockbridge was as eager to return to Cothaire.

Within minutes, they were heading toward the great house.

He quizzed the doctor about what might be wrong with Lucy and what to expect now that she had regained her senses. The doctor answered each question calmly but did not offer any false reassurances.

Cothaire was almost as silent as the grave when he and Hockbridge were ushered into the entry hall. The servants tiptoed past and spoke in wispy whispers. No work was being done that might disturb Lucy. He did not realize how much he had hoped Lucy would be back to normal by the time he returned with Hockbridge, but obviously little had changed. Even Baricoat, when he came to escort them upstairs himself without a word of greeting. Instead, the butler nodded in their direction and began toward the stairs, confident that they would follow.

As soon as the butler opened the door, Lucy called from the bed, "Cap!"

He was surprised to see Mollie sitting on the bed. Her puzzled expression matched what he felt when Lucy pointed to him and repeated the name as if her twin had never met him before.

Lady Susanna glided silently across the floor to stand beside him while Mr. Hockbridge walked to the bed, smiling at both girls as if he were there for a social call.

"Mollie refused to stay with the other children," Lady Susanna said softly. "I agreed that she could come here as long as she was quiet so she did not aggravate her sister's headache. As well, seeing Mollie may help Lucy remember."

"What has Mollie said?" asked the doctor.

"Very little. I think she is accustomed to Lucy taking the lead. At least, it has been that way since they arrived here. Now…" She wrapped her arms around herself as she had in the hall.

"Did I hear good news?" asked Lady Caroline as she came into the room holding the baby and with Gil clutching her skirt. "Good morning, Lucy! We are so happy to see you are awake and smiling."

Seeing Lucy's bewilderment, Drake said, "Lady Caroline, Mr. Hockbridge is here to check Lucy. Let's talk in the hallway."

The lady glanced at her sister, and Lady Susanna motioned for her to go with Drake. Closing the door behind them, he explained how Lucy seemed to have lost her memory of the time before she woke up.

"Oh my!" Lady Caroline rested her forehead against the baby's and murmured a quick prayer for Lucy.

The pose was so loving and intimate that Drake felt as if he had intruded. When she finished her prayer for healing and looked at him, saying, "Amen," he added his own. A pinch of guilt taunted him. Was he saying that to add his prayer to hers or simply because it was the acceptable thing to do?

He submerged the thought and the accompanying guilt. They had had a sleepless night, so he should not be surprised at the peculiar thoughts bombarding his mind.

"How is the earl this morning?" he asked.

Lady Caroline blinked at the abrupt change of subject. "He had a restless night, but his valet assured me that he is resting now. Probably not resting comfortably, though he can forget about the pain when he sleeps."

"Would laudanum help?"

"Certainly, but he refuses to take it. He saw how it helped my mother slip away when she was ill and vowed never to take it."

"He sounds much like your sister."

A faint smile warmed her face. "They are much the same. You are an excellent judge of character, Captain, to have noticed that on such a short acquaintance."

He did not want to say that Lady Susanna had not been far from his thoughts since the moment he first saw her in the smoking room. Nor could he speak of how perfectly she had fit in his arms on the terrace at dawn.

The bedchamber door opened, and Hockbridge followed Lady Susanna into the hallway. The doctor's face was grim, but he said nothing until he had closed the door.

"Will she recover?" Lady Caroline asked before Drake could.

"Her reflexes react as they should," Hockbridge said. "Her eyes follow my finger normally, and she can talk and move as is appropriate for a child her age."

"But?"

Lady Susanna answered, "She cannot remember anything from before she woke, save her own name. And we are not even sure about that. She may have assumed it was her name simply because that is what we called her. Have you noticed she no longer lisps? She speaks quite clearly, but everything and everyone she knew before have vanished from her mind."

As Lady Caroline gasped, Drake said, "I have heard of this before, when a man was struck on the head by a heavy bale. At first, he could not even recall his own name, but, in time, most of his memories returned."

"How much time?" Lady Susanna asked.

"It may be hours or it may be days." The doctor shrugged. "We know so little about how the brain works, so we have no idea how to help."

"There must be something we can do."

Drake heard desperation in her plea. He had already seen that Lady Susanna liked to have everything under control. Now she had been handed the most unlikely of circumstances: an abandoned child who could not even remember her own sister.

"What about familiar things?" he asked. "Would they help her regain her memories?"

The doctor nodded thoughtfully. "Sometimes familiar faces and familiar sights can persuade the mind to find memories that have been lost."

"But nothing here is familiar to her!" Lady Susanna flushed and added in a calmer tone, "Without some idea of where the children lived before they were found, how can we show her anything she would have seen before she was injured?"

Hockbridge looked bewildered, his mouth opening and closing like a fish washed up on the shore.

Drake waited for him to say something, then, when the doctor remained silent, shared what he saw as the obvious solution. "You must help her see as many different items and people and places as possible."

"Yes," Lady Susanna said with a warm smile, "and with God's guidance, may we find a way to help her recall everything she has forgotten." With a laugh, she turned to him and said, "That was a brilliant suggestion, Captain Nesbitt."

When she threw her arms around him and gave him a hug as enthusiastic as her voice, he was shocked. At her action, but not at his reaction to her touch. He already knew that even the brush of her fingers against his arm sent a tingle rippling through him.

No one spoke as she drew back, her face flushed.

"Forgive me," she whispered. "I was so excited that—"

"No need to say anything, my lady."

At his formal address, she flinched. Because he had reminded her of her status or his lack of it? Maybe both.

It was something he could not allow himself to forget. Or let his heart forget, because it would end up hurt as it had before.

Never again.

Susanna was thankful for her family's assistance because someone needed to sit with Lucy, day and night, as the little girl regained her strength and the swelling around her bruises faded. Even Elisabeth was able to get a few hours away from her shop because she had hired Peggy Smith to help at the shop full-time. No doubt, Elisabeth had begun to worry—quite rightly—about how she would take care of the shop and fulfill her obligations as the parson's wife. Elisabeth had worked in the shop alone since her father died three years ago. She never complained about doing the job of two people. She kept the shop open so the villagers did not have to travel over the cliffs and into the neighboring cove to obtain the necessities they could not grow or make themselves.

Susanna understood taking on duties that consumed hours every day. She wished she could say that, like Elisabeth, she had never complained, but that would be false. Every time she saw Elisabeth, Susanna realized how blessed she was that she had her sister and Arthur to help oversee the estate.

But they needed someone to oversee the children in the nursery. Someone with experience and the patience to deal with so many small children. On the days when Raymond or Elisabeth could not watch over Toby, and the little boy returned to Cothaire for a few hours, it was always chaotic. He and Bertie vied to see which one could aggravate the other more, and they ended up setting everyone, adults and children, on edge.

Several inquiries had gone out to families they knew, hoping that someone could recommend a skilled nurse. The few answers apologized for not being able to help. Another batch would have to be sent if they found no one in Cornwall or Devon. Perhaps someone in Somerset or Dorset to the east could assist them.

Susanna tried to keep up with her duties for the household. Mrs. Hitchens had assumed some of them. However, a few, such as menus and arranging for payment to tradesmen, required Susanna's approval. In addition, she would soon be coordinating repairs to the nursery.

Keeping busy prevented her from thinking, and that was good because too many of her thoughts revolved around Captain Nesbitt. How could she have thrown herself at him like a hoyden not once but twice? Caroline had not mentioned her inappropriate actions, which told her that her sister was deeply disturbed by Susanna's lack of restraint. Neither of her brothers nor her father chastised her for her heedless behavior, but she almost wished they would. In the two days since Lucy had awakened without her memories, she had seen her family watching her when they thought she did not notice.

Captain Nesbitt had not returned to Cothaire. Raymond mentioned at dinner that his crew was hard at work doing the final repairs to his ship. Her brother, also, with a great deal of respect in his voice, remarked how Captain Nesbitt worked as long and hard as his crew. He had glanced toward Susanna when he said that, but she had not been able to guess why.

So Susanna kept her days full, sleeping only when she could no longer stay awake. She was one of the first up every morning, and by the time she blew out her lamp, the rest of the house was dark.

Busy, busy, busy.

Lucy was an excellent patient, reveling in all the attention, but about one matter she was adamant. She insisted on calling Susanna "Mama." Susanna admitted, only to herself, that she liked having a child call her that. She had thought often of having children with Franklin, imagining the joy of holding their baby in her arms. That dream had died along with her belief that he loved her.

But none of the children truly belonged to her or her sister or Raymond. Getting attached to them was foolish, but how could she avoid that when Lucy gazed at her with unabashed love? Once Lucy regained her memory, she would know Susanna was not her mother. Perhaps then the little girl might recall something that would lead them to her true mother.

Knowing that she must return to the children as soon as possible so Elisabeth could go back to the shop, Susanna decided to collect some of her father's correspondence and work on replies while Lucy took a nap later this afternoon. Mr. Hockbridge insisted that sleep was the best medicine.

She yawned at the thought, then yawned a second and a third time. Trying to keep her eyes open, she hurried down the stairs and into the entry hall. Papa's correspondence was in the office. Though she could have left such matters to his valet or the estate manager, writing replies would keep her from thinking about—

She hit something hard. Not something, but someone, because her breath and the other person's both came out in a loud *whoof*. A gray cloud surrounded her as if she had beaten a filthy rug.

"Avast there, my lady."

"Captain Nesbitt!" Susanna took a step back. When her gaze met his, an unsettling warmth flooded her face.

Lord, help me understand why I act addled whenever he is nearby. The prayer burst out the way her breath had.

"I did not expect to see you today, Captain," she added.

"At the speed you were going, with your eyes focused on the floor, I doubt you could have seen anyone."

"I am sorry. I did not hurt you, did I?"

He looked down at his chest and patted his brown waistcoat that was flecked with sawdust. "I seem to be none the worst for you trying to plow me over. No dents anywhere."

Susanna laughed. Out loud. Louder than she had in longer than she could remember. For three days, she had fretted about what Captain Nesbitt must think of her. She had planned what she might say the next time she encountered him. All of that had been a waste of time, because she had quite literally run into him and she could not think of a single thing to say that would not sound ridiculous.

A slow, easy grin eased his stern face. "Perhaps it was for the best that your head was down rather than mine. Otherwise, you might have injured yourself by colliding with my hard head."

"If you have come to see Lucy," she said, recalling herself, though she could not stop grinning, "she is upstairs playing with the other children. Now that she is feeling better, she refuses to rest as much as she should."

"Like you, I would guess."

She put her hand up to her cheek. She had hoped

that the gray arcs beneath her eyes would fade as the day passed.

He took her hand and gently lowered it. "You look fine."

"But you said—"

"I drew my conclusion from having learned a little bit about you, Lady Susanna. I know when there are tasks to be done you step forward to do them, and when more tasks arrive in a small boat filled with six small children, you do not hesitate to take on those duties, as well." His smile broadened. "You would make a good ship's captain."

A soft warmth flowed through her, easing the icy cold that had been a part of her for so long that it had come to feel normal. He respected her and not because she was an earl's daughter. He respected her because of what she was trying to accomplish.

Respect. Something she had forgotten how to give herself since she had been embarrassed so publicly.

"Thank you," she said, though she doubted he understood the true reason for her gratitude.

He gently turned her hand over and raised it to his lips. She had been the recipient of such courteous kisses many times, but none of them ever had delighted her as Captain Nesbitt's did. He lowered her hand and released it as if loath to do so.

Susanna understood why when past the open door, she heard many more voices approaching the house. She saw a line of women stretching from the gate almost to the door.

"I had no idea you were the vanguard for a parade," she said.

"Nor did I when I came here to give the earl an update on the progress with repairing *The Kestrel*."

"Have you finished them?"

His mouth hardened along with his eyes. "You would have thought so by now, but…" He stepped away to allow the women to enter the house, but, though each of them smiled, they continued around toward the back of the house and the kitchen.

Curious, Susanna stepped outside. Her eyes widened when Mrs. Thorburn marched past with another woman, both of them complaining about everything from the sunshine to the cost of mutton. Neither of them looked in her direction. Then she saw the Winwood sisters. They were the last ones.

"Miss Hyacinth! Miss Ivy!" She motioned toward the door. "Why don't you come in and sit? It is a long walk from the village."

"It did not seem that way a decade or so ago," Miss Hyacinth said as she paused to let her sister catch up. They both, like the other women, carried wooden pails.

"Much younger legs back then." Miss Ivy motioned with her bucket toward the line of women disappearing around the corner of the house. "But we have come to help, m'lady. We heard that the supplies have arrived so Cothaire's nursery can be made ready for those poor babes."

"Yes, the wood and the new windows were delivered yesterday." Susanna laughed. "I had no idea that we ordered so much. There is barely room for the horses and all the supplies in the stable."

"We wanted to help." Miss Hyacinth held out her bucket. It was filled with rags and thick chunks of soap.

"We will have the walls and windows washed down in no time." Miss Ivy grinned. "Maybe in enough time so we can enjoy a few minutes with the children."

Susanna's smile was so wide her pretty face could barely hold it. "You are so kind, but your own homes—"

"Our own homes can wait. We want to see the precious cargo that came ashore in the harbor," Miss Hyacinth said with a smile.

"Ah, yes. Those wee babes," her sister added before they waved and went to join the other women.

Susanna blinked back tears. "I can hardly believe their generosity. With their own families and housework, they still were eager to come to Cothaire and help make a home for six abandoned children."

"You must own," Captain Nesbitt said from where he stood behind her, "that if the situation were reversed, you would be calling on them to see if there was anything you might do to help."

He did not touch her, but she was aware of him with every particle of her being. All she had to do was lean her head back, and she could rest against his strength. It was so tempting, but she resisted. Unlike Franklin, Captain Nesbitt had never made it a secret how eager he was to leave. Her place was here, woven into the lives within Cothaire's walls and in the village. She must not allow herself to forget that.

No matter what.

"Of course I would help," she said without looking at him. "That is my duty as the daughter of an earl, and I need to get back to those duties straightaway." She added nothing more as she walked off.

Did he watch her go? She refused to let herself turn to discover if he did. When he sailed from Porthlowen, she would be the one left behind. Would he wonder if she watched him go or would he be thinking only of his next adventure upon the waves?

Chapter Six

When Susanna went to relieve Elisabeth, she discovered the children were playing with her sister in the solar, and Elisabeth was already gone. Susanna started to apologize for being delayed, but Caroline waved it aside.

"Mrs. Hitchens told me how the village women have come to help with the nursery," Caroline said as she took the baby from Mrs. Ennis, the wet nurse from the village. Thanking Mrs. Ennis, Caroline put little Joy up to her shoulder to burp her. "Susanna, I can stay with the children if you want to check on the progress they are making in the nursery."

"I will come right back."

"Take all the time you want. The children are playing nicely, and it soon will be time for their naps."

Susanna gave her sister a kiss on the cheek. "I am so happy to see you happy."

"I feel blessed." She laughed when a resounding belch emerged from Joy. "Did I hear that Captain Nesbitt called, too?"

"To see Papa."

"About what?"

Susanna was astonished that she could not answer that simple question. "I don't know exactly. He said he wanted to talk to Papa about his ship, but when I asked if the repairs were completed, he scowled ferociously."

"It could be that he is not as eager as he was before to leave."

"Before he saved the children?"

"Before he met you, little sister." Caroline's eyes twinkled. "I know you have a lot on your mind, but surely you cannot be so busy that you have failed to notice how that man looks at you."

"Half the time, he looks as if he wants to strangle me."

"And the other half, he looks as if he wants to kiss you."

Pretending that her sister's words did not send shivers of anticipation along her—just as Captain Nesbitt's kiss on her hand had—she gave a terse laugh. "I think you are seeing things."

"If you say so, but I am not the only one who thinks that."

"Who else?"

Caroline grinned. "Arthur mentioned something to me when we were talking after dinner a few nights ago."

"Arthur?"

Their brother usually was oblivious to everything but the needs of the estate. He had not, even once, come to see the children. Most nights, he did not join them for the evening meal or for conversation and music and reading aloud after it. Even if he was at the house, he sent his apologies, saying that he had additional tasks to complete.

"If Arthur noticed anything other than reports from

the tenant farms or the gamekeeper, it must be blatant."
Caroline laughed. "Even you cannot deny it, little sister."

"I am not denying it. I am saying you are mistaken.
Captain Nesbitt intends to sail away as soon as his ship
is repaired. Whatever his feelings toward me might be,
I would be foolish to give them even a passing thought."

"That is very logical."

"Thank you."

"I did not mean that as a compliment." Caroline stood
and, carrying the baby, faced Susanna. "I know you
pride yourself on keeping everything around you under
control, but matters of the heart require just the opposite.
Letting go and trusting God's plan for you."

"I don't know what God's plan is, but I know what
Captain Nesbitt's is, and it does not include staying in
Porthlowen to call on me." She groped behind her for
the door and opened it.

"Susanna?"

She halted without looking at her sister. "Yes?"

"Don't be so determined not to be surprised by anything that you miss out on unexpected moments of happiness."

She knew she was being rude when she did not reply
as she went out into the hallway and up the stairs. What
could she say? Her sister should understand why she
acted as she did. Caroline had been a witness to the
mortifying series of events that ended with Susanna losing her betrothed and her best friend in one fell swoop.

Susanna half ran toward the nursery as if she could
leave her own thoughts behind. Maybe she could not,
but she could smother them by keeping busy.

The cheerful voices bursting out of the day nursery
drew her in. She heard more chatter from upstairs. The
Cothaire nursery had rooms on two floors. They were

connected by a staircase that also went down to the
kitchen to make it easier to deliver food to the children.
Both levels were identical, but the lower one was for
playing and lessons. Also, the children would have their
meals in the day nursery. The night nursery upstairs
would have beds for the children. A separate room,
connected by a doorway, was for the nurse.

When she entered the day nursery, it was a busy hive
of women washing down walls and mopping floors.
Greetings were called to her, but the women continued
their work and their conversations.

Mrs. Hitchens walked toward her, wiping her hands
on a cloth. "The nursery rooms will be as clean as a
new pin in no time at all. Once that is done, the men
can come in and fix the stairs and windows. The children can be settled in soon after that. I know those
sweet lambs will appreciate having a place where they
can play without worry that they will hurt themselves
or break something."

"I trust Mrs. Ford has prepared some special food
for our helpers."

"For them to enjoy here and packages to take home
so their families can enjoy the cold roasted chicken supper, as well. They are baking cakes to send with our
volunteers." Mrs. Hitchens smiled. "Isn't it a blessing
how six small children can bring the village together
like this?" She lowered her voice as she added, "Even
Mrs. Thorburn seems to be in an unusually good mood.
She has only complained half the time."

Susanna laughed quietly, not wanting to draw attention to their conversation. For as long as she could
recall, Mrs. Thorburn and Mrs. Hitchens had been at
daggers drawn. She had no idea what had begun the
feud, but other than in church, the two women seldom

were in the same room. Even now, Mrs. Hitchens was in the day nursery and Mrs. Thorburn must be upstairs.

"It appears," Susanna said, "that you have everything under control here, Mrs. Hitchens. With the progress you are making, it would be a good idea to see what furniture is stored in the attic. There may be some pieces we can use. I would like to get the children sleeping in beds rather than on pallets."

"I could have my men rig up some hammocks if there are not enough beds in the attic to go around." A deep laugh halted the women in the midst of their tasks.

She spun to discover Captain Nesbitt stood in the doorway. Her heart pounded so hard she was sure everyone in the abruptly silent room could hear.

Oh my!

Drake had not anticipated his lighthearted comment would make everyone in the room, save for Lady Susanna, freeze. He nodded to the women, then looked at Lady Susanna.

She stared at him for a moment before laughing. "What a jest, Captain!"

"I was quite serious. If the hammocks hang just off the floor, the children can climb in and out by themselves." He walked into the crowded nursery and measured a height off the floor that would be low enough for the younger ones. "Falling out would not be dangerous because they would be inches from the floor. In addition, I would guess that they would find sleeping in a hammock very amusing."

"Maybe too amusing." She walked out into the hallway, and he followed while the women returned to their work. "I can already see Bertie pushing the twins until they all are swinging up to the ceiling."

"There is that."

Behind them, the buzz of voices was low and intense. He suspected his arrival was the primary topic of discussion. Or was it that he had gone with the earl's daughter without explaining why he had come upstairs? He did not want to admit to the village ladies that he had hoped talking with Lady Susanna would help ease his frustration with the repairs on *The Kestrel.*

His hopes that Lord Launceston might be able to give him some insight into the ongoing damage inflicted on his ship had been dashed. The earl had been shocked to hear about the race Drake and his crew had been in to keep ahead of what clearly was intentional destruction. His only suggestion had been to have *The Kestrel* leave Porthlowen and find another sheltered harbor.

Drake refused to consider that. He was concerned that his ship might sink once it reached open sea. That was not the only reason he had hesitated to give such an order. He glanced at the lovely woman walking beside him along the corridor. Once he left Porthlowen, he would sever ties with her and the children. Yes, the Trelawneys would welcome him to call, but it would not be the same. The feeling that they were all working together to help the children would be gone.

Lady Susanna reached for the latch on a door that looked like all the others in the corridor and smiled over her shoulder. "Your idea of hammocks is an idea I shall keep in mind if we don't have enough sturdy beds. Sturdy is vital because *I* can already see Bertie, Gil and the twins jumping on the beds." Her smile wavered. "Not that I would care if Lucy healed enough to join in."

"Aren't you the one who told me to have faith?"

She bristled. "It is not kind to throw one's words,

especially words spoken when exhausted and stressed, back in one's face."

He had not realized how raw her emotions were. He put his hand out to close the door as she started to open it. "I was trying to give you hope. Must you misconstrue all I say?"

"Only when you say something that is easy to misconstrue."

She faced him, and he realized how close they stood. Only the breadth of one of her small hands separated them. He should step away but could not make his feet obey him. Instead, he savored the scent drifting up from her hair. Apple blossoms, if he was not mistaken, an aroma that brought the first lush days of spring to mind.

With her chin jutting toward him and her eyes snapping with indignation, she could have been the model for a ship's figurehead. Even the greatest waves would quell before such a sight. A man would be a beefhead to ignore that warning. How he longed to be that fool and tip her lips beneath his! Her gaze softened, and those full lips parted in an invitation he ached to accept. Why had he not guessed before that she used her prickly tone when she felt most vulnerable? The sudden urge to protect her gripped him.

A throat was cleared behind him, and Drake turned to see a footman standing in the corridor. The same footman who had intruded when Drake stood with Lady Susanna on the terrace, coming with the tidings that Lucy was waking.

"Ah, Venton." Her voice was a bit shaky, and Drake knew he was not the only one overpowered by that fragile connection between them. "What is it?"

"Baricoat thought you might need some help in the attic." Venton did not look in Drake's direction.

"He is right." Lady Susanna opened the door.

Beyond it was a shadowed staircase. When she motioned for the footman to come with her, Drake wondered if she expected him to come along, too. Perhaps accepting Venton's help was her way of letting Drake know that she did not need *his*.

And to own the truth, she did not. He had never met a woman more capable of facing every challenge and besting it than Susanna Trelawney.

Yet, even knowing that, he trailed after her and the footman. He was not ready to return to his ship and his crew, who looked to him for answers to the mess they had found themselves in since their arrival in Porthlowen Harbor. Spending time finding beds for the children would let him accomplish something positive.

At the top of the stairs, Drake stopped, staring around himself in amazement. The attic was not a great-open space. The warren of rooms and corridors was many times larger than all the holds on his ship. Every inch of it was crowded with cast-off furniture and wooden chests and smaller boxes.

He heard skittering and guessed they had disturbed the attic's usual residents. How many boxes and chests had been chewed by the mice and what damage had been done to the contents? The families he had known as a child would not have been able to imagine so many items being left to vermin. He doubted they could even envision a huge attic like this filled with so many boxes and crates.

"The nursery furniture is stored in the third room on the left," Lady Susanna was saying. "There are only three child-size beds from the nursery. We will have to look in the room across the hall to see if any of the bedsteads in there will be suitable for the children."

Drake edged around a stack of boxes that had yellowed labels on them. The ink had faded and was illegible. As he reached where Lady Susanna was peering into the room with the nursery furniture, he could not halt himself from asking, "Do you know what is in every room and box in the attic?"

"Not *every* box." A reluctant smile pulled at her mouth.

"What can I do to help?"

"While Venton is getting the small beds out of this room, why don't we check the one across the hall?"

He motioned for her to lead the way. When she stopped without going in, he looked past her and understood. The room was chock-full of furniture parts. He saw styles that had been popular for the past three hundred years, and the thick dust suggested some of the pieces had been stored, undisturbed, for that long.

Seeing what looked to be part of a low bed, he pushed his way into the room. Dust flew in every direction. He sneezed, sending up a new cloud. A second sneeze, then a third. Then he could not stop.

Slender hands grasped his arm and tugged him out of the room. At the same time, Lady Susanna called to Venton not to touch anything until he opened a few of the windows set high beneath the eaves.

"Are you able to breathe?" she asked.

"Barely," Drake replied. He tried to chuckle, but the sound came out as a wheeze.

"Do you need to sit?"

"That might not be a bad idea." He perched on the edge of a box. When it creaked, he stood quickly. That brought on more coughing.

Again her slim fingers clasped his sleeve. This time, she steered him to a different box. He sat, and it held beneath him. He relaxed as much as he could when she stood so close.

"Forgive me," she said.

"For what?"

"I should not have assumed downstairs that you were mocking me when you urged me to have faith."

"I meant it."

"I know you did. It is just…" She walked to a window and opened it, letting in fresh air.

"Just what?" he prompted.

He was sure she heard him, but she changed the subject and began discussing how she planned to make a wonderful place for the children to sleep. His tongue burned with the question he could not speak: Who had hurt her so deeply that she believed the worst of him?

Lady Susanna gave a sudden gasp and squeezed between two boxes to disappear from sight.

Curious, Drake stood and peered over the boxes. She knelt beside what looked like an odd sort of cabinet. She had the doors open, and inside was a miniature collection of rooms.

"What is that?" he asked.

"My old dollhouse."

Though he had never heard of a house entirely for dolls, he said, "It looks a bit like Cothaire."

"It is supposed to be a miniature of the house." She smiled up at him, and he got a hint of what she had been like before she learned not to trust. There was something so charming about her that brought the twins instantly to mind. Had she been as open and trusting when she was younger?

"But it is a toy?"

"Not originally. When my grandmother had it made, she used it as a way to show what changes she intended to make to the real house. I don't know if my mother ever played with it, but it was in the nursery while I was growing up."

"And you played with it?"

She nodded as she ran her hand along the roof. "I had a family of dolls who had many adventures and held fancy events in the house. My nurse helped me make clothing for the dolls so they could attend balls and entertain at lavish dinners." Her gaze turned inward to memories he could not share.

Toys had been what he and the other children along the street could scavenge and make usable with either their hands or their imaginations. He had spent one whole summer collecting bits of wood and paper to build a ship, which had sunk the first time he put it in water. During the winter that followed, he took the ship apart and put it together over and over until shortly before Easter, the ship had floated. The ship vanished one night while he was sleeping, and he never saw it again, but creating it had inspired his determination to have a life upon the sea.

Now looking at the contented smile on Lady Susanna's face, he guessed she was enjoying memories as precious. He never would have imagined an earl's daughter would learn to sew clothing when her father could hire a seamstress to make her all the gowns she wanted.

"Shall we bring it down for the children to play with?" he asked.

She stood, her face aglow. "That would be splendid, but it must wait until the nursery is ready. Maybe by that time, we will have found a nurse to oversee it."

"These children are fortunate that you brought them here."

"It might not have been possible if you had not come to their rescue."

"I happened to be in the right place at an opportune moment."

She shook her head as she edged between the boxes and came to stand in front of him again. "I prefer to think that God looked for someone to save the children and He found you."

Drake flinched. He had developed such a comfortable relationship with God that centered on neither of them intruding on each other's lives. The idea that God might have chosen him to bring the children ashore suggested that had changed, and he was unsure how to feel about it.

"My lady?" came a woman's voice from the stairs.

"Over here," Lady Susanna replied.

A maid peeked around the top of the stairwell. "Is Captain Nesbitt with you?"

"Yes," Drake said, relieved at the interruption. "I am here."

"'Tis Lucy, Captain. She is asking for you."

"Tell her that I will be right there."

As the maid hurried back down the stairs to convey that message, Lady Susanna chuckled. "Captain Nesbitt, I believe you have lost your heart to a little girl who has you wrapped around her finger. You cannot deny her anything at this point."

"Not if it will help her recover." He followed her down the stairs and offered his arm when they reached the corridor. When she put her fingers on it, he said, "I daresay she has you as firmly affixed around her finger."

"Guilty as charged." Her laugh was sweet music in his ears.

"How is she doing?"

"Better each day. Other than her missing memory, she appears to be healing well. I am actually worried more about Bertie."

"Why?"

"He cannot understand why Lucy acts as if she never met him before a short time ago, even though I have tried to explain to him that she is hurt."

"But she looks fine to him."

Her dark curls bounced as she nodded. "'Tis almost like he believes she has abandoned him as his family did. I had hoped that her memory would return on its own by now, but it has not."

"What about Hockbridge's suggestion that we help her remember by taking her to see people and things she knew before she fell?"

She stopped and faced him, leaving her hand on his arm. "But what do we show her?"

"I think taking her back to the harbor and the jolly boat would be the obvious place to begin."

"Yes, it would be! Why didn't I think of that?"

He tapped her nose and grinned when her eyes twinkled. "You may have a few other things on your mind. Like five of them in addition to Lucy."

"Mr. Hockbridge is supposed to come back and check her on Saturday. Why don't we take her and Mollie to the shore after church on Sunday?"

"After church?"

"Do you have something else to do then?"

He shook his head.

"Then we shall go after church."

He gave a sheepish smile. "If the roof does not cave in when I step foot in the church, we will go."

"Raymond would not allow that." She smiled. "Thank you, Captain Nesbitt."

"You are very welcome." He would have said more, but he found himself sinking into the silver wonder of her eyes. He raised his hand to caress her cheek as he had longed to since they first spoke in the nursery.

A terrible noise erupted through the house, threatening to press his breath out of his chest. He grabbed her and pulled her close, eyeing the ceiling as the floor seemed to rise and fall like the deck of his ship. Was the house caving in? She trembled in his arms and gave a soft gasp as glass shattered in the window at the end of the hallway.

Lady Susanna's face lost all color, turning as gray as the cliffs around the harbor. "The solar!" she cried through the ringing in his ears.

Not sure what she meant, he matched her steps as she ran down the corridor. She tore open a door and shouted her sister's name.

Lady Caroline crouched behind a chair, holding the children close. Glass from the tall windows had exploded into the room and sprayed across the stone floor, mixing with the wooden animals and a couple of dolls the children had been playing with.

He crossed the room in a pair of long steps, squatted and examined the closest child. Gil. The little boy had a cut on one cheek, and glass fell from his hair as he threw himself at Drake. Looking over the little boy's head, he reached for Mollie, but Lady Susanna was already checking her.

Screams erupted from throughout the house.

One rose over all the others. "Fire!"

Chapter Seven

The shriek of "Fire!" was still echoing in Susanna's ears as Captain Nesbitt sped out of the room. She hesitated, looking from the door to her sister.

"Go," Caroline ordered, and Susanna had to strain to hear her because her ears seemed stuffed with cotton. "None of us is hurt, and they will need everyone to put out the fire."

"If it is in the house—"

"I don't think it is." She pointed at the shattered windows. Smoke billowed beyond the house. "Could it be an accident at one of the mines?"

Susanna pushed herself to her feet and ran to the window. Smoke obliterated the back garden. Whatever had exploded was far closer than the mines on Lord Warrick's lands to the south. Saying that to her sister, she gave the children what she hoped looked like a bolstering smile before she ran from the solar.

She reached the stairs and looked down. Below, in the entry hall, Baricoat was waving the footmen outside, ordering them to get shovels and any other tool to fight a fire. He shouted for the maids to grab every available bucket.

Suddenly, Captain Nesbitt pounded down the stairs behind her. Where had he gone? He should have been outside by now. She saw he was holding the handles of four or five pails in each hand. He must have gone to the day nursery and borrowed the buckets from the women cleaning there. He took the stairs at a pace that threatened to send him tumbling as Lucy had.

Susanna ran ahead of him and around the corner of the house. She faltered when she saw flames licking the eaves of a long, low building with a trio of wide doors. The stable! The fire had already reached its upper floor.

She yanked a trio of pails from Captain Nesbitt and shoved them into the hands of servants milling about as they watched in horror. She clapped her hands to get the attention of the ones closest to her. The sound did not carry far over the roar of the fire. Even so, in no time, she had the men and women in two lines that stretched between the well house and the stable. Buckets were passed along the line. As people came from the village, drawn by the smoke, she put them into a second set of lines so the fire could be fought from two directions.

It would not be enough. The fire had gained too strong a foothold in the stable. What could have exploded in there?

Shouts resounded as more villagers arrived. Mr. Jenner, the blacksmith, took his place at the end closest to the burning stable. His thick arms made it look easy to fling water from the full pails. He called to his assistant, Mr. Morel, to take the front spot on the other line. Accustomed to heat in the forge, they should be able to work longer than anyone else before they needed to rest.

A man staggered through the smoke. Sanders! His face was as gray as his hair.

She rushed to the head groom. "Is everyone out?"

Sanders coughed, then nodded.

"The horses?"

He shook his head before collapsing to his knees as he struggled to breathe.

Calling to a stable lad, she motioned for him to move Sanders away from the smoke. She scanned the stable yard. Several horses were being herded into a nearby field, but she did not see Pansy, her beloved bay.

Susanna hesitated only long enough to grab a shawl from a passing maid. Running into the smoke, she lashed the shawl around her mouth and nose. The heat tried to drive her back, but she bent low and kept going.

She thought she knew every inch of the stable, but in the blinding smoke, nothing seemed to be where it should be. She tripped over a shovel handle and winced when her palms struck the rough floor. Pushing herself up, she groped toward Pansy's stall.

The mare neighed as Susanna reached her. Raising her head, she saw two more horses in stalls beyond Pansy's. She could handle only one at a time when they were hysterical with fear.

She wrapped a blanket around Pansy's head before opening the stall door. Seizing the halter, she led the terrified beast toward the door. Something creaked overhead. She did not raise her head. Even if she could see through the smoke, what did it matter which rafter was failing? If the roof fell in, she and Pansy would die.

A hand seized her elbow.

Lifting her head, she could not make out a face through the smothering smoke.

Then Captain Nesbitt demanded, "Have you lost your mind? Get out of here!"

"Two...two more horses," she choked out. "Back... right. Stalls."

"Go!" he ordered. "We will get them."

She had no idea who was with him but nodded. When he slapped Pansy on the flank, the horse broke away and raced out of the stable. She reeled after the horse.

Coughing, gasping for air, half blinded by tears that ran from her smoke-filled eyes, she did not stop until she ran into someone who steadied her before she could fall to her knees. A cup was thrust into her hands. Pulling down the shawl around her face, she gulped the soothing water. The cup was taken and refilled. Again she swallowed it as fast as she could.

Susanna blinked and realized Mrs. Hitchens was helping her. Pain scored her throat as she gasped, "Captain Nesbitt...someone else...still in the stable."

The housekeeper poured more water into the cup and urged Susanna to drink.

Susanna complied only after Mrs. Hitchens said, "They are out. They got the last two horses out."

"Where...?"

"Over there." She pointed to where Captain Nesbitt and Venton knelt on the ground, struggling as she was to breathe. "The horses have been turned out into the field."

Benton raced into the stable yard, shouting his captain's name.

"Over here!" Captain Nesbitt called back, and Susanna marveled at how he could shout when his lungs must be cramping.

His first mate was followed by most of the crew of *The Kestrel*. Benton tipped his cap to her and started to greet her.

She did not let him finish. Coming to her feet, she said, "Help where you can. People are already tiring."

"Unless you want them to start new lines," Captain Nesbitt said as he walked unsteadily to where she stood. His face was black with soot, and she guessed hers looked the same. "You could lose the other buildings unless we soak the roofs."

Though she hated to give up on the stable, she nodded. She told Benton to shift the second group of bucket passers to wet down the roofs for the carriage barn and the icehouse.

Ice!

Susanna called to Baricoat, who was supervising the youngest maids who carried water and a ladle from person to person so the firefighters could drink. Outlining what she needed him to do, she watched him collect a few of the strongest men as well as two nimble lads.

"Excellent idea," Captain Nesbitt said before he took the ladle held out to him and drank gratefully. After thanking the girl, he added, "Those roofs are flat enough so blocks of ice can be set on them. As it melts, the water will protect the roofs from sparks."

"That is my hope," Susanna replied.

Cheers rose as more villagers arrived to help. Susanna directed them and did not see where Captain Nesbitt went. She joined one of the lines swinging the buckets back and forth between the well house and the stable. Out of the corner of her eye, she saw men scrambling up on the roofs. They set large blocks of ice in place, keeping them there by yanking up the roofing and nailing it to make dams that would allow the water to trickle past but prevented the blocks from sliding to the ground.

They finished just as the stable caved in with a shower of sparks that soared in every direction. People ran to put them out with shovels and blankets. On the roofs, more sizzled in the streams of water and went out. The few that missed the water were put out by men who climbed back up. She realized most of them were from Captain Nesbitt's ship. They must be accustomed to being high in the rigging.

Once the stable was no more than embers, Susanna thanked everyone who had come to help. Mrs. Ford and the kitchen maids had trays of cheese and sandwiches, as well as lemonade, so nobody left hungry or thirsty. Mr. Hockbridge had arrived with balms for burns and cuts from broken glass. Her brother Raymond was helping Elisabeth serve food.

But one question was asked over and over, and she had no answer: What had caused the explosion that had broken windows as far away as the village?

Drake stood by the pile of glowing embers. The stable could be rebuilt. No people or horses had been killed. Even the cats who hunted in the stable had been found by the kitchen door, begging for a saucer of milk as they did every day. But the supplies to repair the nursery were gone, and now windows would need to be replaced throughout Cothaire.

He watched as the blacksmith and his assistant turned the glowing coals and poured more water on them. The steam's acrid odor scraped Drake's throat. It did not seem to bother them. In fact, the assistant had been whistling a cheery tune as he worked until Jenner ordered him to stop because it was not respectful to the earl and his family.

Parson Trelawney walked over to Drake and clapped him on the shoulder. "Thank you, Captain, for your help. I had not thought the next fire would be at my family's house."

"Next fire? Have there been others?"

"Nothing like this." The parson sighed and stared

at the charred remains of the stable. "There have been a few incidents in the village, but they appeared to be accidents."

"But now you are not so certain the fires were accidental."

"If a logical reason can be found for this fire, I would feel more comfortable." He looked at Drake. "The fires started shortly before your ship arrived here. I don't know what to think, but I am not the only one praying there will be no more fires."

"Has it been only fires?"

The parson looked at him, surprised. "There have been other incidents. Chickens let out of yards, clothes covered with mud when the rope they were hung on came loose, a broken window. Things like that."

"Is that commonplace in Porthlowen?"

"No." He frowned. "If one person or group of people is causing the damage, it should be reported to the constable."

"No one has been seen?" Drake was astonished. It had seemed as if everyone in Porthlowen knew every detail of their neighbors' lives.

"No one, and now the perpetrator may be growing more bold. Burning a building is a felony and could lead to transportation."

"Or hanging."

"The justices of the peace in the local parishes prefer a sentence of transportation because it gives criminals a chance to remake their lives."

"Either way, nobody is going to step forward to admit to such a crime, and while the criminal roams free, who knows what might happen?"

"We are grateful that so far no one has been hurt

or killed." Parson Trelawney's smile returned. "And I thank you for allowing your men to help us."

"I don't think I could have halted them," he replied with a tired grin.

"Maybe not, but you know as well as I do that some villagers want *The Kestrel* gone. They fear it makes Porthlowen a target for the French privateers."

Both the blacksmith and his assistant stiffened at the parson's words but kept working.

"Have the French been raiding villages along the shore?" Drake asked.

"There are rumors, but none can be substantiated. Yet people fear the French will come ashore as they did in Fishguard years ago. They were beaten back, and I cannot imagine any Cornishman who would not fight to protect his house and family."

"Or Cornishwoman."

The parson chuckled. "If you are referring to my sisters, I can tell you that they are not unique here. The winds and storms off the sea strengthen us."

As if on cue, Lady Susanna came toward them. She had made an effort to clean the soot from her face, but smudges clung to her eyebrows and along one side of her jaw. Even that could not detract from her elegance.

"Raymond," she said, "Papa and Arthur would like to speak with you in the dining room." She smiled sadly. "It is the only room free of glass right now."

"Excuse me, Captain." The parson turned on his heel and walked toward the closest door into the great house.

"How are you faring?" she asked Drake.

"Not much worse for the wear. You?"

"Better now that I have survived the dressing-down Papa gave me for going into the stable to bring Pansy out."

Drake laughed without humor. "I am glad he did that because it saves me from having to tell how caper-witted you acted."

"I was not the only one. *You* went into the stable, too."

"After you! That is something else entirely."

She raised her chin, but her pose was ruined when she coughed. She waved aside his offer of water. Once she regained control of herself, she asked, "If one of your crew had been in there, wouldn't you have risked everything for him?"

"Yes, but—"

"No but. Pansy has been my horse for almost ten years. I could not leave her to the fire."

Drake understood what she did not say. The horse had been a constant in her life when her mother and her brother-in-law died. And there was the event that brought a deep sadness to her eyes. He knew if he asked in the village, someone would explain what had happened, but the idea of going behind her back to gossip about her left a sour flavor in his mouth.

"If you have time, Captain Nesbitt, Papa would like to express his thanks for your help."

He started to answer, then stared at what was left of the stable. The latest holes in *The Kestrel*'s hull seemed to be appearing in groups as if someone had tossed a handful of embers against it. Had any of the crew looked for scorch marks on the wood? He had not. To find even one might be a clue to how the holes had been made and could lead him to the person or people who were trying to keep him and his crew from sailing from Porthlowen.

Parson Trelawney had spoken of the villagers who feared the French would sail into the cove to finish what their imprisoned fellow sailors could not. What if others in Porthlowen saw his ship as possible defense against the raiders? He should excuse himself and return to his ship to discuss these uncomfortable theories with Benton.

"That is not necessary, Lady Susanna," he said, knowing he owed her an answer.

"My father thinks it is." She put her hand on his arm, startling him. "Captain Nesbitt, please do this for him."

"And for you?"

She lowered her eyes. Before she could draw her hand away, he placed his over it, holding it in place.

"My lady?"

When she raised her eyes toward his once more, he was not surprised to see her competent mask had fallen away to reveal the sorrow beneath. In little more than a whisper, she said, "My father's infirmity limits what he can do. Once he could oversee Cothaire from the back of a horse. Now he seldom can leave the house."

"It is a good man who has a daughter who loves him so much that she thinks of helping him keep his pride even when life has laid him low." He put a crooked finger under her chin so she could not look away when he added, "And a good daughter whose thoughts focus on making her father feel useful and needed."

"Will you speak with him?"

Ignoring his eagerness to check his ship for scorched spots, he nodded. "Of course, my lady."

"Thank you, and thank you for coming with us to the shore on Sunday to see if we can loosen some of Lucy's frozen memories. It is a good friend who is willing to share such ideas as well as his time."

"Friend? Is that how you see me?"

He had pushed too hard. She drew back, looked away and smoothed her hands over her smoke-stained apron.

With a prim farewell, she hurried toward the house. He watched her go, as he had so often. He wished he knew how to convince her to stay when he knew he could not remain in Porthlowen much longer.

Chapter Eight

Drake entered the small stone church along with his first mate and several members of his crew. Even though the sun was eclipsed by clouds, the light coming through the four stained-glass windows along the sides and the large one behind the altar splashed colors onto the simple wooden pews.

He looked at the ceiling. Oak rafters rose to a peak over the center aisle. Flowers and vines had been carved into two of them, but otherwise they were as plain as the ribs of his ship. He grinned as he noted that no cracks appeared to warn him that the roof was about to collapse because he had entered the church.

Heads turned as he followed Benton toward the front since the rear pews were occupied. When he saw smiles, he was startled. While the residents of Porthlowen were willing to help obtain supplies to repair *The Kestrel*, they had treated the crew like unwelcome outsiders.

Now smiles suggested he was a prodigal son, being drawn back into the fold. The moment he and Benton had pulled the jolly boat up on the shore, he and his whole crew had been redeemed in the villagers' eyes.

That the ship's crew had helped fight the fire at Cothaire made them even more a part of the village.

He sighed as he thought how disappointed he had been when he went to speak with Lord Launceston. Lady Susanna had not been in the room. Only her older brother, the very correct Lord Trelawney. Her sister and even the parson and his betrothed had wandered in to bring their father updates. Of Lady Susanna there had been no sign, and that surprised her family as much as it did him. It was unlike her to be absent during such an important discussion.

The earl had sent a message to the ship before Drake left for church. It was straightforward—so straightforward he suspected Lady Susanna had written it. In the past three days, no progress had been made in learning anything about how the fire had started in the stable. Whether something exploded to trigger the fire or the fire itself had started first, no one seemed to know. Lord Trelawney insisted there had been nothing in the stable that could cause a detonation. The head groom had confirmed that. It could not have been an accident.

A quick search of *The Kestrel* did not turn up any scorched wood, but many of the spots had been sanded when the boards were plugged. He had no proof one way or the other, so he was as stymied as the earl.

Sitting in the second row, Drake heard a low rush of whispers. He turned and saw Lady Susanna coming in along with her sister and the children, who waved to people they recognized. So many of the villagers in recent days had come to help at Cothaire that the children had met just about everyone in the church.

His gaze settled on Susanna. Her gown had tiny blue flowers on a cream background, and she wore a small straw bonnet with a matching blue ribbon. Her cheeks were a lush pink, and he guessed she had struggled persuading the little ones to hold each other's hands. Her own were encased in gloves that might once have been white but were stained with chocolate.

She glanced in his direction, and her eyes widened. Had she expected that he would not come to church as he had agreed? Or maybe she had assumed he would meet her on the beach once church was over. As she looked away, he noticed gray circles under her eyes. She was surrounded by uncertainty, which must be especially difficult for a woman who preferred to have everything under control.

When Gil ran over to where the Winwood sisters sat with Miss Rowse and her assistant, Peggy, he crowed something about his baby. That brought soft laughter from every pew. Lady Caroline took his hand and urged him to come with her toward the family's pew, which was marked by the Launceston crest.

"They like us?" asked Mollie, pointing to the Winwood sisters.

Lady Susanna smiled. "Yes, they are twin sisters. Just like you and Lucy."

"I like them," the little girl announced, and more laughter rippled through the church.

"We like you, too," one Miss Winwood said. He believed it was Miss Hyacinth Winwood.

"Indeed, we do," added the other Miss Winwood.

Mollie pleaded to sit with the Winwood sisters, but Lady Susanna told her that they could spend time with Miss Hyacinth and Miss Ivy after the service. That calmed the little girl before she could give in to tears.

"I hope we do not have such antics every Sunday," muttered a female voice behind him. "I may be the only one who has not forgotten that this is God's house, not an orphanage."

He did not have to turn. He recognized Mrs. Thorburn's cool tones. He considered mentioning that such words did not show Christian kindness. He could only imagine how she would respond to that.

Hearing a thump, he looked past Mrs. Thorburn's pursed lips to where two men were helping Lord Launceston into the church. His left foot was wrapped. Drake stepped out of the pew, motioning to Benton. He and his first mate took over from Lord Trelawney and another man, who must have carried the earl from his carriage. The older man could not put any weight on his swollen foot.

"Anywhere is fine, Captain," Lord Launceston said. In spite of his obvious pain, he chuckled. "It appears the family pew is overflowing. One does not expect one's family to increase so abruptly."

"Watch his foot there, Benton." Drake guided the earl into a nearby pew, which was hastily vacated by a younger couple who moved to the pew across from where Drake and his first mate had been sitting.

They assisted him to sit. Going to where about a dozen kneeling cushions had been stacked, Drake brought four back to prop under the earl's foot so he could stretch out his left leg at a comfortable angle.

"An excellent solution," the earl said, the strain on his face easing. "Sometimes it takes a newcomer to find a solution to an old problem."

"I would be happy if I could solve your new problem, my lord."

The earl motioned for him to sit with him while Benton returned to the pew near the front and Lord Trelawney went to speak with his sisters. Quietly, the earl said, "I assume you mean the children. How goes the search for information on them?"

He listed where he had sent inquiries throughout western Cornwall and the disappointing response. No one knew of six missing children or had any idea why they had been put in a jolly boat. "You could say we have been lucky, even though it has been only bad luck so far."

Chuckling again, Lord Launceston scanned the church before his gaze focused on Drake once more. "I do not believe in luck, Captain. I believe in the will of God. When the time is right for the truth to be known, you shall find it."

"I wish I could be as sure."

"No wonder you get along so well with Susanna. You are two of a kind, trying to control the unfolding of the world in God's time rather than accepting that everything happens for a reason. Maybe a reason only God is privy to, but a reason nonetheless."

A twinge of something that felt like longing pinched at Drake. He admired the faith that was as much a part of the Trelawney family as their love for each other. But it was a disquieting reminder that he had not had either. Now…he did not know how to respond to the earl, and he was glad to be spared by excusing himself to return to his own pew when a door opened near the pulpit, signaling the beginning of the service. When he walked past Lord Trelawney, he received a curt nod. Was the man ever anything but deadly serious?

Drake realized the man who had entered through the door by the pulpit was not Raymond Trelawney. This parson was older. His silver hair was painted by the light coming through the stained-glass windows.

He was startled to see Parson Trelawney sitting with

his betrothed, Elisabeth, across from his sisters. Was the parson unwell? He looked quite hale, but there must be some reason why Raymond Trelawney had stepped aside to offer his pulpit to a man who introduced himself as Parson Lambrick.

Drake rose as the others did for the first hymn. He was grateful that it was one he recalled from the short time he had attended church regularly. As the voices lifted around him, he smiled at Lucy, who had turned around to wave at him. She called out, "Cap!" as the song ended. Gentle laughter came from all around them, save for Mrs. Thorburn's sniff.

When they sat, Lucy refused, calling out to him again. He held out his arms. Lady Susanna gave him a rueful smile as she passed Lucy to him.

He set the child on his knee and put his finger to his lips. She nodded, abruptly as solemn as if she stood at the pulpit. She leaned her head against his chest and, within seconds, was asleep with her thumb in her mouth. Her other arm wrapped around his, trusting he would keep her close.

He looked at his first mate, who gave him a wide grin and a wink. Benton clearly thought it was funny to see his captain cradling a little girl, but Drake enjoyed her nestled close to his heart.

Lady Susanna glanced at them. A gentle smile lit her face. She reached back and stroked Lucy's hair. The motion seemed to link the three of them in a special moment when time stood still. On one thing, he and Lady Susanna agreed wholeheartedly: they would do the best they could to make sure the children were safe and loved.

When she looked at the pulpit, he turned his attention to Parson Lambrick. He understood why there was a substitute when Parson Lambrick began reading the

banns for the marriage of Raymond Trelawney and Elisabeth Rowse. Shifting his gaze toward where the couple sat, he was startled that nobody else was looking at
them. Instead, every eye seemed focused on the pew
in front of him. There was a soft intake of breath when
the parson stated the announcement was the first reading of the banns that would be repeated two more times
before the couple could wed.

What was going on? Why was the congregation acting as if the very words drove a dagger into each of
their guts? Even Mrs. Thorburn had gasped behind him.

Ask Lady Susanna. At that thought, he looked at
where she sat in front of him. His eyes widened as he
noted the stiff tension across her shoulders and realized that the congregation's attention was on her and
her sister.

Beside him, Benton whispered, "What is amiss?"

Drake gave him a stern glance. The time for such
a discussion was not during the church service. Did
this have something to do with the pain Lady Susanna
tried to mask?

Raymond Trelawney went to the pulpit to lead the
rest of the service. He thanked the other parson, who
took a chair beside the pulpit.

Putting his hands on either side of the pulpit, Parson Trelawney smiled at his congregation. "I would
like to begin with a reading from the fifth chapter of
Ephesians." His voice resonated off the sounding board
hanging over the pulpit. *"'Now are ye light in the Lord:
walk as children of light; for the fruit of the Spirit is in
all goodness and righteousness and truth.'"* He raised
his eyes and smiled at the congregation. "When we do
good, we do it in God's name, and we can feel His hand
upon our hearts. We walk closest with the Lord when

we heed the lesson to do unto others as we would like them to do unto us, when we do something for someone else without the thought of reward."

Each word took aim at the wall Drake had built to protect his too-oft disillusioned heart. He tried to persuade himself that the parson was not speaking only to him. Other heads nodded in agreement. Maybe the lesson was meant for them.

"But there are rewards," the parson went on. "The ones we find are beyond what we can imagine. Rewards of love and the satisfaction of achieving something that is not measured in pounds and shillings but in joy." Parson Trelawney continued sharing his thoughts on how goodness needed to come from the heart and from the soul, not simply be an appearance of good deeds and kindness.

The words spoke to Drake as if they were the answer to a question he had asked. Or the answer to a prayer he had not even known was lying quiescent deep in his heart, waiting for him to send it forth.

As he bowed his head, his chin brushing Lucy's soft hair, he listened to the parson lead them in the morning's final prayer. Thoughts whirled through his mind, but he was not ready to examine the questions they posed.

The worshippers stood and began to go toward the door to the porch. Many of them stopped to greet Lord Launceston and express how they were praying for his pain to ease. Drake was impressed that he thanked each one by name. It was another indication of how closely connected the lives in Cothaire and the village were.

"Good morning, Captain Nesbitt, Mr. Benton," said Lady Susanna as she reached to take Lucy.

"Cap!" An excited voice came from beside her. "We go beach now. Go play. Fun, fun."

He was surprised at how Mollie prattled while Lucy watched with her thumb in her mouth. It was unsettling. Before the accident, Lucy had been the chatterbox. It was as if they had changed places.

Stepping aside to let Benton out, Drake motioned for Lady Susanna and her sister and the children to precede him. They emerged into the breezy day. The clouds had blown away, and the sun turned the waves to diamonds. The church was set at the inner curve of the cove. With the tide out, *The Kestrel* was not the only vessel balanced on her keel. Fishing boats were moored to long ropes connected to iron rings driven into the rock beneath the sand. The fresh salt air tantalized him.

He turned his back on his longing to return his ship to the sea and a life with few complications. Instead, he looked around the churchyard with the history of the villagers written on the tombstones. Most of the parishioners gathered around the parson and his future wife, congratulating them on the first reading of the banns.

Lady Caroline went to join her family with the three little boys and the baby, but Lady Susanna hung back, holding Lucy's and Mollie's hands.

"Go beach now?" asked Mollie.

Instead of answering her, Drake looked down into Lady Susanna's eyes as he asked, "What was all the gasping about when the banns were read for your brother and Miss Rowse?"

"It is nothing of import," she replied in a clipped voice. "Not now at any rate, when we need to help these children."

She was avoiding giving him an answer, but he did not press her. Shadows from the past dimmed her eyes.

Was she thinking of her sister's marriage that had left Lady Caroline a young widow? Or was it her own pain that she avoided speaking of? It could be anything, and prying could add to her sorrow.

"I had Benton bring a jolly boat to the shore before we came to church," Drake said. "I can row us out into the cover and—"

"No!" Her face lost all color.

"What's wrong?"

"I have an appalling fear of the waves."

"The waves in the cove?" He started to laugh at the idea of being scared of such small waves. He halted when he saw she was sincere. "What about them frightens you?"

She shrugged. "Everything. I have been afraid of them for as long as I can remember. When I stand on the sand and feel the water pulling at me, I can think only of being pulled out and under."

He wanted to take her hands and fold them between his, but he could not when they stood in public. Rather, he said, "Then we shall stay on the shore."

"Don't think I am bird-witted."

"When I think of you, my lady, *bird-witted* is not a word that comes to mind. Lovely, wise, warmhearted, perhaps, but never bird-witted."

A soft pink flush climbed her cheeks as she whispered, "Thank you."

He motioned toward the lych-gate. "Anytime you are ready, my lady."

"As they say, there is no time like the present."

"Who is this *they*?"

As he had hoped, she smiled at his ridiculous question. She tilted her head and eyed him from beneath her pretty bonnet. "*That*, my dear Captain Nesbitt, is a question for another day."

"Agreed." He bent to pick up Mollie to prevent Lady Susanna from seeing how her calling him "my dear Captain Nesbitt" had sent a bolt of dangerous excitement into him.

He needed to put an anchor on his thoughts, holding them from drifting on dangerous currents. Now was not the time for musing about a family of his own. A family with a pretty wife and two adorable little girls. Odd, he had never considered being the father of girls. That had changed when a set of twins grinned up at him.

Halting his wandering thoughts, he focused on other important matters: finding who had put the children in the jolly boat, reuniting the youngsters with their families, and last, but certainly not least, discovering who was intentionally damaging *The Kestrel*.

But who had damaged Lady Susanna's heart? Again he told himself he could ease his curiosity by asking anyone in the churchyard, but he respected her too much to do that.

And you are in too deep here already. You know what happens when you get involved with women.

Never again.

That was a vow he had made to himself, and it was one he needed to keep. When he motioned for her to lead the way from the churchyard to the beach, he was glad her back was to him. That way, his expression could not betray his thoughts.

Susanna was pleased that Captain Nesbitt walked behind her and Lucy. She needed every second of the short walk to the beach to regain her composure. It frayed

every time he looked at her with those dark eyes that hid
so much and yet displayed his longing to hold her again.

As she had so many times before, she chastised herself
for finding solace in his arms the morning after Lucy's
fall. If she had resisted then, neither of them could have
known how wonderful it was to stand so close.

She had made an awful mistake when she dared to
trust Franklin and her bosom bow, Norah. She could
not do that again.

No matter what.

"Pretty," Lucy chirped, breaking into Susanna's
thoughts.

"What is pretty?" she asked.

Lucy pointed at the waves breaking by the bend in
the cove, and Susanna gave her an unsteady smile. She
could not infect the little girl with her own foolish fears.
She pointed out how, with low tide, the rocks that would
be hidden at high tide were topped by gulls and other
birds feasting on small creatures caught in the pools.
Their raucous cries and flapping wings resounded between the two walls of cliffs.

Another sound resonated like distant thunder across
the cove, and Susanna looked at the tunnel that had
been carved in the outer cliff by aeons of water. The
opening went all the way through, and the tide washed
in and out, not quite emptying with each wave. When
enough water built up within the tunnel, it burst out
like a cannon firing. An arc of spray shot partway up
the cliff, then fell back into the sea to start the cycle
all over again.

"Whoosh!"

"That is right, Lulu," she said.

Mollie chuckled. "Lulu? Her name Lucy."

"But don't you think Lulu is a fun name for her?" Susanna asked.

"Lulu?" Mollie considered it, then said, "Cap! Lulu and Susu." She pointed at Susanna and her sister and giggled.

Captain Nesbitt chuckled, the sound a deep rumble like the water rushing through the tunnel in the cliff. "I think those are great names, Moll."

"Me Moll." The little girl tapped her chest before pointing again at Susanna. "She Susu. She Lulu." With a grin, she patted Captain Nesbitt's chest. "Cap."

Susanna smiled. "Well, that is settled. We all have special names."

"Me Moll."

Captain Nesbitt mimicked her childish voice. "Me Cap."

"Susu," Susanna said with a laugh, then looked down at the little girl beside her.

Lucy said nothing, just continued to suck her thumb.

Susanna knelt beside her. "Do you like the name Lulu?"

She nodded.

Acting as if she were not bothered by how the child had changed, Susanna stood with a smile. She lifted Lucy—Lulu—into her arms as the path down to the beach grew steep. She did not want the little girl to fall again.

The beach was empty, save for a few gulls walking along the sand, much to the delight of the girls. Moll chattered about the birds while her sister listened with a contented smile.

All that changed when they came around the curve of the cove and saw the jolly boat pulled up on the sand. Moll gave a shriek that sent the birds fleeing into the sky. She buried her face against Captain Nesbitt's neck and tightened her arms around it. He loosened her hold gently but did not shift her. Great sobs shook her small body.

Susanna put Lulu down and reached for Moll. The little girl screamed again and clutched him even more desperately. Thick tears rained down her face.

Lulu regarded her sister with puzzlement. "She cries."

"Yes," Captain Nesbitt said in a gentle tone as Susanna rubbed Moll's back in slow circles. "She is afraid."

"What 'fraid of?"

"The boat."

Lulu walked up to the jolly boat and patted it. "Good boat. See? Good boat."

Moll began to sob more loudly.

Brushing Moll's damp hair back from her face, Susanna stood on tiptoe to kiss the child's wet cheek. Only then did she say, "We should go."

"Yes." He nodded. "Bring Lulu."

She looked over at the little girl who was examining the boat as if she had never seen one before. What had left her twin weak with terror intrigued her.

Walking over to Lulu, she squatted. "You like the boat, Lulu?"

"Good boat."

"There are a lot of good boats like this one. Have you ever gone for a ride in one?"

The child considered that, then shook her head. "Go ride now?"

"Maybe another time. Mrs. Ford will have our luncheon ready, and we do not want to be late, do we?"

She patted her stomach. "Hungry."

Susanna somehow kept smiling. Their experiment had been a failure. Lulu remembered nothing of the journey in the jolly boat, while Moll remembered too much.

Forgive us, Father, for adding to her suffering. I know how malicious memories can be. She shuddered at the thought of the eyes on her when the banns were read for Raymond and Elisabeth. Being pitied was painful.

"My lady?" Captain Nesbitt stood next to her.

When she did not move, he put a hand on her elbow to assist her to her feet. A peculiar buzz again surged up her arm and into her head, making it spin. The feeling originated beneath his fingers.

As she stood, still holding Lulu's hand, she gazed up at him. She had never seen a sight more adorable than this strong man holding Moll, as he had her sister during the service.

Her eyes were caught by his, and all thoughts of the children vanished as she imagined his mouth nearing hers. What would his kiss be like? Powerful like the sea he loved or gentle as he was with the children? She edged toward him, needing to know.

He whispered something. Her name? She could not tell as her pulse thundered. He released her arm, and her wordless murmur of protest became a happy sigh when he cupped her chin. His fingers splayed across her cheek, urging her to lean against his palm.

"Good day!" interrupted a cheerful shout, quickly followed by, "I am sorry. I did not mean..."

Susanna pulled away from Captain Nesbitt, the connection between them broken once more. Yet, a fragile filament remained, a thread that could draw them together again if she dared to explore the feelings he brought forth within her. All she needed to do was forget the mistakes of her past, something she had told herself she would never do.

No matter what.

Belatedly she realized Mr. Morel, the blacksmith's assistant, had called to them. "Forgive me," he said. "I did not mean to startle you. Everyone in Porthlowen knows you dislike surprises, my lady."

She stiffened at his words, then forced the tension from her shoulders. Mr. Morel had already garnered a reputation in the village for being willing to help anyone with a difficult task.

"That is true," she managed to say.

"Aren't you Jenner's assistant?" asked Captain Nesbitt darkly. "I saw you at the fire at Cothaire, didn't I?"

She risked a glance toward Captain Nesbitt and saw he was not hiding that he was annoyed with Mr. Morel's arrival. The blacksmith's assistant struggled not to quail before the frown.

"You are right. This is Robert Morel," Susanna said. "He came to Porthlowen a few months ago to work in the smithy in the village. Mr. Morel, this is Captain Drake Nesbitt."

Mr. Morel eyed Captain Nesbitt, then offered his hand. "I have heard a lot about you, Captain."

"I am sure every member of *The Kestrel* is the talk of the village."

Mr. Morel chuckled. "You must admit, Captain, that having your ship linger in Porthlowen for so long is a nine days' wonder."

"I would have gladly spent only nine days here."

"Mr. Morel may be able to help," she said. "If some of the boards need more support, he could prepare iron bands to hold them in place."

"Whatever I can do to help, Captain, let me know."

"Thank you." Captain Nesbitt's vexed tone eased slightly, and he frowned as Mr. Morel walked away, whistling.

In the silence that followed, she said, "He is a good man. He has settled in well here in Porthlowen."

Captain Nesbitt continued to stare after Mr. Morel, then walked back in the direction they had come.

She remained where she was, holding Lulu's hand. Whatever had been between her and Captain Nesbitt was now gone as if it had never existed. All his thoughts were elsewhere. Something about Mr. Morel disturbed him, but what? Was he upset because she suggested Mr. Morel help repair his ship? Maybe he thought she was eager for him to leave Porthlowen. A week ago, she would have said yes, but now...

She had no idea what she wanted now, except to regain some say-so over her life before she lost all control of it as she had five years ago.

Chapter Nine

Susanna looked at the woman seated across from her. Her blond hair severely pulled back, Maris Oliver wore a warm smile, though it was tentative while Susanna interviewed her for the position of supervising the nursery. Her most striking feature was her jade-green eyes, which she kept lowered, except when she was answering a question.

Receiving a letter inquiring about the position had been a relief to Susanna. She had replied immediately, asking Miss Oliver to call at Cothaire at her earliest convenience. Two days later, the woman had arrived. Susanna guessed Miss Oliver was closer to thirty than she was, which should mean she had quite a few years of experience handling a nursery.

Mrs. Hitchens had already interviewed her and perused the letter of recommendation that Miss Oliver had supplied upon arrival. The housekeeper had given Susanna a good report. Susanna suspected Mrs. Hitchens wanted to return to her own duties and let someone else tend to the children.

"There seems to be only a single question left to

ask," Susanna said. "Why did you leave your former employer and now are seeking a new one?"

"The reason is simple, my lady." Her voice was soft and calm, perfect for dealing with the five youngsters who would move into the nursery as soon as it was ready. "The children in that house grew too old for a nurse, and the family had hired a governess. I was pleased when they offered me a wonderful letter of recommendation as well as the information that Cothaire was seeking the services of an experienced nurse."

Susanna could not help being impressed with Miss Oliver's obvious education. She understood why the woman had chosen to become a nurse rather than a governess. A governess was neither part of the servants' hall nor the family's household. A nurse held a position of greater respect in a house because she oversaw the children through their first years. She was expected to set them on the path they would walk their entire lives.

"It sounds as if you enjoy your work," Susanna said.

"I find it very satisfying. I am always happiest around children." She raised her head, and a shy smile tilted her lips. "Sometimes I find I prefer their company to that of adults." Her eyes widened. "Lady Susanna, do not mistake my meaning. My words were not intended to insult anyone."

"You have no need for an apology. There are times when I find the company of children more comfortable, too. With a small child, one always knows where one stands. Not so with adults."

"Thank you for understanding, my lady."

Susanna waved aside her words and leaned forward, clasping her hands in her lap. She told Miss Oliver how the children had come to Cothaire. "I want you to understand that once we find the children's families, we will have no further need for a nurse. I don't know how long the position will last."

Miss Oliver smiled. "The idea of living in Cornwall appeals to me, so I am willing to take that chance if you offer me the position."

"The position is yours."

"Thank you, my lady." Tension fell off her shoulders, and Susanna heard her sigh of relief. "If it is not too much of an imposition, could you tell me about the children themselves?"

Susanna smiled and began to describe each, from oldest to youngest. She was astonished how much she could share with Miss Oliver. In the two weeks the children had been at Cothaire, she had learned a lot about their idiosyncrasies, even Toby, who was seldom at the house because he had become Elisabeth's shadow. The perfectly named baby, Joy. Gil, who was determined not to let his baby sister out of his sight. Bertie, gentle and always concerned that the others were happy…except when he was sparring with Toby. The twins, who seemed to have switched personalities because they depended so much on each other. Then she told Miss Oliver about the accident that had left Lulu without her memory.

"Lulu is not the only one who is lost," Susanna said with a sigh. "All of them are. They cannot tell us where they lived before we found them, and, though we are searching the countryside, nothing yet has turned up to explain why they were in that boat."

"You want them to have a calm haven where they can be children again."

Susanna chuckled. "I daresay they have not forgotten how to do that. With so many young ones, what trouble one does not think up, another does. We have been grateful that women from the local church have offered their time."

"Will they continue?"

"Until you hire a staff for the nursery. Some of the women have expressed interest in continuing to work here."

"That will be good while the children become accustomed to me. If you will excuse me, I should like to see the nursery now."

Susanna nodded, and Miss Oliver stood. With a surprisingly elegant curtsy, the new nurse took her leave.

Getting up, Susanna stretched and smiled. She was glad to have that vital task completed. Maybe she could get her life back to normal again. Arthur would be remaining closer to home while the stable was being rebuilt and the broken and cracked windows replaced. She had already given him and Papa an account of what she had ordered. Including: replacing the materials for the nursery that had been stored in the stable, and the names of skilled laborers in the village who would be glad for the work. She needed to prove to them—and herself— that she could keep the household under control despite the arrival of the children and the events since then.

A knock came at the door, and Susanna smiled as she saw her older brother in the doorway.

"Arthur, I was just thinking about you," she said.

He nodded a greeting as he walked in. "I wanted to see if the interview went well."

"It did. Miss Oliver has accepted my offer of employment."

"Really? Did you mention that the job might end tomorrow?"

Susanna frowned. "Of course I did. I would not be false about such an important issue."

"And she still was willing to take the job."

"Yes."

"Why? Did you ask her?"

"I did, and she said she wanted to live in this part of Cornwall."

He raised a brow. "An easy answer."

"You sound as if you believe she is lying. Have you spoken with her?"

"No, but I find it highly unusual that an experienced nurse with an excellent recommendation would settle for such uncertainty."

Putting her hand on his arm, she said, "Arthur, she was forthcoming in her answers to my questions."

"No one is *completely* forthcoming."

"That is cynical, even for you. Is something wrong?"

He rubbed the bridge of his nose. "Forgive me, Susanna. I should have known you would be thorough. I need to leave these matters in your competent hands. I have more than enough to keep me busy."

"And if," came their sister's voice from the doorway as she walked in with Joy in her arms, "we have any worries about the new nurse, we can ask Mrs. Hitchens to keep a close eye on her. Or, better yet, Baricoat. He could sneak up on a hawk."

"Where is Gil?" Susanna asked, glad for Caroline's arrival, which had lightened the conversation. Something was bothering Arthur, but he clearly was not willing to explain now. She thought of his comments about nobody being completely forthcoming. So often, he kept everything he was thinking to himself.

"Greeting Captain Nesbitt."

"He is here?" She whirled to look toward the door before she could halt herself.

Caroline laughed. "I don't recall you being this excited when we have other callers."

"Hush!" She did not want Captain Nesbitt to hear her sister's teasing. He might get the wrong idea.

Or would it be the right idea? Her heart no longer seemed to be listening to good sense, and it had begun an excited dance when Caroline mentioned his name. She needed to get it—and the rest of herself—under control before she encountered Captain Nesbitt.

She wished she knew how.

Gil was babbling about his baby sister while Drake carried him toward the room where Lady Caroline had told him to bring the little boy. Drake admired how devoted he was to his sister. Would he have been the same if he had a younger sister of his own? As a child, he had dreamed of having a real sibling. The fraternity aboard ship had fulfilled that longing for brothers, and he could not imagine staying ashore. Not since his dream of becoming the proud owner of a fleet of ships had taken shape.

Yet when he saw these adorable children with Lady Susanna, his thoughts turned to a family of his own. A true family, not just a crew with the common goal of getting their cargo from one place to another profitably.

A deep male voice came out of a room ahead, silencing Gil. The little boy looked at Drake as they heard "Captain Nesbitt? Isn't he the master of that listing ship in our harbor? I thought it would be gone long before now, but it is still cluttering up our pier."

He recognized the voice. It belonged to Lady Susanna's older brother, the viscount.

"Arthur, that is not kind." That was Lady Susanna,

and warmth spread through him as she came to his defense. "He not only rescued the children—"

"And dumped them on our doorstep."

"But he helped to fight the fire that destroyed the stable."

"True, but the stable was lost anyhow."

"Surely," said Lady Caroline, her voice sharp, "you do not blame him for that."

"Of course not, but…"

Drake was curious what else Lord Trelawney might have said if Gil had not let out a squeal about his baby. Drake put the child down. Gil ran immediately to Lady Caroline.

Lady Susanna stood by her sister, her color high. Even though she wore a pale yellow gown beneath a practical white apron, her stance suggested she was a warrior ready to go into battle on his behalf. She had never looked so beautiful.

"Captain Nesbitt," she said with an unsteady smile, "do come in and join us."

As he walked in, Lord Trelawney asked, "How are the repairs on your ship coming, Captain?"

"Slowly," he said.

"That seems the situation in too many places, I fear."

"Which is why we appreciate your help with the children more than ever, Captain," Lady Caroline added, flashing another frown at her brother.

"It has been my pleasure." He said nothing more as Lord Trelawney excused himself and left.

"Pay him no mind," Lady Caroline said. "He has been extra grumpy ever since the fire." Her smile faded. "He takes too much upon himself without asking for help."

"Sounds like a family trait."

Both women laughed, and Lady Susanna invited

him to sit while they discussed what had brought him to Cothaire. Lady Caroline chose a comfortable chair where she could lean her elbow on one arm as she continued to hold Joy, as she had just about every time Drake had seen her.

When Lady Susanna chose the settee facing her sister, he sat beside her, leaving enough room for propriety's sake. He was unsure if he could have kept from draping his arm over her shoulder if he were closer to her. If only Morel had not interrupted them on the beach after church...

"To what do we owe the pleasure of your call this afternoon?" asked Lady Susanna.

Did she smile a bit more sweetly when she said "pleasure of your call"?

"Since the failure of our experiment with the jolly boat, I have been trying to think of other sites that might help bring back Lulu's memories." He clasped his hands between his knees and leaned forward so he could look at both women at the same time. "If you recall, the note mentioned that the person or persons who put the children in the jolly boat wanted to make sure they did not grow up to work in a mine. Maybe we should visit a mine."

"There are certainly plenty along the north shore of Cornwall," Lady Susanna said. "There is one not far from here. It is on Jacob Warrick's land."

"Is that Lord Warrick?" He had heard a few rumors about the eccentric baron who had what people called outlandish, newfangled ideas about mining.

"Yes, he inherited the title from his uncle along with the estate. There are more than a dozen mines still being worked, though he has closed several because groundwater was rising faster than it could be pumped out. I am sure, if you ask, he will allow us to visit one of the mines."

Lady Caroline shuddered. "I cannot imagine why you would want to take poor Lulu to such a wretched place."

"Only because the note mentioned the mines," he said, choosing his words with care. "Because the person who wrote it was so adamant about keeping the children out of the mines, it is possible the note writer is from a mining village and truly knows how hard that life is."

"It is possible that the children will recognize someone, or someone will know them," Lady Susanna said, her voice unsteady. "By going there, we could be making the first step toward reuniting them with their families."

"Yes." Lady Caroline lowered her eyes, but not fast enough.

Drake saw pain in them. Like her sister, Lady Caroline had taken the children into her heart as well as into their home. To return them to their families now, even though she knew it was the right thing to do, would be difficult.

"Excellent." He set himself on his feet. "We will need a cart large enough to carry all the children."

"All?" breathed Lady Caroline.

Her sister stood and went to her. Putting a consoling hand on Lady Caroline's shoulder, Lady Susanna said, "We cannot know if the children are from the same place. Having one child recognized may be the key to finding out the truth about all of them."

Lady Caroline rose, mumbled something and rushed out with Gil's little legs pumping to keep up.

Drake sighed, then heard Lady Susanna do the

same. As he started to apologize, she waved his words aside.

"My sister realizes this is something we have to do." Tears bubbled into her eyes. "We both do, but it is not easy."

"I know."

"Yes, I think you do." She tilted her head back to look up at him as she said, "Thank you for another good idea, Captain."

"Will tomorrow be too soon for us to take the children to Lord Warrick's mine? Benton has the day watch, so I can spare the time to come with you."

"Don't you have to find a cargo for your ship?"

"I may find what I am seeking when we call on Lord Warrick."

"I wish you good luck with that, Captain. Now, if you will excuse me, I will see to arranging—"

He put out a hand to halt her from turning away. At her astonished expression, he resisted the urge again to apologize. This time for his boldness. Instead, he said, "We are working together to help the children. They have shortened our names to nicknames. Would it offend you if we followed their lead and set aside such formal address?"

"You want me to call you Cap?"

"I had hoped you would consider calling me Drake."

A dozen emotions fled across her face, both positive ones and negative ones. Again he had to fight the temptation to ask her the name of the person who had betrayed her trust. Had she loved a blackguard who had treated her as heartlessly as Ruby had him?

"I don't think that is a good idea." She whirled away and rushed to the door. "Good day, Captain Nesbitt."

Then she was gone, and he was left wondering if one simple request had ruined everything.

Chapter Ten

Angry voices echoed through the forward hold. Angry and frustrated.

Drake understood both emotions too well. Why had Lady Susanna turned down his reasonable request as if he had asked her to elope with him to Gretna Green? As much time as they spent together in their efforts to help the children, addressing each other with their titles had become tiresome. The children called her Susu, but with him, she was as correct and strict as a patroness at Almack's.

And shouldn't he be relieved? As soon as *The Kestrel* was seaworthy, he could leave Porthlowen and Susanna Trelawney far behind. No tearful farewells, no worry that he would be betrayed again by another faithless woman.

She is not faithless, his conscience argued.

No, she was not. She had a strong faith, so strong that it awed him and made him question his own casual relationship with God. He did not want questions in his life. He wanted his only worry to be if the wind would get them to the next port on time.

Pushing his uneasy thoughts aside, a skill he had perfected in the years since he had heard of Ruby's betrayal, Drake went belowdecks to see why there was so much shouting. His crew knew he would not tolerate fistfights on *The Kestrel*, but he accepted that there were times when they had to let off steam before they burst like an overheated engine.

Drake could not believe it. More holes had been found deep in the hold. As his crew set to work patching and ridding the hold of water, he examined several.

He frowned. The holes they had repaired after the battle with the privateers had been jagged with splinters sticking into the ship from where the shot had struck the hull. These newly discovered holes were smoother.

Kneeling in the briny water, he ran his fingers over the hull. He could see no clue to what had caused the damage. He raised his fingers and rubbed them together. Was that sawdust he felt or something else? The hold had been filled with grain, and the chaff had not been cleaned out while the crew concentrated on fixing the ship.

Drake rinsed his fingers, then stood. He gestured for his first mate to follow him up on deck. There they could talk without every ear listening.

Benton outlined what he intended to do once he found out who was behind the damage. It started with drawing and quartering and got worse from there.

Paying him no mind, because his first mate was not a vengeful man, Drake stared across the harbor to where fishermen were dragging their boats onto shore. Others repaired nets, and a trio of old men sat smoking pipes, the smoke a straight line from the pipes as the bracing wind snatched it away.

"Tell me what you think is causing this damage," Drake said.

"Maybe the largest woodworm in history has taken up residence in *The Kestrel*."

"I am not in the mood for weak attempts at humor."

Benton folded his arms on the rail and looked toward the village. "All right. I'll be serious. If we don't leave soon, the lads may jump ship. They are too bored. Several were asking if they could have leave for the parson's wedding so they could look forward to going to the celebration."

"The banns have been read just once. I hope we are not still moored to this pier in a fortnight." He turned to watch the crew going up and down the ladder to the front hold. "We cannot pretend that these holes are caused by French shot. There was no damage in that hold when we arrived in Porthlowen Harbor, and now it is riddled with holes. I had thought that perhaps the holes might be caused by some embers thrown against the hull, but these newest ones were drilled."

"From which side?"

"The inside."

Benton shook his head. "Impossible. No one is allowed on board without permission."

"I doubt our woodworm, as you call him, is going to ask permission."

"Who would want to keep us in Porthlowen?"

"Maybe one of those village lasses who has her eyes on our crew?"

He shook his head. "The lads like to flirt, but they will be just as happy to flirt in another harbor. Other than you, Captain, nobody seems to be building any ties here."

"If you speak of the children—"

"Not only of the children."

Drake pushed back from the rail and crossed the

motionless deck. He would not discuss Lady Susanna with his first mate.

"There is no choice but to divide up the crew into thirds," he said, "so we can have more men on watch day and night."

"I will see to that, Captain, though perhaps we should have four teams, so the lads have a break."

"A good suggestion. Having them fall asleep on watch defeats our purpose. Select which men will be on which shift and have the list ready for me when I get back."

"Get back?"

Drake explained the plan to take the children to the mining village. Benton's nose wrinkled in disgust.

"I know," Drake said. "We have put off going there, hoping that the children don't belong there. But we have found no sign of them being from a fishing village or a farm settlement. I hope they don't belong there, either, because I do not want to consign any of them to such a life, but we have to know the truth."

"Why?"

"Because..."

Why *did* they have to know the truth? The children had been sent away for a reason, so why were he and the Trelawneys trying to take them right back to where their journey began? He thought of Lady Susanna's sparkling eyes when the children made her laugh and how a little baby was banishing her sister's grief. Should they keep looking or leave well enough alone?

Which should it be? Would stopping be selfish or doing what is best for the children?

His steps faltered as he realized he had aimed those questions at God. Why was he calling on Him now after so many years? Did he really expect a response?

The questions roiled through his head, and he stamped

away, leaving his first mate to stare after him. He could not give Benton an answer to his question when he did not have any for his own.

One look at Captain Nesbitt's face when he arrived at Cothaire, and Susanna knew he was in an evil temper. When she greeted him, he grumbled like a bear with a sore head.

That did not halt Lulu from squealing his name and holding out her arms to him. He picked her up and, after being introduced to the new nurse, placed her beside Miss Oliver in the cart before helping Moll and Bertie and Toby in. The nurse wisely separated the two boys before they could begin pinching and poking each other.

Caroline had insisted that neither Gil nor Joy go on the outing. Gil was sneezing and had a runny nose, and her sister did not want to risk his health on what might be a fruitless journey. Even though Susanna believed her sister was grasping for any excuse to keep the children close, she had agreed to let them remain at Cothaire.

Not waiting for Captain Nesbitt to assist her, Susanna climbed onto the narrow plank at the front of the cart. She picked up the reins and waited for him to settle himself beside her.

The cart had never seemed so cozy before. Captain Nesbitt's broad shoulders brushed against her as she drove out of the stable yard and onto the road to the village. She focused her eyes on the horses pulling them.

Or she tried to.

Her gaze kept slipping to the man beside her. He appeared far more comfortable than she was. One elbow rested on the edge of the seat, and his left boot balanced on his right knee. He had taken care that the sole did not brush her skirts.

But he did not say a word to her. She could understand why he was furious with her. His request to address each other more informally had been a reasonable one. After all, she referred to him as Cap when she spoke to the children. Yet, the formal titles helped keep her heart in line. Even to say his given name might give her heart carte blanche to open itself further to him.

She was grateful for a bit of traffic in the village because she had to concentrate on weaving the cart between other vehicles and pedestrians. From the back, the children called out with excitement to people they recognized, but Captain Nesbitt remained silent.

At the edge of the village, Miss Hyacinth Winwood stepped out of her stone cottage that was covered with rose vines. "Good afternoon," she called.

Her sister, Miss Ivy, appeared at the door, then ducked back inside. A moment later, she rushed out, carrying a jar. She waved to the children. "Look at the lot of you! Out to take the fresh air on such a lovely afternoon."

Susanna drew back on the reins, slowing the horses before they ran Miss Ivy down. The Winwood sisters took that as an invitation. Miss Ivy held the jar, and Miss Hyacinth plucked out candied fruit for each child. Within seconds, the children had sticky faces and fingers, and Miss Oliver was kept busy making sure they did not touch each other's clothing.

"They look so much better with every passing day," Miss Ivy said. "Soon they will be as chubby and rosy as babies should be."

"Not a baby," Toby said, jabbing his thumb against his chest. "Big boy. Raymond say so."

"Well, if our parson says that, it must be true." Miss

Hyacinth winked at her sister, then added, "And now that I look at you again, I can see you boys are getting really big." She looked back at Susanna. "Where are you bound?"

"To one of the mines on Lord Warrick's estate."

The two sisters exchanged an abruptly unhappy glance before Miss Hyacinth asked, "Why would you take them *there*? I thought the note said not to let them go into the mines."

"How do you know what the note said?" Captain Nesbitt asked.

"Nothing stays secret long here." Susanna chuckled to counteract the sudden suspicion in his voice. Though he had been in Porthlowen for weeks, he still did not understand how tightly knit the villagers were. What one of them knew everyone soon knew.

Miss Ivy said, "Miss Rowse probably mentioned something when we were in her shop. Was it something we should not know?"

"It is of little consequence," Susanna replied, wanting to smooth any ruffled feathers. For both the sisters and Captain Nesbitt. "The note spoke of when the children were old enough to work in the mines, which they are not yet. We are going to the mine in the hope that seeing it will help Lulu remember her life before the fall down the stairs."

"That accident was a horrible thing," Miss Hyacinth said.

"We cried when we heard of it," added her sister, who reached into the jar again to offer more candied fruit to the children.

Susanna halted her by saying that they must be going and promising to let the sisters know if anything came of the visit. As soon as the cart was out of earshot from the Winwood cottage, she said, "They mean well."

"Tell Miss Oliver that," Captain Nesbitt replied in the same dark tone.

Susanna laughed and heard a smothered chuckle from Miss Oliver in the back. Whether the nurse found his words amusing or she was laughing with the children, it did not matter. The happy sound propelled them up the steep road onto the moorlands beyond the village.

The land stretched out before them, undulating like a sea that had been frozen in midmotion. Few trees intruded upon the bare expanse of the moor. Its vast openness was unsettling. She was accustomed to the cliffs and thick hedges around her home. She found the sea off to her right a far more comforting sight.

As did Captain Nesbitt. She could tell when she saw him staring out at the water.

"You miss it, don't you?" she asked.

"The sea? Of course I miss it. The life I chose for myself is out there, not here on land. If we could solve the puzzles of the children and my ship, *The Kestrel* could return to the work she is meant to do." He paused and cocked an ear, trying to catch a sound.

She strained her own ears to hear over the excited youngsters. Upon the swift breeze came the distant baas of sheep that grazed on the common land. A dull repetitious thud sounded beneath the flock's plaintive bleats.

"What is that?" asked Captain Nesbitt.

She glanced at him in astonishment. "I thought you were from Cornwall."

"Actually, I grew up in Plymouth."

"Oh, that explains why you don't recognize the sound of a beam engine draining water from a mine. There are places on the moors where there are so many mines so close together that the racket is louder than a thunderstorm."

"I look forward to seeing the beam engine."

She shook her head. "I don't look forward to seeing anything at the mine."

Whether he agreed or not, he lapsed again into silence. They continued along the road that was little more than a rough track with grass between the wheel ruts. The monotonous beat of the beam engine grew louder as they neared the mine.

Beside her, Captain Nesbitt inhaled sharply. She understood why if he had never seen a beam engine house up close.

The stone building was more than three stories high, but no longer or wider than the dining room at Cothaire. A great round chimney rose another two stories above the peaked roof. Three windows, the uppermost one arched, marched up the outside as if following a staircase. The front wall was far thicker and more than half the height of the other walls. Over it, a great iron beam rocked in and out like a pendulum.

From the back, the children pointed in awe and began calling questions. Susanna stopped the cart and got down, going around to the back. She asked the children if they knew what the building and the beam were. Bertie suggested it was a great drum, which was why it made so much noise, while Toby, who was interested in shopkeeping from his time with Elisabeth, argued it had to be a way to lift large crates up to a high shelf. Lulu and Moll had their hands over their ears.

Captain Nesbitt lifted Lulu out while Miss Oliver gathered the children to take them for a walk toward the village that was set past the mine entrance. It was no more than a collection of several terrace houses that were only a shade lighter gray than the piles of refuse outside the mine. Susanna came around the wagon and took the hand Lulu held out to her.

As she walked with the little girl and Captain Nesbitt toward the door of the beam engine house that was up a wooden staircase with four steps, Susanna looked back to make sure none of the other children were following. She glanced down at Lulu and sighed. The little girl was gazing around herself with avid curiosity as if she had never seen a beam engine house.

Just as Captain Nesbitt was.

She wished she could be as fascinated, but it was not easy when she was torn between the hope of finding someone who recognized the children and wanting to keep them at Cothaire. She could not be selfish, even though her heart urged her to turn around and return home.

Lord, You brought these children into our lives for a reason. I cannot understand it, but You do. Help me accept Your will and do Your good work here in finding the homes where these children truly belong.

"This is astounding," Captain Nesbitt said, raising his voice to be heard over the steady thump of the engine. "I know nothing about steam engines."

"They have put some on ships."

"So I have heard, but I look forward to feeling the wind driving *The Kestrel* once we repair the new damage."

"You have had more damage?"

He looked over Lulu's head to her. "Yes. New holes appear to have been drilled by some sort of auger. It will take us at least a week to plug them and make them watertight."

"I am sorry."

He gave her a faint smile. "I appreciate that."

Susanna hesitated. Then taking a deep breath, she said, "As it appears you shall not be gone as quickly as you wish, maybe I should rethink the decision I made yesterday."

"Which one?"

She was disappointed that he had forgotten their discussion. Sneaking a glance in his direction, she realized he had not. He simply had not forgiven her for turning down what he had seen as a reasonable request.

And it had been reasonable. She had been the unreasonable one.

Captain Drake Nesbitt was not Franklin Chenowith. He had not made her a promise that he would stay forever and then disappeared without explanation. She had known from the first second she met Drake that he would be leaving Porthlowen as soon as his ship was ready. He was honest with her, and there would be no surprises waiting to humiliate her again.

"About using our given names rather than our formal titles," she said.

He stopped. Because he held Lulu's other hand, she had to stop, too, so she did not jerk the little girl. He turned to her and slowly smiled.

Something deep within her uncurled in tempo with his lips tilting. Even though such thoughts were foolish, she could not keep from imagining those lips brushing hers.

"Will you call me Drake?" he asked.

"Yes, and you can call me Susanna if you wish."

"Not Susu?"

"I restrict use of that name to those under the age of six."

"No Susu?" asked Lulu, who had been listening intently.

"Susu for you," Drake said with a laugh as he bent to tap the little girl's nose. Looking up, he added with that enticing smile, "Susanna for me."

Susanna liked the sound of that. Far more than she should.

Glancing away, she asked, "Shall we take a look at the beam engine? We may find Lord Warrick there because he enjoys tinkering with mechanical things."

"Is it louder inside?" Drake asked.

She smiled when she noticed Lulu had her hands over her ears. Drawing one down, she took the child's hand. Drake picked up the tiny girl, and she clamped her hands over her ears again and grinned.

Susanna led the way up to the door. She did not bother knocking to see if they could enter. No one inside would hear her.

Inside, she looked up at the beam. It was a great iron arm that rocked back and forth above the engine, raising and lowering the metal shaft that fit precisely into another section. The steam-powered engine moved faster than the water-driven one that had been in use when Susanna visited about five years ago. The beam rocked up and down every two to three seconds, never going faster, never slowing.

Drake held Lulu close as he peered over the wooden rail at the water being pumped from the mine. He said something to the child, and Lulu nodded eagerly, then pointed at the beam. He stepped back so she could not touch any part of the engine. He was so patient with the children.

She turned away before she started thinking what an excellent father he would be for her children. She had thought of Franklin in that role. He was a father now, but his children were not hers, too. Quieting her heart, she told it not to ask for the impossible.

"Lady Susanna?" came a muffled shout over the engine's clattering, and she looked to her left to see Jacob Warrick coming to his feet from where he had been squatting by the engine. "What are you doing here?"

If one were to judge by appearances, Susanna would have guessed Lord Warrick taught at a college in Oxford. He wore brass spectacles that arched high over his nose. Even though the sides extended to fit tightly behind his ears, he pushed the front up his nose again and again.

Susanna did not know him well, but her father had visited the mine before his gout worsened. He told her Lord Warrick possessed a nimble and curious mind. The baron had invested in the mines on his estate, buying modern equipment to keep the miners as safe as possible when they were more than fifty fathoms below the surface.

She began to shout back an answer, but he motioned toward the door. Tapping Drake on the shoulder to get his attention, she followed Lord Warrick outside.

The baron asked, "Were you waiting for me long? I get so fascinated by the steam engine that I fail to notice most comings and goings in the beam engine house."

"We were not there long," she replied, then introduced the men before giving an abbreviated explanation of why they had come to the mine. When she finished, she asked, "Did she recognize any of it, Drake?"

"At first, I thought she might, but it was more excitement at the movement and the water than anything else."

"You might want to try the village," Lord Warrick said. "Someone there might know the children."

"That is our next stop," Drake replied, then looked at the mine entrance. It led into darkness. "How deep is the mine?"

"Close to ten fathoms at its deepest, but some of the other tunnels are shallower." He glanced at the engine house. "Hmm…that sounds wrong. Excuse me."

Though Susanna could hear nothing different in the beam's rhythm, she stepped aside as Lord Warrick bolted up the stairs and inside.

"Did he say fathoms?" asked Drake, drawing her attention back to him.

She nodded. "The depth of a mine is measured in fathoms."

"It is measured at six feet to a fathom like at sea?"

With a laugh, she answered, "Yes, so the distance the shaft has been dug should be easy for any sailor to calculate."

"At six feet to a fathom, they have dug down sixty feet. Impressive."

"I am sure Lord Warrick would arrange a tour for you if you wish."

"No, thank you. I prefer measuring fathoms while on my ship rather than surrounded by unforgiving earth." When he offered his arm, she slipped her hand onto it and smiled at Lulu, who kept her arms around his neck.

Together, they went to where Miss Oliver and the other children waited for them. The nurse aimed a silent question at them and sighed when Susanna shook her head. Like everyone at Cothaire, Miss Oliver wanted to discover why the children had come to Porthlowen.

The youngsters' chatter faded as they reached the village. Their eyes got big, but, though Susanna watched and knew Drake and Miss Oliver did, as well, there were no signs that they had ever been in the village before. They did not react to anyone as they did in Porthlowen. Bertie, clearly frightened, edged closer to Susanna, and she lifted him into her arms.

"There is nothing bad here," she whispered against his soft cheek.

"Want go home." When he repeated the words more loudly, Toby and Moll picked up the refrain.

Hushing them, Susanna looked along the single street. On either side, the terrace houses each had eight doors. The apartments within must be tiny and cramped. The stone walls were stained with dust from the mine, but unlike her previous visit, glass glittered in the windows. Lord Warrick must have invested in the houses as well as the mine.

Women and children in clean but worn clothing peeked out doors and windows. Susanna called for them to come out. As they gathered around her, she asked, "Do you recognize any of these children?"

The women studied the youngsters' faces. Then, one after another, they shook their heads. One asked if these were the children who had washed ashore in Porthlowen, and Susanna's heart sank. If they had heard of the extraordinary events, then surely they would have come to her father's house to share any information they had.

But they had none.

Lord, she prayed again, needing to remind herself over and over that the children were not in her life to stay, _help me to keep from faltering on my journey toward the truth._

She thanked each of the women and was able to keep smiling when they wished her good luck in her quest, but tears burned the back of her throat. She had no idea where to try next. Should they take the children to some of the other coves along the northern shore? That seemed a waste of time when those villages had already been checked and no one claimed to know anything about the children.

As she turned to go back to the cart, Drake said, "Maybe their husbands might recognize one or more of the children."

"That is unlikely. The women spend time with the children while the men are in the mine. Lord Warrick has maintained the tutwork system here."

"Tutwork? What is that?"

"The miners bid for the right to excavate and extract the tin. Because those who bid the lowest are the pair who win, the men have to work long hours to find enough ore to pay for their supplies and provide for their families. Sometimes they do not get to spend much time with their families because they are working in shifts around the clock to dig out the ore."

"It hardly sounds fair."

"Maybe to you or me, but the miners were pleased when Lord Warrick announced he would continue the system. Other ways of bidding for the work can be far riskier."

Drake looked back at the village as they helped the children into the cart. "There are plenty of other mines and other villages along the shore."

"How far do you think that boat went before you rescued the children?"

He shrugged. "I have no idea."

"No?" She pointed to where the boys were already wrestling and giggling. "How long do you think *they* would have sat still in the boat? Even assuming that their mothers gave them a sleeping draught to keep them quiet for as long as possible, which might have kept them from tipping over the boat for a few hours."

"But none of the children showed any signs of taking a sleeping powder."

"My point exactly." She climbed up onto the seat. Once he was sitting beside her, she turned the cart around to return to Cothaire. "I doubt they were in the boat very long before you chanced to see them."

"Long enough for them to drown with nobody watching them."

"We cannot be certain that nobody watched them until you reached the boat. Did you see anyone else on the strand?"

His brow furrowed as he thought. "To own the truth, I don't remember who was there before I brought the boat ashore. After that, it was crowded."

"It would be simpler if you could remember seeing someone."

"By now, you should know that nothing about these children and their secrets is simple."

She laughed. "No truer words were ever spoken."

"Unless," he said, his voice fading to a whisper, "it is that I have enjoyed spending time with you."

"Me, too. I—"

The cart jerked to one side. A loud crash came from the back. The children screamed. The horses whinnied and broke into a run. She fought the reins to hold them back. The cart bounced oddly beneath her. What had happened? She did not dare to risk looking back.

Broad hands seized the reins in front of hers, pulling back sharply. Drake shouted to the horses to stop, his foot braced against the dash. More screams came from the back. The cart made a strange crunching sound and tilted to the left.

Then they stopped. For a moment, there was silence; then shrieks erupted from the children.

Susanna jumped down from the tilting cart and ran around the back. Miss Oliver was helping the children out and past the broken axle. The missing wheel was spinning to a stop on the road behind them. She ignored it as she hugged one child after another and assured herself that none had suffered more than a few small bumps and scrapes. Miss Oliver cradled her wrist but said she would be fine.

Drake came back carrying the wheel, which he leaned against the higher end of the cart. Past clenched teeth, he said, "We were lucky. If we had gone a few more yards and been on that nearly vertical section down to Porthlowen, the cart would have been impossible to control."

"I'm grateful the accident happened when it did, then."

"Accident? Do you think this was an accident?" He pointed at the wheel where the metal had been smoothly cut almost the whole way through. Beyond that, the break was sharp and uneven. "Whoever did this miscalculated, and the wheel broke earlier than it was supposed to." He looked at the nurse, who was kneeling on the ground with the children around her. "Because of Miss Oliver. Whoever did this did not figure that an adult would be riding in the back with the children. She is slender, but her weight was enough to break the wheel early."

"But who would want to injure the children?" She could not pull her gaze from the wheel.

Drake's finger against her cheek turned her eyes toward him. His expression was hard when he said, "That, my dear Susanna, is what I intend to find out before whoever did this tries something else."

Chapter Eleven

Susanna put two more dolls on the pile of fabric and blankets, then wiped her hand against her sweaty brow and pushed her hair out of her eyes. Her fingers came away streaked with dirt. Her face must be covered, as well, but the past few hours of working in the stuffy attic had been fruitful.

This morning, the children had been introduced to the freshly painted day nursery. The night nursery should be done early next week; then the children would sleep in comfortable beds instead of on pallets. They looked forward to it as much as Miss Oliver looked forward to having a space of her own.

After seeing the cramped and dirty conditions in the mining village and knowing that Lord Warrick was trying to make them better, Susanna had wondered what she could do to help. She had thought about the extra toys and other things stored in Cothaire's attic. Once she had Papa's permission to collect as many as she wanted and have them delivered to the mining village, she went to work. She also had accumulated a smaller pile for Raymond to distribute to children in Porthlowen.

Maybe Papa had seen that she needed to do something so she could forget the terrible events of the afternoon they went to Lord Warrick's mine. The children had been terrified when the wheel came off the cart, and Miss Oliver had twisted her right wrist. She wore a sling to protect it, much to the delight of the girls, who thought it was the perfect way to carry a doll. So the nurse had created slings for them out of handkerchiefs.

But who would want to injure the children? Was it the same person who had set them adrift? All along they had assumed that whoever did that was the one who wrote the note, begging for the children to be cared for. What if it had not been?

Her mind went around and around pondering the questions, but never got any closer to an answer. There must be something she had overlooked, the something that made the puzzling pieces fit together in a logical answer.

Coming up to the attic had been a way to escape her thoughts. She looked at the stack of blocks, dolls and wooden animals that she had made. It was her third. It would have to do…for now. Dust was glued to her skin. She could have had a footman help her move the crates, but she needed the hard work to silence her mind. Once she had a chance to speak with Lord Warrick, she would implore him to search his own attic to help the families who worked in his mines. For now, there were enough toys in the piles so the children in the mining village would receive one or two toys each.

Susanna hurried down the stairs, sucking in the cooler air at the bottom. Knowing a visit to the stable would leave her covered with cinders and soot, she decided to check on the cleanup out there before she washed and changed. She slipped out a side door and was astonished to discover the sun was setting over the western

cliffs. She had lost track of time in the attic. She needed
to hurry if she wanted to be ready for the evening meal.

As she rushed across the back garden, her hair bounced
on her shoulders. It fell down her back as the last two pins
tumbled out. She bent to pick them up and slid them into
her apron pocket. Reaching up, she started to braid her
hair to keep it out of her face.

"Susanna!"

Hearing Drake call her name, she looked down at her
filthy dress and hands. She hastily twisted her hair into
place, pulling the pins back out and hoping they would
hold her hair in some semblance of a proper style. She
thought of the streaks of dirt she had rubbed off her face.
To speak with him when she was in such a sad condition was unthinkable, but rushing into the house when
he was already walking toward her would be even ruder.

She straightened and turned in his direction. All
thoughts of retreat vanished as her eyes drank in the
sight of his strength as the breeze brushed his shirt-
sleeves against his brawny arms. Without his coat, and
with his waistcoat unbuttoned to float out to the side as
he walked toward her, he was the picture of a man she
would love to have in her life.

If only...

"Good evening, Drake," she said, knowing she was
setting herself up for more heartbreak if she followed
her heart to him. After all, if she could not take control of her own heart, how would she keep other parts
of her life in order? "I did not realize you were here."

"I wanted to check the cart again."

"Oh." A sudden cold brushed across her skin as if
she had been doused with ice water. "Did you find anything new?"

"The wheels on the other side appear to be untampered with, though there are marks on the front wheel on that side of the cart. However, those may be nothing more than wear from the road. It is impossible to tell."

"Anything to tell you who might have done this?"

He shook his head. "It had to be someone who had the proper tools, but that could be almost anyone in Porthlowen. Even the fishermen have very sharp knives that could slice through the axle if one had enough patience."

"Or wanted to damage the wheel enough."

"Yes." He gave her a lopsided grin. "You look as if you have been digging ditches."

"I have been working in the attic." She told him what she had gathered and her plans to have the toys distributed. "I thought while I looked like a complete rump, I would check on progress with the stable."

"Nothing has changed. The men assigned to pull debris out of the ashes have been put to work strengthening the roof on the building to be used for the horses. Just in case someone gets the idea to attack Cothaire again."

She shivered when he said "attack," but could not deny what the fire had been. "What about your ship? How are the repairs coming along?"

"We have had no further damage since we set a guard on every deck." Grim satisfaction matched his expression. "The repairs are slower than I would like, but we must make sure no leaks will sink her when we get to sea."

Another shiver ran an icy finger down her back. "What a horrible thought!"

"I agree." His smile returned. "Is there something less horrible we can discuss?"

"I cannot promise it will be less horrible, but the

next time I saw you, I was told to ask you to join us for dinner."

"Dinner?"

"Caroline's idea. She thought the conversation would be more productive if we were well fed."

He looked down at his salt-stained boots. "I am not dressed for such a gathering."

"It is en famille. The four of us, and you and Elisabeth. Papa has decided not to come down and asked me to send you his apologies. Will you join us?"

Drake was astonished how nice sharing a meal with family sounded. How many times he had dreamed of sitting down with a real family. To sit with a family that loved and respected one another and worked together for the good of the earl's estate and Porthlowen. It was a heady thought. How many times during his childhood had he imagined doing just that, instead of sitting on a cold, wet kitchen floor eating what was left in the bottom of the pots? Not that the others in the family who had taken him in ate much better, but they supped together. Once he was old enough to feed himself, he was left to fend for himself in the kitchen. The first time he had to use his fists to defend himself occurred when a stray dog sneaked through the back door and tried to steal his food.

How long had he dreamed of having a family of his own? He could envision himself sitting at the head of the table, and at the far end, where he could admire her beauty in the candlelight, would be his wife, a woman as lovely and charming and delightful as Susanna Trelawney.

Have you lost your mind? What are you thinking? Such a life was not for him. Hadn't he seen in the past that becoming closely involved with a woman led to waters with potential hidden shoals? He was a man of the sea, a man who someday would have multiple ships trading in and out of the ports of Cornwall and farther east. Susanna was a woman with deep roots in Porthlowen.

"Will you join us, Drake?" The sound of his name on her lips was a treat he savored.

"Yes, but I must change my clothes first."

"But—"

"Do you intend to go into dinner looking as you do?" He laughed when she reached up to check what looked to be a hasty bun. "'Tis not your hair. You have a streak of dirt here." He ran his finger along her forehead and felt a quiver. His quiver or hers, or both of them reacting to a simple touch? Knowing he was a fool but unable to halt himself, he asked, "Will you leave the smudge here?" He brushed her left cheek before his fingertip edged along her lips.

Her soft breath was warm and inviting against his skin. He drew his hand back, and he stepped away before he could no longer resist kissing her.

His words tumbled over each other as he said he would be back within an hour. She said nothing. Only nodded, but he could see the uncertainty in her silvery eyes. Would she have let him kiss her? Perhaps.

That knowledge seared his gut like a canker while he returned to his ship. He tried to ignore it while he spoke with Benton in the wardroom about who would be on watch overnight. When he told his first mate that he was joining the Trelawneys for the evening meal, he paid no attention to the knowing twinkle in Benton's eyes.

"I want the men informed so they don't challenge me

when I approach *The Kestrel* after dark," he said. "If I have to call back our password, our enemy may hear it and use it to his advantage."

"I will let them know, Captain."

"And stop grinning like a fool. Why are you grinning like that?"

Benton scratched his side as his smile grew even wider. "The question is why you are not. Pretty Lady Susanna has invited you to join her family at their private table."

"Actually, the invitation was her sister's idea."

He knew he should not have shared that when Benton roared a laugh and said, "So her family approves of a sea dog like you? I find that very interesting. Don't you?"

"I find nothing about this conversation interesting." He stamped across the deck and sat at the table. "Report, Mr. Benton, on the progress of the repairs."

When his first mate snapped to attention with a quick salute and began spouting off facts as if they were both in His Majesty's navy, Drake grew even more annoyed with himself. He should not take out his frustration on his first mate, who always gave exemplary and loyal service. It was not Benton's fault that Drake was torn.

"Thank you, Benton," Drake said, halting him midword. "We will follow the same procedures every day until the last hole is plugged and we set sail."

"Aye, Captain." He saluted again and turned on his heel with military precision to leave the wardroom.

"And no more saluting," Drake called.

Benton's good-natured laughter remained behind when the first mate was gone.

Pushing himself away from the table, Drake went

into his tiny quarters. There was room for his narrow bed and a small trunk. Nothing more. He changed into his best waistcoat and coat. Both were unadorned dark navy wool. He tied his cravat in the simple knot he always used. He tried to clean his boots, but the stains left from when he had waded out to the jolly boat refused to come out.

Finally he could put off returning to Cothaire no longer. He was too eager to spend time with Susanna, and he would have to curb his impulse to tug her into his arms and kiss her until she melted against him. If he cared about her, and he did—far too much—he needed to protect her as closely as he did his heart. Nothing had changed. Nothing would change. As soon as *The Kestrel* was ready, he would leave Porthlowen. As kind as Susanna had been to him, he would not break her heart by letting her think he would stay.

The great house was lit against the dark when Drake returned. He nodded to the footman who opened the door. Then hearing the rustle of satin and lace, he turned to see Susanna approaching.

Could this be the same woman as the rumpled one he had spoken to an hour ago? Her shining hair was piled on her head, and her face shone almost as brightly. Instead of dust and cobwebs, her lavender-and-white-striped gown was covered with lace.

"You are staring," she accused with a smile. "Did I clean up well?"

"Very well. Good evening, Lady Susanna. You look even lovelier than usual." He took her hand and bowed over it. When he stood, he saw he had shocked her with his greeting. He winked before asking, "And do I look more appropriately dressed without a layer of ash on me?"

"You look wonderful."

Again he had to exert all his resolve to release her hand so he did not draw her closer. He thanked her, keeping his tone light, saying he hoped he was not late.

"Actually, the meal has been delayed because of some crisis in the kitchen," Susanna said. "Mrs. Ford reassured me that it was nothing, but asked if they might serve a half hour later than planned. The others are in the back garden, but I thought you might like to see the children while we wait."

Though he would have preferred to spend that half hour alone with her in the garden, it was not an option. He nodded and realized he was anxious to see how the children fared in the wake of yesterday's excitement. As they climbed the stairs, he asked if Lulu had recovered any memories after visiting the beam engine house and the mining village.

"She has not recalled anything important." Susanna sighed as they reached the next staircase to take them up to the nursery floor. "Maybe nothing at all... Moll has been telling her about the jolly boat and other things that happened in the days between their arrival and her fall."

"Did you learn something to help us?"

She shook her head, her smile wavering. "No. Moll was telling her how you and your first mate pulled the boat to shore and..."

"What?"

"She said something about the lady who pushed them out into the waves."

"Did she describe the lady?"

"I did ask, but Moll became alarmed." She gripped the newel post, and he recognized her determined expression. "But we have time now. Maybe if we ask again…"

Drake took the steps two at a time to keep up with her as she ran up the stairs. Catching the sight of a slender ankle made his breath catch, and she glanced at him. He looked away, not wanting her to see the longing that must be on his face.

He was surprised when she opened the door to the day nursery. Walking in, he could not believe the change. The walls had been freshly painted in sunshine yellow, and white shelves were filled with books and toys. The dollhouse from the attic was set between two windows. A rug that must have once graced a room downstairs was worn enough so that children playing on it or dropping food on it could not do any damage.

The children were seated around a small table, finishing their supper. Bertie was the first to realize they had arrived. He jumped up, much to Miss Oliver's dismay, and ran to the door.

"Cap!" he shouted before he threw his arms around Drake's knees.

Drake picked him up and tossed him in the air before catching him. The little boy squealed with delight, and the other three came running, begging him to do the same to them.

"Maybe later," Susanna said before he could reply. "Cap has changed his coat once already this evening."

The children looked puzzled. Drake, however, understood her warning not to jostle the children too much when they had just eaten.

When the youngsters began to whine, he knelt and said, "I have a good idea. How would you like to visit *The Kestrel*?" They looked at him, baffled, until he added, "My ship."

"Go boat?" asked Moll, her eyes wide with sudden fear.

He grinned at her but looked past her to meet Susanna's eyes. "No little boat. I don't want to hear any more talk about a little boat now. Let's talk about the big ship. We can walk out on the pier and climb aboard it."

Moll's lower lip stopped trembling, and she began to smile.

"What do you say?" he asked, looking up at Susanna. "Would you like to visit *The Kestrel*?" He was astonished how much he wanted her to accept his offer to visit his world, so she would see why he loved his life upon the sea.

She glanced from him to the eager children. "If we would not be in the way..."

"No need to worry about that. Nor do you need to worry about getting in a jolly boat. You can walk out on the pier and avoid the waves."

Smiling gratefully, she said, "I am glad to hear that."

"Go ship, Susu!" shouted Gil. The other children repeated it, jumping up and down.

"Go ship, Susu?" Drake asked as he came to his feet and took her hand again.

She smiled at them. "How can I say no? Yes, we will go to visit the ship."

"Now?" asked Lulu.

"Soon," Drake replied. "Now you need to finish your supper."

As the children rushed to the table, chattering like excited magpies, he continued to hold Susanna's hand. She did not pull it away while they made plans with the children. It was, he had to admit, the perfect beginning to the evening.

* * *

Smiling at the children who were gathered in a half circle by her feet, Susanna hoped her anxiety and anticipation did not show on her face. She clasped her hands on her lap as she sat on the small nursery chair.

Drake stood behind her. He put his hand on her shoulder, and she was grateful for his understanding that she felt as if she stood on the sea cliffs and was about to step off. If the children could give them a good clue, they might be able to find the truth. She tried not to think about what would happen then.

"Moll," she said, "you were telling Lulu this morning about the little boat you were in when Cap found you."

All the children but Lulu cringed at the memories of that day.

Moll nodded, then stuck her thumb in her mouth.

"You said a lady put you in the boat."

All the children but Lulu nodded. Lulu looked around, clearly fascinated that everyone else seemed to be playing a game, and she wanted to discover the rules.

"Did you know the lady?"

All the children shook their heads. Lulu shook hers belatedly, but Susanna was certain she was copying the others.

"Was she young or old?" Drake asked as he came around her chair to kneel beside her.

"Old!" shouted Bertie and Gil at the same time.

His smile faded when Susanna asked how old, and the children spouted back answers from twenty to a hundred. She looked at him and shrugged. The children's perceptions could not be trusted.

As if to prove her point, she asked them what color hair the lady had. Two said brown, one said green, and

Lulu suggested it might have been purple. Giving each a kiss on the cheek, she bade them a good night.

"So much for that," Drake murmured as they went toward the stairs. "For all we know, they may be talking about a lad instead of a lady."

"True." She ran her fingers lightly down the banister. "Thank you for inviting them to visit your ship, and thank you for keeping me from dreading the waves."

"It is a shame you feel that way, when you love looking at the sea."

"Visiting the ship might be just the thing to help Lulu remember."

"Or maybe it will help one of the others. We still have to hope that we can find out where they really belong."

They belong here. With us, she almost said, but halted herself. "Have faith, right?"

When he did not reply, she saw he was looking down the stairs. She did, as well. Her siblings and Elisabeth, who would soon count among them, were waiting at the bottom.

"We wondered where you had gotten to," said Arthur, his tone stern.

As they reached the bottom of the stairs, Susanna said, "Drake wanted to invite the children to visit his ship." She saw her brothers exchange a quick glance when she used Drake's given name. She decided saying nothing of it was the best plan.

Caroline smiled broadly. "What a lovely idea! I am sure they are very excited."

"You have no idea." At Drake's droll answer, her sister laughed and the tension washed away.

Susanna turned to Raymond while they walked into

the dining room. "If you don't mind, I would like to drop some donation boxes at the parsonage when we go to the harbor."

"You may want to keep them here a little bit longer." He grimaced. "The parsonage is a bit pungent at the moment."

"Pungent?"

"Someone put a bucket of fish in a back closet that is seldom used. The stench began slowly, but by today it was intolerable. I sent Toby to Elisabeth at the shop, and then I searched the parsonage from top to bottom. That is when I found the rotting fish."

Drake asked quietly, "Do you know who would play a hoax on you, Parson Trelawney?"

"Call me Raymond, if you would." He did not pause as he added, "And, no, I do not know anyone who would do that. I cannot recall the last time I opened that back closet."

"Is there anything we can do to help?" Susanna asked. "Mrs. Hitchens—"

"I have many volunteers from the village already, but thank you. Some of the fishermen's wives have assured me they have old family recipes for getting rid of the stench of rotten fish."

"Good." She glanced at Drake as Caroline urged him to sit between them at the mahogany table in the smaller dining room.

His mouth was in a straight line when he drew out her sister's chair and then hers. As if he spoke them aloud, she knew his thoughts. He wondered if the incident at the parsonage was related to the others. Young Toby lived there with her brother, so if someone truly was eager to hurt the children, the boy was an easy target. When he was with Elisabeth at the shop, there were probably too many people coming in and out.

But why would anyone want to hurt six darling children?

Chapter Twelve

A soft sound woke Susanna. It had been a restless night
as the questions plaguing her played endlessly through
her mind. As she went through the incidents over and
over, she began to wonder if the children were the only
targets. The fires in town and the one at Cothaire's stable
had no impact on the youngsters, save for the delays in
renovating the nursery. And then there was the damage
inflicted on Drake's ship. That could have begun even
before the children were rescued.

So her mind went around and around, keeping her
from sleeping until long after the moon set. Even asleep,
she dreamed of chasing someone and never catching him
or her.

The soft sound came again.

Susanna opened her eyes, seeing the gray light of
the hour before dawn coming around the bed curtains,
which were too far apart. Who had opened them?

Turning onto her back, she almost yelped in shock
when she saw three children sitting at the foot of her
bed, watching her. Bertie was flanked by Lulu and Moll.
None of them spoke as they waited for her to say something.

At first, vexation swelled within her. She squashed it. The children had not meant to make her upset by surprising her. They had no idea how little sleep she had gotten.

"How long have you been here?" she asked.

"Long time," Bertie said. "Long, long time."

She smiled as she pushed herself up to sit against the pillows. By now, she should know better than to ask such a question. A long time for Bertie could be hours or minutes.

When Lulu yawned, quickly followed by the other two, she held out her arms. They crawled up the bed and under the covers beside her.

"Why don't you sleep awhile longer?" she suggested. "It is still very early."

Bertie nestled down beside her. "Mama let me pillow with her, too."

"Tell me about your mama," she whispered as she tucked the covers around him. "What does she look like?"

He closed his eyes, and a dreamy smile lifted his lips. "Pretty. My mama pretty."

"My mama pretty," murmured Moll as she snuggled on Susanna's other side.

Stretching out her arm, Susanna drew both twins closer to her. In another few nights, they would be moving to the refurbished night nursery. There would be no more delightful opportunities to cuddle together before the day began.

"Does your mama have yellow hair or black or red?" Susanna asked. If they could get a description of the missing mothers, they might have a better chance of finding the children's families.

"Mama pretty." Bertie added nothing more before he fell asleep.

Moll's eyes were closed, her thumb in her mouth. Beside her, Lulu raised a hand to Susanna's face and smiled. "Pretty. My mama pretty."

For just a moment, Susanna let herself savor the idea that these adorable children were hers. But she was not Lulu's mother. She was the woman who had been left to sit alone in church during the first reading of the banns for a wedding that never happened.

She closed her eyes and leaned back into the pillows. As the children's soft, slow breaths grazed her cheeks, she ceded herself to the fantasy she had evaded for almost five years. The fantasy of her and the man she loved and the children they were blessed with, living in joy and growing old together in the house that Papa had built on the far side of the harbor. It was to have been a wedding present for her and Franklin, and it had a beautiful stone terrace where they could have watched the sun set beyond Land's End.

But as, in her mind, she walked out onto that terrace and into her husband's arms, for the first time, it was not Franklin Chenowith holding her. She raised her eyes to look into the loving face of the man she had married. The loving face of Drake Nesbitt. His head lowered to kiss her...

With a gasp, she forced her eyes open and sent the traitorous fantasy back where it could not tease her with what she could not have. Oh, she could have a few of Drake's kisses. The longing in his eyes when he looked at her lips told her that he would happily kiss her. Yet, how could she kiss him when she knew that he would soon be gone? He might never come back to Porthlowen. She had to keep her heart safe, no matter what.

Lord, she prayed silently so she did not wake the children, *help me remember what is important is making sure these children are safe. My own yearnings You know, because You know my heart. Help me keep them from getting in the way of doing what is right for the children.*

Burrowing into her pillow again, she slid down beneath the covers. The children shifted, then nestled against her once more as she fell asleep, too. This time, her slumber was dreamless.

The shouts rang along the shore. Feet pounded on the deck over Drake's head. Coming out of his quarters, he pulled on his coat. His cravat was half tied, and he stuffed the ends into his waistcoat.

"Benton, where are you?" he called as he came up to the main deck and saw his crew clustered near the starboard rail.

"Here." His first mate pushed through the rest of the crew as more shouts and sharp curses sounded from the beach.

Drake saw a group of fishermen, maybe twenty in all, clustered where their boats usually floated at high tide. None of the boats were visible.

"What is going on over there?" he asked.

"Something is amiss with the fishermen," Benton said.

"I can see that. Any clue what?"

He shook his head. "Nothing I can tell from here."

Making a quick decision, Drake said, "Very well. Get the crew back to their tasks. Then you and I will go find out what is going on."

"Aye, Captain." Benton trotted across the deck.

Drake finished tying his cravat and watched the fishermen. They were gesturing with emphatic arms. Some motions seemed to be aimed at *The Kestrel*, though he could not figure out why.

As soon as Benton returned, they left the ship and strode along the beach.

Even before they reached the fishermen, he could see their nets had been slashed to pieces. Three of the boats had planks torn from their sides, and the rest looked as if someone had struck them with an ax.

Beside him, Benton murmured a prayer for God's help in finding and punishing whoever had inflicted such damage.

Truly wishing he could be as certain as Benton that God would turn His attention to the matter, Drake continued along the sand. He was not surprised to see Raymond Trelawney among the men. Someone must have alerted Susanna's brother.

"Good morning, Parson," he said before nodding in the direction of the fishermen.

All he received from the fishermen were glowers, but Raymond said, "I am glad you are here, Captain Nesbitt. I know *The Kestrel* has suffered damage caused by unknown hands. You can see what has happened here. Whether or not it was caused by the same person may be something you can determine for us by looking at the mess left behind."

"My ship has had holes drilled into her. This damage is far more extensive. What I can do is ask my men who were on watch last night if they saw anyone coming along the strand, though they would have reported it immediately if they had."

A man muttered something under his breath, and the parson stepped forward. "If you have something to say, Oates, say it so we all can hear."

"I will." The man jutted his chin toward Drake. "I said that *The Kestrel*'s crew was the only one in the harbor last night."

"Along with whoever did this," Benton said stoutly.

Drake put a hand on his first mate's arm before he could drive one of his clenched fists into the fisherman's face. Starting a brawl would make matters worse. That the fishermen believed his crew had a hand in the destruction showed that, despite an outward welcome in church, his crew remained unwelcome in Porthlowen.

"Are you sure of that? No one saw any strangers." Oates glanced at his fellow fishermen. Many of them nodded, but others waited to see which way the wind was blowing before they committed themselves.

"That means it had to be someone from Porthlowen." Drake folded his arms in front of him. "Someone who has a reason to be angry at you. That is not me nor my crew. We have no quarrel with you. In fact, we will gladly leave your harbor to you once we fix the damage done to *The Kestrel*."

"Course you would defend'm."

Refusing to give in to his yearning to shout back that the fishermen had lost their minds, he said in the calmest voice he could manage, "If you will not take my word, then ask yourselves why my crew would wreck your gear."

The men who had said nothing looked at one another, then at Oates and his cronies.

Oates hesitated, then said, "Maybe they were bored. Maybe they wanted to do some mischief. Maybe—"

"We don't need maybes. We need facts." Drake swept the group with his gaze. The crowd had grown. A few women had come down to the water, as well as Peggy from the village shop, and the blacksmith and Morel, his assistant.

He focused on the fishermen. They were, despite their bluster, afraid. Not of the person who had wrecked their boats and nets, but of how they were going to provide for their families until repairs could be made or replacements found. He could not offer them sympathy. These proud Cornishmen would see that as pity.

"What facts do we have?" the parson asked.

"My boat is worthless now! That is a fact," shouted one man from the center of the group.

"We know," Drake replied as if the fisherman had not spoken, "that someone is causing havoc in Porthlowen. It started out as a few mischief fires, but it has gotten worse. The earl's stable burned, holes drilled in my ship, a wheel sawn nearly through on a cart carrying the babies who were pulled from the sea, and—"

The parson's hand halted him as he was about to mention the rotten fish left at the parsonage. As soon as he mentioned the children, appalled gasps erupted. Questions came at him and the parson from every side. Was anyone hurt? Who did they think was behind these crimes? The first was easy to answer, but not the last.

Drake watched the faces in the crowd. People were looking at each other in suspicion.

Raymond must have noticed, too, because he said, "It is important we keep our trust in each other and work together to stop this. Don't let fear tear us apart." He held up his hands. "Let us pray for a quick deliverance from this misguided soul who aims to bring tumult to us."

Bowing his head along with the others, Drake listened to the parson's prayer for God's guidance to keep cool heads. He added a few of his own to keep the children and Susanna's family safe, hoping his prayer would be lifted up along with the parson's.

"Amen," he said along with the crowd, who then began to disperse, comforted by the prayer.

The fishermen, now silent, began collecting the broken pieces of boats and equipment before the rising tide could pull them out of the cove. Benton headed back to *The Kestrel* to supervise the work there.

Drake and the parson remained on the sand. When Raymond motioned to the path leading toward the church and Cothaire beyond, Drake walked with him.

"I want you to know that my crew would never destroy another man's livelihood," he said when Raymond said nothing. "We understand how hard it is to wrest a living from the sea."

He nodded. "I know your men are not behind this." He halted at the top of a rise. "Here is where we must part, and I must ask a favor of you. I need to minister to the village now when there is so much uneasiness. Will you take word of the destruction of the fishermen's boats to Cothaire? My father needs to hear of it immediately."

"What if he believes, as some of the fishermen still do, that my crew was involved? Will he think I 'doth protest too much'?"

"You do not strike me as a man who is fond of Shakespeare." He grinned.

"Is that Shakespeare? The master of the first ship I sailed on always said it when someone was trying to avoid being caught in a mistake. The time I have ashore is usually spent unloading my cargo and arranging for another. I don't have time to visit a playhouse." He clasped the parson's shoulder. "I will be glad to deliver the message."

"I thought you might be. Caroline has mentioned that you seem happy for any excuse to visit Cothaire to see Susanna and the children."

"Your sister is an insightful woman."

"Both of them are."

"A warning?"

Raymond laughed. "A fact."

Looking back at the fishermen, Drake asked, "What about them? Who will repair the boats?"

"Each group of men who work on a boat divides the profits from their catch evenly among themselves and the boat."

"The boat?"

"To pay for repairs and new equipment, but I doubt any of the boats have earned enough to pay for such massive repairs. Often when a boat is heavily damaged, the other boats will work out a way to help replace it. But when more than one boat is damaged, no amount of generosity among the fishermen will provide." He squared his shoulders. "Under extraordinary circumstances like this, my father has stepped in to help in the past."

"The earl or your heavenly Father?"

"Both." His smile returned. "My earthly father has provided funds and food while God gives us the strength to go forward. God can offer you the same, Drake. All you need to do is open your soul to Him and let Him in."

"I am trying."

"I am glad to hear it, and God is, too. Thank you for taking the message to my father."

As Raymond turned to go, Drake said, "One question. Why did you halt me from telling them about the fish left in the parsonage?"

"They are upset enough. They don't need to worry

about what was only a temporary inconvenience. I have made a few quiet inquiries but have not learned anything. I pray we can find the person responsible."

"It must be someone who has a grudge against everyone in this cove."

"That is a lot of hatred for one soul to carry in it. Such hatred can consume the one who holds it within him. We must keep him in our prayers. Not only that he will confess, but that he can set aside the hate that drives him. One of the first lessons we teach children at church is the one our Savior preached: *'Love your enemies, bless them that curse you, do good to them that hate you, and pray for them which despitefully use you, and persecute you.'*"

"Not an easy lesson to live in a time of war."

"No one promised it would be." With a wave, Raymond took the path toward the village.

Drake turned in the opposite direction, pondering what the parson had said about the attacks on Porthlowen and what he said about God. He had a lot to consider about both.

Handing a book to her father, whose gout was easing enough that he could come downstairs, Susanna turned at the sound of vigorous footsteps. Her heart began to thump within her chest, even before she identified the person approaching her father's office.

Drake walked in but slowed slightly when his eyes met hers. Her breath caught over her excited heart, and she was unsure if she could draw another while she was held by the warmth of his gaze.

He continued across the room and bowed his head to her father. "Lord Launceston, I wish I could say I was arriving with good news, but that would be a lie."

Susanna lowered herself to the closest chair and clutched its wooden arms. More bad news?

No hint of her father's pain was in his voice as he asked, "What has happened, Captain? Bad news does not get better by delaying."

She listened, appalled, as Drake outlined what had been done to the fishermen's boats and nets. No matter how hard she tried, she could not imagine a single reason why anyone would want to jeopardize the livelihoods of more than a dozen families in Porthlowen.

"I intend to speak with the men who were on guard duty last night," Drake finished. "Your son Raymond plans to do the same in the village, because there are some who believe my men might have done the damage."

"That makes no sense," Susanna said. "The villagers are striking out in any direction because they are in shock." When both men looked at her, she felt heat rise up her cheeks. It was not appropriate for her to speak when Drake had come to see her father.

"You are right," Papa said, stretching to pat her hand reassuringly. To Drake, he added, "My daughter has a way of getting to the very heart of a matter."

"I have noticed."

Papa chuckled. "I believe you know, Captain, that this destruction was meant to drive a wedge between your crew and the villagers." He motioned to a chair next to Susanna's. "Make yourself comfortable, Captain. Shall we ring for some refreshment?"

"I would be grateful, my lord."

Susanna rose and picked up the bell sitting on a nearby table. Before she could ring it, Baricoat appeared in the doorway, offering to fetch an early tea. She wondered how he managed to be there whenever they needed him.

While they waited, she listened to Drake and her father discuss who could be behind the crimes and why. She was very pleased when Papa listened to Drake's theories. Each in their own way, the members of her family were showing they respected the man she was falling in love with.

Falling in love with? Where had that thought come from? She knew the answer even before the question formed. In spite of the safeguards she had put around her heart, Drake had discovered a way to slip past each of them. As she watched him with her father, she was fascinated by the emphatic motions of his hands as he suggested another idea or the way he sat with quiet intensity while her father spoke. She imagined those hands cupping her shoulders as he gazed down at her with the same intensity.

Baricoat returned with a tray, which he placed on the table beside Susanna's chair. She thanked him, then smiled when she saw the pitcher of cool cider set to the far side of the meat and cheese. She stood to pour a glass for each of them.

"No," her father said sharply, and she almost spilled the cider. "There are no roving bands of criminals in this part of Cornwall. If there were, I would have been alerted by the constable or the justice of the peace."

"What about the French?" Drake asked as he took a glass from Susanna with a warm smile. "They would delight in disrupting our lives and livelihood. I know that all too well."

"Any that have dared to step foot on shore have been caught, because they find it hard to pretend to be Cornish. If their accents don't betray them, then the fact they are strangers makes them stick out in any village.

Once caught, they are sent to Dartmoor Prison. Just as the ones you captured were."

"If one escaped…"

"There have occasionally been escapes, but no prisoner gets very far. The moors are not kind to a man who has been on restricted rations. Few of them get more than a short distance from Princetown before they are recaptured. One is reported to have gotten all the way to Plymouth. While in his cups celebrating his escape, he shared his adventures with other patrons of the tavern, who wasted no time turning him over to the constable in exchange for the reward for his capture."

Drake chuckled and chose a selection of food to put on his plate. "There is a lesson in that for all of us."

"True," her father said. "I have to say I don't agree with the prison officials who are allowing a few prisoners of war out each day to build a parish church for Princetown. Neither the French nor the Americans have any love or respect for this country and its people."

"I agree with erring on the side of caution, but bored men are men easily tempted into trouble. If the work crews are heavily guarded and the villagers are willing to accept the risk, then the reward is great."

"But what reward is that criminal expecting for the damage he is doing in Porthlowen?" Susanna asked as she offered the plate to her father.

The two men looked at her, then at each other before affixing their gazes on her again.

Papa chuckled. "I warned you that she gets to the heart of the matter." He took the plate. "Captain Nesbitt, if we can guess what reward he hopes for, we may find the man."

"You make it sound simple, Papa," she said.

"It is," Drake said, giving her one of the scintillating

smiles that made her sparkle inside, "once we make the right guess." He raised his glass of cider. "Let's hope we are right very soon."

Chapter Thirteen

Bertie was so excited he leaped from one step to the other as Miss Oliver brought the children downstairs. "Boat! Boat! Boat!" he shouted on each step.

Lulu and Moll held hands and wore wide grins. In their matching bonnets and new pink dresses with darker pink sashes, they looked even more adorable than usual.

As she pulled on her gloves, Susanna greeted each of the children. Miss Oliver had done an excellent job getting them ready and keeping them neat.

"Boat!" called Bertie, bouncing from one foot to the other. "Go boat!" He sneezed once, then another time.

Before he could wipe his nose on his sleeve, Susanna squatted and handed him the handkerchief Miss Oliver held out to her. She told him to blow his nose and he did, making more noise than was necessary and eliciting giggles from the twins.

Returning the handkerchief to the nurse, she said, "Yes, we are going to *The Kestrel.*"

"Cap's boat," Mollie said, and Lulu nodded, her eyes bright.

The children had talked of little else for the past week. Even though Drake had planned on a visit the day after he invited them, first the damage to the fishing boats and then a storm that settled over the cove with days of unending rain had postponed it. When morning dawned with a sky so blue it almost hurt to look at it, Susanna had sent a footman to ask if the children might get a tour of the ship that afternoon.

Drake's quick response had delighted her because the note he had dashed off told her that he was looking forward to having the children on *The Kestrel* and even more eager to see her. When her heart bounced like Bertie as she read those words, she had told herself to be thankful for the time she could spend with him. It would soon come to an end.

"Where is Gil?" Susanna asked. "I thought he was coming with us."

Miss Oliver shook her head. "He is still coughing. Lady Caroline does not want him to take a chill from the sea."

"That makes sense." She tied her bonnet ribbons under her chin. The simple basket bonnet with its light-green-and-white-checked ribbon would be perfect for a visit to Drake's ship.

Mr. Jenner promised the cart would be fixed as soon as possible. The smithy was busy replacing fishing hooks and other equipment the fishermen had lost in the destruction to their boats. As well, when she went to check on the repair's progress, Mr. Morel had been pouring iron into a round mold. Making cast-iron pots was one of his regular tasks.

Susanna chose the closed carriage. That way, there was no chance of a child popping out on the way to the harbor. They stopped at the parsonage long enough to collect Toby, who wore new shoes, which he proudly showed off until *The Kestrel* came into view; then every child crowded to look out the windows.

She insisted that she and Miss Oliver get out of the carriage first. Each of them took two children by the hand. Miss Oliver grabbed the boys' hands and warned them that no fisticuffs would be acceptable on board the ship. As Toby and Bertie solemnly agreed, Susanna led Lulu and Moll along the pier. On every step, one twin or the other said, "Look, Lady Susu! What is that?" Because she could not answer many of their questions, she told them to ask Drake once they were aboard.

She gazed at the ship. The mighty masts were even taller than she had realized. The rigging created a path to the very top of the masts. The sails were folded like a hawk's wings, and she could understand why Drake had chosen the name *The Kestrel* for his ship.

"May we come aboard?" she called from the bottom of the plank.

Drake and his first mate stepped into view, and her breath caught. Both wore spotless navy blue coats over light brown breeches. Their flat-top, wide-brimmed black wool hats were different only in the color of the braid at the bottom of the crown. Rising to their knees, boots shone like the sun itself, though she could see the salt stains on Drake's boots.

Stepping forward, Drake doffed his hat and bowed. "Please come aboard, ladies and gents."

The twins giggled but gripped Susanna's hands as they climbed the steep board that swayed gently.

"Good afternoon, Captain Nesbitt," she said, unable to pull her eyes away from his commanding appearance. "Thank you for letting the children see the ship."

"Go boat!" yelled Bertie as he jumped onto the deck.

Miss Oliver tried to hush him, but the little boy was too excited. Drake motioned for the children to follow him.

Susanna watched Drake cross the deck to where Obadiah, if she recalled the cook's name correctly, offered a tray of sweets to the children. As they swarmed around him, she realized Drake was more at ease than she had ever seen him. There was a lightness in his step, and a broad smile threatened to split his face.

When Benton stepped forward and offered to escort Master Bertie and Master Toby, who were keeping their promise to behave—at least so far—the little boys squealed and grasped his hands. Questions flew at him from both sides as they went to look at the scuppers. Miss Oliver trailed behind them, smiling as the first mate tried to answer one question before the boys had another.

"And I get to give a tour to three of the prettiest ladies I have ever seen," Drake said, coming back with the twins.

Moll giggled. Lulu stuck three fingers into her mouth, but a chuckle escaped around them.

"While we are fortunate to be escorted by such a fine gentleman," Susanna said, her smile as lighthearted as his.

"Shall we?" He offered his arm to Susanna. When she put her fingers on it, he held out his hand to the twins. Moll grabbed it first, and Lulu skipped to take Susanna's other hand. "What would you like to see first?"

"Boat!" the twins said together, then laughed.

"Then we shall see all of it."

"Or as long as their legs hold out," Susanna said quietly.

Drake escorted them around the main deck and

showed them the mighty wheel that controlled the rudder, then took them belowdecks to let the little girls try the sleeping hammocks that hung in an open section midships. She and Drake gently pushed the hammocks to rock the girls, much to their delight.

"How are the repairs going?" Susanna asked.

"We keep finding holes where we do not expect them." He leaned one hand on a beam that held the deck over their heads. "It is maddening."

"New holes?"

"To us, yes, but from the water seepage and discoloration of the boards, it would appear that they may have been there a day or two. If the water was not so shallow here, allowing *The Kestrel* to balance on her keel at low tide, the boat would have sunk by now. When my crew is not plugging holes or standing watch, they are bailing out the lower holds." He shook his head and sighed. "I doubt they can go much longer at this pace."

Looking closer, she saw deep shadows under his eyes and new lines etched across his forehead. "When did you last sleep?"

"I have no idea." He smiled, then yawned. "It is better when I don't talk about sleep, because once I do, I don't want to do anything but take a nap for a month or two." He started to reach into the hammock to lift out the twins, then laughed quietly. "It looks as if someone else had the same idea."

Susanna moved to where she could see into the hammocks. The little girls were curled up into balls, their thumbs in their mouths, asleep.

When Drake took her by the elbow, she tiptoed away. Then she realized heavy footfalls came from every direction as well as over their heads, and neither twin reacted.

He led her into a room where a table was bolted to the floor. Beyond it a single door was closed. He pulled a pair of chairs off hooks on the wall and set them by the table.

"It is not as grand as the dining room at Cothaire, but try not to notice," he said.

"I think it is very clever how you keep items from sliding around when you are at sea." She sat in the chair he drew out for her. "Thank you, Drake. The children, as you saw, have been so excited about coming here."

"You have already thanked me. No need to do so again."

"I wanted you to know how happy we were to get your note this morning."

He sat next to her. With gentle fingers, he tucked a strand of hair back beneath her bonnet as his gaze caressed her face, lingering on her lips. His voice was low and uneven as he asked, "All of you were happy?"

"Yes." No other words formed in her mind as waves of delight rose through her at his tender touch.

"The children?"

"Yes."

"Miss Oliver?"

"Yes."

"You?"

"More than the rest of them together," she breathed.

A smile teased his expressive mouth. "That is saying a lot. I thought Bertie was going to jump right through the deck."

"I know how he feels."

"I do, too." He paused for so long that she thought

he might not say anything else, but then he whispered, "Susanna..."

"Yes?"

Drake faltered again, searching for the right words, then realized he had no idea what he wanted to say. So many things teased him to speak, things that came from the heart. He could not—he *would* not—let himself become so vulnerable.

Never...again.

He stumbled on the pledge he had been able to make so easily—and so proudly—before he guided *The Kestrel* into Porthlowen Harbor. It should be a warning that while his ship lingered in shallow waters, he was getting in far too deep with Susanna. And the children, as well.

He continued to look at her face, unable to pull his eyes away from her loveliness. She was not Ruby. Once she made a vow, she kept it. But nothing had changed in his life. He needed to return to the sea, to fulfill the dreams of his soul.

His soul... Since his arrival in the cove, he had begun to sense its need to reconnect with the faith that once sustained him through so many tough and hungry days. Could he? After all of this time of keeping God distant. He was unsure, and he hated feeling that way.

"I missed seeing you this week," he murmured when he realized he could not keep her waiting while he mulled over the changes he had experienced in the past few fortnights.

"Oh, that reminds me. Papa asked me to invite you to the ball on the night of Raymond and Elisabeth's wedding."

Shock riveted him. *She* was asking him to a formal assembly at Cothaire? Did she mean as her escort for the evening and dinner partner? For a moment, he imagined holding her as they danced, oblivious to the rest of the guests. Good sense returned immediately.

"That is very kind of you and Lord Launceston, Susanna, but I cannot attend a ball. The clothes I am wearing now are my very best. They do not meet the strict standards of the *ton* for such a formal event."

She eyed him up and down. "You and Arthur are close to the same size. I am sure he would be willing to loan you what you need."

"Me? In a viscount's clothing?" He chuckled and shook his head. "That would cause great amusement in the low streets where I grew up."

Instead of laughing along with him, she put her hand on his forearm and leaned closer. His own laughter vanished as he gazed into the silver eyes that had fascinated him from the first time he had seen her.

"You are not impoverished any longer, Drake. You are the captain of a fine ship."

"A fine, *leaky* ship." He smiled ruefully.

Her expression did not change, and her voice remained earnest. "If you think I am going to lament that you have not succeeded in plugging every last hole on *The Kestrel*, you are mistaken. While the work goes on, you remain in Porthlowen. And while you are here, I see no reason why you cannot attend my brother's wedding and the celebration afterward. If the only reason is that you do not have appropriate clothing, I have already told you that is easily rectified." She drew her hand away. "You are welcome anytime at Cothaire."

"I know, but—"

"Your ship and crew need you." She stood and went to where a porthole gave her a view of the inner curve of the sea cliffs. With her back to him, she said, "I think I

am coming to understand why your voice always softens
when you speak of *The Kestrel*, why you are so protec-
tive of her and so eager to see her repaired."

"And why is that?"

She faced him with a gentle smile. "To you, she is a
living entity. A friend, a protector, a fellow adventurer."
She hesitated, then whispered, "She is your family."

"She and the crew, yes. The best I have ever had.
Of course, I had no choice but to choose a life upon
the sea."

"Why?"

"My father was a sailor, and he ordered that I be
named for the greatest sailor England ever had. Sir Francis Drake."

"He could have named you Francis." She chuckled.

"I have thought of that, and I am grateful he did not.
A boy with a fancy name like that is asking for some-
one to punch him in the nose." He stared at the table.
"It was the only good thing he ever did for me."

"The only good thing?"

"Other than leaving. From the stories I have heard,
I was better off than I would have been if he and my
mother had stayed around."

Her eyes widened. "Your mother left you, too?"

"They tell me that she took me to a neighbor and
never came back. Maybe she went with my father. I
don't know."

"Drake, that is abominable."

"Far better than what was done to these six children.
At least I was not set adrift upon the sea."

Clenching her hands, she said, "Sometimes when I
think of that, I get so angry I cannot see straight."

"I know. One day the children will appreciate how

your family has provided for them. Not every abandoned child is so blessed."

"What happened to you, Drake?"

"The neighbors took me in with their brood, which was large enough that they never seemed to notice one more."

"So they became your family?"

"No. They were never cruel to me, but I was always an outsider. I was never allowed to call them 'Mother' and 'Father.'"

"Oh, how horrible! You must have been so alone and so lonely, even in such a crowded house."

His brows arched. "No one else has ever said that." He quickly looked away. A flush of heat warned his neck must be turning as red as if he were a new crew member who had spent too much time in the sun.

"If I have pried too much…"

"No, it feels good to have someone understand." He shook his head with a grin. "I told Raymond that both you and your sister are able to see the truth others miss, so I should not be astonished. But that all happened long ago. As soon as I could, I lied about my age and signed on the first merchant ship leaving the harbor. I did not care what work I had to do as long as it was not in Plymouth and as long as it was at sea. For as long as I can remember, I wanted to ship out to sea. I was not going to let that chance pass me by."

Before she could ask another question, the twins called to her. As he stood, she went to swing the girls out of the sleeping hammocks. They had slept only a few minutes, but were now wide-awake and eager to see more of the ship.

He could sense that Susanna was just as anxious to leave the solitude belowdecks. As for himself, he would be glad to return to where they would not be able to talk about the past and what he had planned to do in the future.

A future when the rolling waves of the sea would come between him and Susanna.

No, he definitely did not want to think of *that*. Not until he had to.

Chapter Fourteen

The boys were just as excited as the twins were, babbling about what they had seen. Drake thanked Benton for taking them and Miss Oliver around the ship, then said, "I have a treat for you."

"What? What?" asked Moll as she and Lulu danced around him like eager puppies.

Drake took the bag his first mate held out to him before telling the youngsters to follow him. Susanna and Miss Oliver grabbed little hands when he headed for the pier.

He grinned when the children asked him over and over what the treat was. When he reached an empty expanse of sand, not far from where he had pulled the children's jolly boat from the water, he set down the bag. He stooped down and undid the thick string keeping it closed.

He pulled out a miniature of *The Kestrel*. Its sails were unfurled, and the wood shone. Balancing it on his palm, he smiled as the children inched forward, their eyes fixed on the ship that was as long as his hand.

"Pretty," Bertie said.

"Boat," added Lulu. "Pretty boat."

He stretched past them and placed it on Susanna's hand. His fingers grazed hers, and a storm exploded through him. Her silvery eyes sparked. He smiled as she held the little ship with care and examined it.

"Drake, this is amazing," she said as Miss Oliver peered over her shoulder. "Who made it?"

"It rained a lot this past week, and while we were waiting for the holes to seal, several of us started whittling. You see the result." He chuckled. "A ship really belongs in the water."

"Won't the water ruin it?"

"It is sealed." He laughed. "Better than the real one, to own the truth."

He put the little ship on the sand. Opening the bag, he drew out four more. He handed one to each child.

They shouted with excitement and raced to the water's edge. Before they could put them in the water, Miss Oliver called them back, insisting they take off their shoes and socks. With his help as well as the nurse's and Susanna's, they were soon barefoot.

He showed them the strings connected to the sterns of ships. "A good captain always makes sure his ship is secure so it will not be taken away by the sea." Over his shoulder, he gave Susanna a grin as he added, "That would be highly embarrassing."

Within minutes, the little ships were floating in front of them. Miss Oliver went from one child to the next and tied the end of their ship's string around each child's wrist.

"Shall we do the same for you, Susanna?" he asked when he carried the first boat to where she watched.

"I don't think that is necessary." She smiled as she listened to the delighted children. "Drake, this is wonderful. Such a fine flotilla of ships, and they will not tire of playing with them quickly."

"This one is for Gil. I hope you don't mind sharing."

"Some things, like happiness, are meant to be shared."

"I agree." He lightly brushed his knuckles on her cheek and watched her silver eyes light up again.

Putting the little ship on the bag where it would not be stepped on, he crooked his elbow toward her. "Shall we take a stroll while the children are busy?"

"I should—"

"Miss Oliver is watching them as closely as a sheep-dog guards the flock."

"That is true." She put her hand on his sleeve.

He slipped his own over it as he walked with her toward where the cliffs rose straight up from the beach. When they passed where fishermen were working on their nets, she stopped to talk to them. She asked not just about the damage, but about their families, seeming to know the name of everyone in the village and even some of their relatives who lived beyond Porthlowen. Her questions were both kind and aimed at gathering information and opinions, which he guessed she would share with her father. Lord Launceston was fortunate his children had assumed his duties with skill and dedication.

A frustrated cry rang through the air. He looked back to see Miss Oliver grabbing for the children. They were too close to the water's edge. Toby was shrieking.

What was happening? A single glance at the waves gave him his answer. The tide had risen high enough so it could surge around the curve of the sea cliffs and rush into the cove. He ran back and grabbed Toby, trying to pull him back. The little boy yelped in pain when his arm was stretched to its limits.

Susanna dropped to her knees and looped one arm around each of the twins, keeping them from getting pulled in. "Can you untie the strings from their wrists?"

He tried, but the knots had tightened. Pulling a knife from under his coat, he slashed through one string after another. The children fell to the ground, then began screaming for their boats that were sailing away on the tide.

"I will get them!" he shouted. "Keep the children on the sand."

"Drake, no! Just let the ships go. It is too dangerous."

He bent, tugging off his boots. He tossed them behind him. "It will only take a minute."

"Drake, don't!"

He waded in. Maybe if he showed her that the waves did not hurt him, she could set aside her fear of them. The undertow tugged at his legs, and he used it to propel himself forward. Grasping the trailing strings, he wrapped them around his hand. He moved to return to shore, but the current was powerful. Even though the water was not as high as his waist, it tried to drag him away from the beach.

He fought the current. He thought he was making some headway until he looked up and discovered he was actually farther from the shore. Now he understood why Susanna had warned him to stay out of the water. Gritting his teeth and wishing his feet would stop sliding on the slick rock under the water, he struggled to reach the shore.

"Grab hold!"

He raised his head to see a hand under his nose. He slapped his own against it, seizing the man's arm.

The man grasped Drake's and shouted, "Got'm! Back us out."

Only when Drake felt himself being pulled against the tide did he realize the man was at the end of a long line of men who clasped each other's arms to make a human rope. He saw his crew members interspersed among fishermen. Even Raymond Trelawney had joined the line. Two large men anchored the far end of the queue.

Someone began counting cadence, and they all moved as one. More than once, a man lost his footing and fell. He was always grabbed by the men near him, pulled up and linked into the line again.

Though Drake had been less than ten feet from shore, it took more than fifteen minutes until he stepped on the sand. Cheers came from all around. He collapsed to solid ground. He nodded his thanks to his rescuers before holding out the little ships to the children. Everyone smiled and clapped as the youngsters rushed forward to collect them.

Several men clapped him on the shoulder before returning to their interrupted tasks. He heard Susanna thank each one before asking Miss Oliver to take the children back to Cothaire. With a sigh, he lifted his head to see Raymond walk toward the parsonage with Toby.

Susanna came over to where he sat. She handed him his boots. As he pulled them on, she sat on a nearby boulder.

"Go ahead," he said. "Give me a good dressing-down. I deserve it."

Susanna stretched out a hand and put it on Drake's shoulder. "Why do you think you deserve a scold? You saved the children's toys."

"And then I needed saving."

"We all need saving once in a while."

His dark brown eyes pierced her. "What do you need saving from, Susanna?"

For a moment, she considered giving him a frivolous answer; then she decided on the truth. "Myself."

Coming to his feet, he brushed sand off his coat and breeches. She could hear water in his boots as he moved. He tilted her head back so she could not escape his gaze. Not that she wanted to. She could happily spend the rest of her life looking into his eyes, exploring the potent emotions within them.

"Why do you need to be saved from yourself?" he asked.

"Because I am a fool."

He ran a finger along the ribbon holding her bonnet on her head so the fickle breezes did not snatch it away. When she leaned into his caress, he said, "Susanna, when I think of all the ways I might describe you, *fool* is never a word that has come to mind."

"That is because you don't really know me."

"I know you. You care deeply for your family. You hold your responsibilities dear. You did not hesitate to open your heart to six abandoned children." He smiled. "You don't like surprises, though I am curious why."

"Why are you curious?" she asked before she could halt herself.

He chuckled. "I cannot imagine not enjoying a surprise now and then. If I knew what was going to happen every single day, I would become bored in no time."

"I simply like to be prepared so I am not taken unaware."

"Again."

When he did not make it a question, she nodded and closed her eyes. The familiar feelings of humiliation threatened to drown her.

Drake whispered, "Tell me. Please."

"Very well." She opened her eyes. "I will tell you, though I have no doubt you will tell me I was a fool not to see what was coming." She stepped away, unable to look at him as she explained how she had been betrayed by her two best friends on the very day she should have been celebrating. "I thought I could trust Franklin Chenowith and Norah Yelland."

When he wrapped his arms around her, she stepped into his embrace, glad for his sturdy comfort. She paid no attention to the water seeping through her dress from his drenched breeches.

He murmured into her hair, "Now I understand the reaction in church when the banns were first read for Raymond and Elisabeth."

"I worried about what might have happened to Franklin for the next week," she said against his damp waistcoat. She unfolded her fingers across his chest and heard his heart skip a beat. Just as hers did when she breathed in the fresh scent of him, a mixture of salt and wood and lacquer.

"You never heard from him?"

"Not for what seemed like a lifetime. We sent messages to his home but received no answer. Finally, after almost a fortnight, word came that he and Norah had married by special license the very day the banns were first read for us." She lifted her hands. "Surprise!"

Drake's brows rose as he whistled a single long note that wafted across the cove. "And now I understand why you hate surprises."

"They never seem to bring anything but sadness. I know I should forgive Franklin and Norah. That is what the Bible teaches, but I have failed because... I don't know how."

"Weren't you supposed to be married shortly after your mother died?"

"Yes." She kicked a piece of broken shell into the water. "But the tragedies my family suffered does not excuse me for not being able to forgive them. It has been five years. Since then, Franklin and Norah have had two children, and I understand they are expecting another."

"Understand? You have not seen them?"

"No." Tears washed into her eyes. "I received a couple of letters from Norah, but she only said that she was sorry if I was hurt. *If?* Then she went on to say that she was sure I understood. I had no idea what she meant, and I was not ready to beg for an answer."

"I cannot imagine you begging for anything."

She shook her head. "Do not make me sound proud, Drake. That is not a good way to live one's life."

"You are far from proud, though you have every reason to be. We all make mistakes, Susanna, but you also make a difference. Not just to your family and the people of Porthlowen. You are ready to help anyone who needs help. I know how you went through Cothaire's attic and selected items not only to give to Raymond's parishioners, but also to send to the families in the mining village we visited."

"How did you know that?"

"Shall I say that a little Bertie told me?"

She brushed away the single tear falling down her cheek. "I should have guessed. Everything in life is exciting and new for him, and he wants to share everything with everyone."

"Susanna," Drake said, abruptly somber again, "I have to ask a question. Is it Franklin Chenowith and his wife whom you cannot forgive? Or is it that you cannot forgive yourself, because you feel you should have had the situation under control so you were not surprised?"

She stared at him for a long minute, then slid her arms around his waist. As his arm came up to enfold her again, she whispered, "I don't know. Drake, I honestly don't know."

He pressed his lips to the top of her bonnet. Then he pulled her even closer. He kissed her cheek with a tenderness that made her heart pound before he trailed kisses along her jaw. Her breath rasped in her ears before his lips found hers. As he explored them gently, she could no longer deny this was what she had been waiting for. *He* was what she had been waiting for.

He raised his head to say, "You have no idea how long I have been waiting to kiss you."

"Probably as long as I have been waiting for you to kiss me." She stroked his cheek, thrilling in its roughness from storms upon the sea.

"Then it seems silly to wait any longer for another."

"I agree." She slid her arms up to curve around his back as he kissed her again, more deeply and more intensely.

She returned the kiss, hoping he could understand what words would never be able to say. She had rediscovered happiness with him and did not want that happiness to end.

Chapter Fifteen

The sun shining through the tall windows struck Susanna's closed eyes, waking her from a dream that dissolved instantly. All she could recall was that Drake had been in it. She smiled into her pillow, longing to grasp what had faded away; then she realized her happiness was real. Since Drake had kissed her on the beach, everything seemed more splendid.

Too bad they had not had time alone since. He had come to Cothaire one evening to dine with the whole family, and she had admired how he could argue with her father when their opinions differed, but always offered her father the respect he was due as an earl. Raymond and Caroline welcomed him wholeheartedly, but Arthur was a bit more tentative. Her older brother always felt it was his position, as heir, to be cautious. Even so, by evening's end, he had become slightly more relaxed with Drake. She assured Drake that, for Arthur, it was equal to a hearty embrace.

She treasured every moment with Drake. A single glance from him left her smiling for hours. The brush of his fingers made her dizzy with delight. Seeing Drake playing with the children, who adored him, touched her heart in ways she could not have imagined.

Was that how Raymond and Elisabeth felt? Today they would become man and wife. If she looked in a glass, would she see that same glow of love around her? Her joy became almost too sweet to bear. So much happiness in a house that had been dreary for so long. She never had guessed that the love between a man and a woman was a lamp that lit people from the inside out, just as God's love did.

When the sun pierced her eyelids again, Susanna turned away and opened her eyes. She looked over her shoulder. The bed curtains had been pulled aside, allowing the morning light to wash over her bed.

Having that happen was no longer a surprise, though the children had not sneaked into her room since they moved into the night nursery. Susanna sat, taking care not to jostle the bed. The twins and Bertie were curled up together in innocent sleep. No doubt, Miss Oliver was frantic trying to find them without disturbing the family.

Reaching for her dressing gown, Susanna slipped out of bed and drew the bed curtains closed, leaving a finger's space so the children would not be in the dark if they woke. She buttoned her dressing gown as she went to the door. With a glance back at the bed, she closed the door and crossed the sitting room.

It did not take long to find Miss Oliver, who was peering into one open doorway after another. Hurrying to the nurse, Susanna said, "They are in my room."

"I had hoped that was so, but I did not want to disturb you, my lady, so I was checking elsewhere. Just in case."

"Rightly so. Those imps could have been anywhere, from the attic to Elisabeth's shop in the village."

Miss Oliver dipped in another of her curtsies that were more elegant than any Susanna had ever achieved. "I will collect them now and remind them that they should wait until everyone is awake before they go exploring."

"They are asleep. Leave them be."

"But you need to ready yourself for the parson's wedding. They are certain to interfere."

Susanna smiled, knowing she was being overindulgent. "I am sure they will not sleep much longer. They always wake in time for breakfast."

"That is true." A rare smile warmed Miss Oliver's face. "Send for me when they wake, and I will get them fed and ready for the service and the wedding."

"I will."

Susanna returned to her room and the whirlwind of last-minute preparations. The assembly would be crowded, and she and Caroline had worked with Mrs. Ford, Mrs. Hitchens and Baricoat to make sure no detail was overlooked. She was partway through the breakfast tray delivered to her room when the children woke. Sending them to the nursery, she gave herself to the ministrations of the head maid, who also served as her lady's maid.

When Caroline came to tell her that they were ready to leave, Susanna pulled on her gloves and bonnet. She tossed her favorite dark blue paisley shawl over her shoulders. It had belonged to their mother, and the fringe was gold silk. In this small way, she could make her mother part of the wedding.

Papa was able to walk with a cane to the closed carriage with the family's crest on the door. He and Arthur would ride in that to the church, while Susanna would follow with Caroline, Miss Oliver and the children. With the sun shining and only a wisp of a breeze off the sea, she was glad to ride in the open carriage.

As soon as she stepped in, Lulu and Moll both scrambled to sit on her lap. Miss Oliver halted them, reminding them that no one wanted to arrive at the church with her dress mussed. When they acquiesced, nodding enthusiastically, Susanna was astonished. The nurse was an excellent influence on them.

She leaned back against the black velvet cushions and gazed down at the harbor. *The Kestrel*'s bare masts were tall and proud just like her captain. Clasping her hands together on her lap, she smiled as she thought of seeing Drake again.

It was going to be a wonderful day.

"'Tis a wonderful day for a wedding," Benton said as he took off his hat and followed Drake into the church.

"Made to order." Drake looked for a place to sit.

Most of the pews were filled to overflowing. The front two were almost vacant. An elderly couple sat on one side. The bride's parents? Grandparents? He would ask Susanna later.

Just the thought of her name sent anticipation pulsing through him. He could not believe so many days had passed without him having a chance to kiss her again. If he had not tasted her lips once, his annoyance at how events had contrived to keep them apart might not be so strong. Yet, having sampled them once, he yearned for them even more.

Perhaps tonight when others are dancing. He almost chuckled. Drake Nesbitt attending an assembly at an earl's great house. No one would believe that in Plymouth. He had hardly believed it himself, even though a footman from Cothaire had delivered an elegant black evening coat and black waistcoat to *The Kestrel*. Hanging with them in his quarters were his freshly laundered white shirt and cravat. The footman had also brought what Drake guessed were the proper shoes. He had worn nothing but boots for years, and he found the low shoes with their thick heels amusing. He might be able to walk in them, but dancing was certain to be impossible.

Unless he danced with Susanna. It would not matter what he wore then, because his feet would have wings. Just as his heart did. It had been held to the earth for too long by the spike Ruby's betrayal had driven into him. But his bitterness was gone. It had been pushed aside by Susanna's sweetness and gentle but strong faith. She had healed his heart, and her acceptance of God in her life as wise counselor was helping him repair his own connection with Him.

A parishioner walking past jostled Drake out of his reverie. He saw space left in a pew about halfway to the front. Elbowing his first mate, who was eyeing a pretty lass, he walked to it. He was surprised to see there was room for him and Benton and perhaps one other.

Sitting, he looked around the church. He was astonished how comfortable he had come to feel in the small stone building. Not just worshipping with others, but the feeling of community as he watched people greet their neighbors. Many offered him a cheerful "Good morning." Until he came to the parish church, he had not realized there was a family to be found within it, as well.

The irrepressible Winwood sisters gave him a wave, and he nodded in their direction. Mrs. Thorburn, who seldom looked happy even in church, was wearing less of a frown than usual. More people were entering the church and gathering at the back, some sitting on chairs they must have brought themselves. Others stood. He thought about motioning to them that there was room in the pew where he sat with Benton and a fisherman he recognized and the man's wife.

Then the earl and his family arrived. While they went to take their seats in the front pews, warm greetings met them.

The voices faded when Drake's gaze settled on Susanna. She wore a simple pink gown, the exact shade of her cheeks. If she had been carrying a bouquet of fresh flowers instead of Moll, she could have been a bride walking down the aisle. The sunlight glistened in her hair, burnishing it with auburn fire, and her smile was as bright.

Her eyes searched the congregation, and they crinkled in a smile when she found him. Moll waved wildly in his direction. He returned it as Susanna carried her past their row, then paused when it became clear there was not enough room for the whole family, including the bride and groom and the children, in the front pews.

"There is space here," Drake said, standing and stepping out of the pew, giving Benton a half shove toward the fisherman and his wife. "You are welcome to take our seats."

"I believe there is room enough for all of us if you gentlemen can spare a lap."

"Anytime. You need only ask."

When Susanna blushed prettily, Drake was sure she thought, as he did, of her perched on his knees, her arms around his neck and her lips meeting his.

He lowered his voice and repeated, "Anytime, Susanna."

Hearing a sniff behind him, he nodded toward Mrs. Thorburn, who wore a vexed expression. He could not guess if she was upset at him, Susanna or the children. Probably all three.

"Good morning, Mrs. Thorburn," he said with a smile.

"Yes, yes." She looked away, then turned to speak to the people in the pew behind her.

Benton scooped up Bertie and put the little boy on his lap. Bertie crowed with excitement when the first mate slid farther along to leave room for Drake and Susanna.

"My lady," Drake said as he motioned for her to go ahead of him. When Susanna did, holding Moll close, he bent and held out his hands to Lulu.

"Cap!" she yelled, throwing herself at him.

"That is my girl." He ignored Mrs. Thorburn's frown along with the chuckles from the Winwood sisters across the aisle as he sat beside Susanna.

Lulu opened her mouth to say something more, but Susanna put her finger to the child's lips.

Drake was surprised that she would halt the little girl, who was too quiet, from speaking. He was about to say so, but, her eyes twinkling with amusement, Susanna moved her finger from Lulu's lips to his.

Even though he had been dreaming of her touch all week, he was unprepared for the sweet sensation of her teasing touch. He could not look away. The amusement in her eyes metamorphosed into wonder. Her lips parted in an unspoken invitation to kiss her right there and then. Each fiber within him urged him to accept, but he drew back, unable to forget that they sat in her family's church, waiting for her brother's banns to be read for the third time and for Raymond and Miss Rowse to take their vows.

Envy surged through him, as powerful as the yearning was. Envy that today was the wedding day for Raymond

Trelawney and Elisabeth Rowse rather than Susanna Trelawney and Drake Nesbitt.

Was he insane? He had made the mistake of falling in love once before, and what had it gained him? Heartache and disillusionment and the determination not to be stupid again. He should count his blessings that he had not spoken vows with faithless Ruby.

Parson Lambrick had returned to read the banns for the third time, and he oversaw the whole service. His lesson was dry and without little hints of humor as Raymond's had been, but as Drake bounced Lulu on his knee gently, he heard the wisdom in the words.

Then Parson Lambrick called Raymond and Elisabeth to come to stand with him by the altar rail. He held a simple brown leather book.

Susanna leaned toward Drake and whispered, "It is so strange to see my brother with his back to the congregation."

"I suspect it is odd for him, too."

"He loves Elisabeth and cannot wait for her to be his wife."

Drake smiled. "I don't doubt that, but look at his hands. If he clenches them any more tightly, he is going to drive his fingers right through his palms."

Susanna put her fingers over her mouth and coughed, but he was not fooled. She was trying to conceal her laughter.

He was not the only one grinning broadly when Raymond gave Elisabeth a kiss to seal their vows. Cheers broke out through the church when the couple turned and, the bride's hand on the groom's arm, began to walk up the aisle.

Elisabeth's smile made her plain face glorious. She paused by the front pew to give Toby a kiss and offer

her hand. He grabbed it and marched beside the newlyweds. He grinned at her with the same adoring, loving
expression as Raymond wore. Anyone watching would
guess that Raymond, Elisabeth and Toby were a family. In all the important ways, they were.

That realization gave him pause. The children had
been in Porthlowen for almost two months. No one had
come forward to ask about them. All their efforts to discover where they had come from and who had put them
in the rickety boat had come to naught.

His thoughts continued in that direction as he carried
Lulu out of the church. He paused once he was outside
and turned to wait for Susanna, Benton and the other
children. When his first mate put Bertie down and made
his exit at top speed, Susanna took the little boy's hand
and steered both him and Moll to where Drake waited.

Instead of Susanna talking about the wedding cer-
emony, the first thing she said was "Drake, I have been
thinking. Maybe we should stop looking for the children's parents."

"You have?" He set Lulu down beside her twin.

As the children chattered to each other, Susanna said,
"Look at my brother and his family. They *are* a family.
How can we tear them apart?"

He glanced toward where Raymond and Elisabeth
were accepting congratulations. Each held one of Toby's
hands, and the little boy wore a smile as big as the bride's
and groom's.

"Is halting the search what you truly want?" Drake
asked.

Susanna hesitated. How easy it would be to say yes!
A small hand tugged on her dress, and Moll asked,
"Go see Toby? Play with Toby?"

"Yes, but go no farther than where Toby is now." She crouched down and looked directly into the twin's eyes before glancing at the boys with the same serious expression. "If you go farther, you will have to come back and stand here with Cap and me."

They ran off.

Drake asked, "Do you think they will listen to you? They are young."

"They won't, but Miss Oliver will keep a close watch on them." As the two little girls paused to talk to the Winwood sisters and other people they knew, she sighed. "Look at that, Drake. The children have become a part of our community. These six small children have brought so much happiness to Porthlowen and to Cothaire. Only Arthur, who is always so serious about everything, seems immune to their charm."

"And my crew has made them more toys out of bits of wood than any score of children would need."

"They are at home here, and we are glad to have them here." She watched Caroline join the children. After giving her hugs, they rushed away, and she continued talking to the Winwood sisters, holding Joy.

When had she last seen her sister so happy? *Before Mama became sick and before Caroline's late husband, John, made his final voyage.*

Susanna frowned. How could she have forgotten how down-pinned her sister had been in the weeks before John's ship set sail? Even before their mother died, Caroline had lost her smile. Only now did Susanna realize that something else must have happened, something as horrific as that double loss. She could not imagine what, but it had changed her sister…until Caroline took Joy and the baby's brother Gil into her arms and heart.

If the children stayed, Caroline would not sink into

such a depression again. For that reason alone, even if her own heart had not been warmed by the children, she wished they could halt the search for where the children had come from.

"All you need do is say the word, Susanna," Drake said, "and everyone will stop searching."

"You have been thinking of this, too."

"I have. When I saw your brother and his new wife with young Toby, like you, I could not miss how much they looked like a family."

"A family like you wish you'd had."

"Yes." He rested his elbow on a nearby gravestone and smiled sadly. "That is why I would hate to see these children sent back to families who obviously don't want them."

"But what if their families *do* want them. If the children were stolen, whoever took them might have found it impossible to take care of all six at once."

"They can be a handful."

"Many hands full." She smiled for a moment. "It is selfish of me to believe that nobody else cares where they are. That is why I cannot call off the search."

"Good."

"Good?" she repeated, astonished.

"I want to find whoever set the children adrift in a wobbly jolly boat. That person or persons condemned them to death and should pay for such a crime. I would like to be the one who makes sure they do."

Not caring that they stood in the churchyard amid family and friends, she laced her fingers through his and slanted toward him. "If anyone can, it will be you, Drake."

"You have that much faith in me?"

"Yes. You took on French privateers who must have

had cannons on board. A trading ship like *The Kestrel* does not. You fight for what you believe in, no matter the odds."

"And we were able to ram a hole in their ship because we were lighter and more maneuverable."

"You followed the tactics of the man you were named for. Sir Francis Drake's fleet faced such odds when they defeated the Spanish Armada."

His laugh rang through the churchyard, making heads swing toward them. When the twins came running, he bent and lifted one up under each arm. The girls giggled as their legs and arms dangled. He swung them back and forth gently, eliciting more laughter. At the same time, he gave Susanna that special smile he reserved for her. She smiled back, knowing that, if only for that moment, they must look like a family, too.

Just like the one she had dreamed of so often.

Had Franklin and Norah dreamed of that, too? She would not want anyone to stand between her and the realization of this dream. Maybe they had felt the same.

As she took Moll from Drake and cuddled her close, a weight lifted off her heart. She had, she realized, forgiven her two erstwhile friends for cutting her out of their lives. She now was able to understand why they made the choices they did.

Drake plucked Moll back out of her arms and laughed when she knocked his hat off. In that instant, the last bindings of betrayal fell away from Susanna's heart, and she acknowledged how deeply she loved Drake Nesbitt.

Her gaze moved from him to his ship in the harbor. Soon he would be sailing away, leaving her broken-hearted again. And this time, she feared, the hurt would never heal.

Chapter Sixteen

In the twilight, Cothaire was brightly lit. At every window, a lamp shone, and all along the road to the great house, lanterns had been placed to create a glowing path for the guests.

Drake strode up the driveway, stepping aside again and again as fancy carriages drove past. A few had crests on their doors, denoting nobility rode inside. Even those without crests were brilliantly polished from the top to the wheels. Servants in every possible color of livery drove or rode on the back, ready to jump down and open doors the moment the wheels stopped turning.

Drake threaded his way among the carriages waiting to discharge passengers and went to the front door. He nodded to the footman who had his hands filled with hats and walking sticks.

"How are you doing, Venton?" he asked.

"Busy, Captain. I think everyone in Cornwall is celebrating tonight."

Giving the footman a friendly pat on the arm, Drake drew off his gloves. He would need them later if he made the mistake of dancing but, for now, the white kid gloves were hot and pinched his fingers. He would not have worn them except Benton insisted he must. Though he had no idea how his first mate had become acquainted with the canons of Society, he had relented because he was determined not to give Susanna or her family any reason to regret inviting him.

He followed the other guests toward a wing of the house he had never entered. Stepping aside to allow two elderly ladies and their escorts to pass, their canes tapping the floor, he was surprised to hear footsteps to his left. He looked along a small corridor and saw Raymond walking toward him. He had assumed the bridegroom would be welcoming his guests in the grand chamber where the ball would be held.

"Drake, I am glad you decided to come." He winked. "And I know my little sister will be, too." He looked out into the main hallway. Raising his voice to be heard over the multitude walking by, he said, "Quite a crowd, wouldn't you say? Elisabeth and I would have preferred a smaller, more intimate gathering, but her great-aunt, a true old tough, would not hear of it. Great-Aunt Grace refused to be denied her opportunity to hold court tonight. Elisabeth loves her great-aunt dearly, so how were we to say no? You know how families can be."

Even though he did not, Drake smiled. "Now you have two."

"You need not remind me. I probably should make sure that Elisabeth is prepared for the crowd."

"A good lesson for a parson's wife."

"True."

As Raymond started to walk away, Drake called, "Do I have time to tell the children good-night? I would not want to miss your grand entrance with your bride."

"I am sure you are more eager to see Susanna."

"I would never speak falsely to a parson. Not a good habit to get into."

Raymond laughed. "These events never run on time, even with Baricoat in charge. Go ahead. If you are not down by the time the orchestra begins the first set, I will send someone to the nursery for you."

"Excellent."

Drake felt like a ship tacking against the wind as he made his way through the crush of people. He was relieved when he climbed up and away from the guests who were eager to reach the ballroom and claim a good place to stand for the newlyweds' entrance. He gladly left the cacophony behind. He knocked lightly on the door to the day nursery, hoping the children were not yet abed.

Miss Oliver opened the door and smiled. "Captain Nesbitt, I did not expect you to give us a look-in this evening."

"I thought—" His words vanished as the children realized he had arrived.

They were sitting on the floor, playing happily together. He was glad to see Bertie and Toby and Gil building with wooden blocks without pinching or poking each other. As the children had become more comfortable with the Trelawneys, they no longer fought as much. With a shout of "Cap!" they ran to him. He put his arms out and gathered them into a big hug.

Moll took his hand and tugged him toward the dollhouse. "Look!"

He did, but could not see anything different about it.

Miss Oliver came to his rescue when she said quietly, "The dolls are gathering in the best parlor on the center floor to celebrate Parson Trelawney's marriage to Miss Rowse."

"Oh, yes," he said, though all he could see were dolls arranged haphazardly in the room.

Bertie reached in and pulled out a doll. "This is Lady Susu."

"Oh, yes," he replied again, even though he could see little resemblance other than the dark hair. "Who are the others?"

Moll pointed to two dolls sitting at a table. "Me."

"And me," Lulu added before sticking her thumb back in her mouth.

Toby stuck out his chest. "Bertie and Gil and me are out riding horses."

"Like Lord Trelawney?" Drake asked.

The boys nodded, excited. As they debated what color horses they would choose, he squatted by the dollhouse. His muscles began to protest, but he ignored them. A bit of an ache was worth seeing the boys smiling and playing together and growing pudgy. In the short time they had been in Porthlowen, they had changed from scrawny waifs to happy, healthy youngsters.

Gil lifted another doll. "You, Cap."

He struggled not to grin. The rag doll wore a dress and had braids, but that did not seem to bother the children. "Am I having tea, too?"

"No," Bertie said as if that was a stupid question. "You are here to dance."

"Dance?" He stood and looked down at his feet with an exaggerated frown. "I don't believe these feet know how to dance. Can you show me?"

The children began twirling and jumping about and wiggling their hips and waving their hands. In fact, every part of them was in motion as they danced to a nonsense tune they sang together, each of them in a different key.

It did not matter. The song was one of pure excitement and happiness.

Miss Oliver came over to stand beside him. "Thank you for coming to visit the children, Captain Nesbitt. You are very good with them. Do you have children of your own?"

"No. I am a bachelor through and through."

"You seem to have good instincts when it comes to children. You listen to them, and they appreciate adults who do that. They have been excited all day. I did not think I would convince them to take naps, but finally they fell asleep on the floor here waiting for Lady Susanna and Lady Caroline to come to see them. Lady Caroline has visited, but Lady Susanna has not yet." Miss Oliver arched her brows. "I daresay she is extremely busy with the details for the evening."

"I cannot imagine anyone more capable of handling every facet of the evening and making sure it runs smoothly."

"Why, thank you, Captain," a laugh-filled voice came from behind him.

He turned to see Susanna framed by the freshly painted molding on the doorway. She flowed toward him as if she were being washed to shore on a gentle wave.

He found it difficult to breathe when she offered her gloved hand that was not holding the folded fan tied with a ribbon to her wrist. Bowing over it, he resisted the yearning to bring it to his lips. He raised his head and drank in the sight of her in her pure white gown. The lace decorating the modest décolletage had probably cost more than the profit he made on a half-dozen voyages.

It was well worth the price, for the elegant design,

as fragile as a spiderweb, added to her ethereal beauty. With her hair piled up on her head in a glorious confection woven with the same lace, her slender neck was bare, save for a single strand of pearls.

"*My* lady," he murmured, unable to keep from putting the emphasis on the first word. How he longed to make those words a reality! To spend the rest of his life knowing this incredible woman was his.

Oh, Lord, if only that could be true. The prayer came from the very center of his heart, the place that had been ravaged by Ruby's treachery. Susanna's kindness and sweet smile had healed him.

"You look very nice, Drake," she said, that hint of laughter still in her voice.

"In my borrowed finery?"

"It suits you well."

"*You* suit me well." He smiled when she dimpled at his compliment.

Tiny footsteps came toward them, and he bent and stretched out his arms, halting the children from reaching her. To mar the perfection of her appearance with smudges from little fingers would be a shame.

"Look with your eyes, not your hands," Miss Oliver cautioned.

Drake made sure the children would heed their nurse before he lowered his arms. He stepped back as Susanna spoke with the children, promising that she would make sure cake was saved for them to enjoy at lunch the next day.

"I will tell you about everything that happens then." She held up her hand. "But only if you stay in your beds all night. If you try to sneak out, I shall not tell you for three days."

He smiled at the crestfallen faces. For the children,

three days might as well be three centuries. When they nodded solemnly, she gave each a kiss on the cheek, then gave Gil a second one for "his" baby.

Susanna put her hand on Drake's proffered arm, and he led her out of the nursery. The children crowded the door, waving and talking about cake. Both he and Susanna turned to wave back before they went down the stairs.

Noise came up to meet them, and he asked, "Are these events always so loud?"

"It has been so long since we have held an assembly at Cothaire, I was barely more than a child looking through the railing to watch the people pass. No one felt like celebrating after Mama died and John died and... and everything else."

"I am sorry to remind you of that."

"Don't be. We have all begun to learn again how important being happy is." She gazed up at him so sweetly that his heart skipped a beat and his foot almost skipped a stair. Her hand tightened on his sleeve. "Whoa, there!" She laughed. "Or should I say 'Avast, there'? Are the shoes giving you trouble?"

"Not as much as your captivating eyes, Susanna."

The dusty pink on her cheeks deepened. "Such pretty talk, Captain Nesbitt."

"The truth. I have learned that it would be as foolish to be false with a parson's sister as with the parson himself." He chuckled at her baffled expression, then explained that he had said something similar to Raymond, though he omitted the fact they had been talking about her.

They were still laughing when they reached the ballroom. Drake became silent as he stared around in awe. Cothaire's ballroom was magnificent. The arched roof was painted in vivid colors. He saw the sea curving off to the right and realized the mural was supposed to represent a view of Porthlowen and the mighty cliffs from the moors beyond Cothaire. Past a trio of crystal chandeliers that shimmered in the candlelight and sent color in every direction, he saw a depiction of the country house sitting amid its flower gardens.

The walls were decorated with raised pilasters and wreaths that had been painted the pale green of spring's first grasses. White marble edged the wooden floor where guests would dance. At opposite ends of the long room, huge hearths of the same marble were decorated with life-size statues of shepherdesses. No fires burned on them, for the room was already overwarm.

Lord Launceston's guests were even more elegant and colorful than the room. The villagers stood to one side, talking to each other, while the wealthier and titled guests congregated on the other. That changed when the newlyweds entered the ballroom. All the guests began to clap and surged forward to offer congratulations.

"I must leave you now," Susanna said. "I am sorry, but I offered to help with the receiving line."

"Hurry back as soon as you can."

She squeezed his fingers, then was swallowed by the crowd.

Wandering around the ballroom, Drake listened to conversations. The villagers were discussing how soon the fishing fleet would be repaired and back to sea, while the members of the *ton* spoke of politics and investments and the latest fashions. One topic crossed the line between classes. The war. More than once, he heard complaints about how the war had dragged on too long, allowing the Americans to build up a small navy to distract the British government from putting all its efforts into preventing Napoleon from amassing a vast empire on the Continent.

"And now they are letting those blasted sailors— pirates, the lot of them—walk free in Princetown," complained one short and wide man who was at least a decade older than Drake. "There must be better ways to build a church than allowing those scurvy French dogs a taste of fresh air."

"Why not get some work out of them in exchange for the food we put in them?" asked another man.

"Busy men are ones who are too tired to plot escape," Drake said when the two men glowered at each other.

The second man nodded. "You are right, sir. Make them do an honest day's work, and they will be grateful for what they are fed and a place to sleep instead of harrying our ships off our own shores."

"Bah!" The first man was not ready to cede his stance so easily. "Drop them in the deepest pit and forget about them, especially the American colonists. How many times will we allow them to revolt against the Crown before they accept it is futile?"

"They did win their war of independence," Drake said.

The first man needed no further invitation to tell anyone willing to listen to his opinions on the subject and anything else to do with the "American colonies," as he insisted on calling the United States. He allowed no one else a moment to speak.

When the second man slipped away, saying he needed to offer felicitations to the bride and groom, he shot Drake a sympathetic glance.

Drake wished for his own excuse, but when he tried to disengage himself from the conversation, the arrogant man clamped a hand on his sleeve. Drake could have pulled away easily. However, that would be rude, and he had to remember that his behavior reflected on Susanna and the rest of the Trelawneys. Where was she? If she would come along, he could easily end the torture to his ears.

"Sea battles," Drake said when the man made an outrageously mistaken comment, "are far different from a general setting his troops on the battlefield, though position is vital in both."

"A navy man, are you?" The man eyed him as if seeing him for the first time.

"No, sir," he hurried to reply before the pompous man could launch into another long tale. "I am the master of the ship in the cove."

"The one that has been badly listing for so long?"

"Yes." Annoyed by the man's arrogance, he added, "From a battle with a French privateer. We triumphed by God's good grace and were able to reach Porthlowen with our prisoners."

He made a sniff that could have belonged to Mrs. Thorburn. "More mouths for our taxes to feed in exchange for them doing nothing but fighting among themselves, trying to escape, refusing the rations given them. You should have done us all a favor and left them to sink with their ship."

Drake was shocked. "It is not the way of honest seamen to abandon one another to the sea. No one should be set adrift to drown, whether he is French or English or American or a tiny babe."

"If you are speaking of the children who were found in the cove…"

"I am."

"It is a shame the earl is burdened with them simply because his children want instant families. There are places for abandoned children, and they should be there with those like themselves instead of being paraded through decent company like pampered pets."

Affixing his iciest smile on his face, Drake said, "Not everyone shares your opinion, sir."

"I would not expect *you* to understand the reasons."

"I understand them all too well. I wonder if you understand that none of us is more valuable than any other in God's eyes."

The man's face turned a bilious shade before he mumbled and walked away.

"That was rude, even for Mr. Miller," Lady Caroline said as she came to stand beside Drake. "But it might help you to know that, since he became the justice of the peace for a parish farther up the coast, he treats everyone as if they are dirt beneath his feet."

"Even your father?"

She laughed, and he realized how odd it was to see her without baby Joy in her arms. Dressed in an elegant gown of pale yellow, she looked barely older than the young misses flirting with men their mamas approved of and a few they did not. "He fawns on Papa and assumes Papa believes all his Spanish coin."

"So he is, in truth, a twit."

Her eyes sparkled as she tapped his arm with her ivory fan. "Now, Captain Nesbitt, you know me well enough to know that I would never agree aloud with a statement like that."

"Ever the diplomat, I see."

"I prefer to think of it as being a peacekeeper."

"*'Blessed are the peacemakers, for they shall be called the children of God,'*" said Susanna as she linked her arm with her sister's. "That is our Caroline."

Drake smiled. "I would say that is a role all the Trelawneys have learned too well."

"Memories are long in Cornwall, and grudges last even longer, so it is better not to let one start."

The orchestra began to play, and Caroline smiled. "Do not let me keep you from dancing." She kissed Susanna's cheek, then moved away to talk to two older women who greeted her with warmth.

Again that flattering pink rose along Susanna's cheeks. It startled him—and also charmed him—how she could be so forthright but also fetchingly shy.

"Let me see if I can do this correctly." He bowed his head to her, then asked, "Lady Susanna, would you do me the great honor of standing up with me for this set?"

"Why, Captain Nesbitt," she replied, flicking her fan open, "it is I who is honored by your invitation." She wafted the fan, then gave him the familiar grin that set his heart to racing like a storm across the waves.

"I cannot promise not to embarrass you," he said, "but I have managed to foot it a time or two without crushing my partner's toes."

"How could any woman turn down such an elegant invitation?"

"That was the plan." He winked at her and was delighted at her girlish giggle. "And I know how you like plans, Susanna."

"Only when they are good ones."

"I believe this is one of our best." He held out his hand to her.

Closing her fan, she raised her hand to place it on his palm. He closed his fingers around hers as he led her out to the middle of the floor. She gazed at him as they waited for the first notes of the quadrille to begin, but his heart already was dancing with joy to be there with her. She did not move, and he was utterly lost in her silver eyes that glistened like the sun frosting the waves.

Belatedly he realized she had drawn her hand out of his and was curtsying. He bowed, hating that in his haste, he looked as awkward as one of the children would have. She gave him an adorable smile when she took his hand again in the first steps of the dance.

Together and apart they moved in the pattern of the dance. He knew he should offer the other women in their group a smile, but his eyes were focused on Susanna. Each time she returned to him, he wanted to pull her into his arms and spin about—just the two of them—to the sweet song created by their hearts.

Too soon the orchestra stopped. He could not bear for the wondrous moment to be over, so he asked, "Will you stand up with me for the next one, Susanna?"

Her eyes widened. "I shouldn't."

"Why not?"

"For us to be partners for a second dance in a row is tantamount to making a public announcement that we are..." Her face flushed red.

He was torn between laughing at her charming reaction and saying he did not care what anyone else thought. He did not want her dancing with another man tonight. For this one so very special evening, he wanted her to be only his.

"You shouldn't," he whispered, "but will you?"

"Yes," she answered just as softly.

He smiled and offered his hand again. Her fingers froze in midair as her gaze swept past him. All color faded from her face before she whirled, the lace on her hem grazing his shins, and fled.

Drake stood, his hand upraised like a footman without a tray. What had happened? He scanned the room but saw nothing but the guests.

He recognized fear and dismay. What had put those expressions on Susanna's face? Or who?

Susanna closed the door of the room where the ladies could come to fix a torn hem or replace hairpins. No one was inside, and she dropped to sit on the tufted green satin bench. She covered her face with her hands.

How could she have fled when she was about to dance again with Drake?

The sight of Franklin and Norah Chenowith walking into the ballroom had sent her back to that day when she was lost in hurt and fear. Hadn't she forgiven them? She had, but maybe Drake was right.

She had not forgiven herself for failing to see that her betrothed and her best friend had been falling in love. No matter how many times she replayed the preceding weeks in her mind, she could not discern any signs that they were about to betray her. Yes, Norah had been quiet and had looked a bit gray, but she had reassured Susanna that she was not ill. Had guilt of what she planned to do with Franklin stolen the pink from her cheeks?

That was the past, and Susanna yearned to put it behind her. The only way was to confront it, not hide here for the rest of the evening. Raymond and Elisabeth were depending on her.

What to do?

Susanna tossed away idea after idea on how to excuse herself for the evening. If she claimed to be ill, Miss Oliver would insist that she stay out of the nursery so not to carry the "illness" to the children.

Even avoiding Franklin Chenowith and his wife was not worth such a high cost.

Why had they come tonight? Who had invited them? She recalled Raymond mentioning a few weeks ago that Elisabeth's great-aunt had asked them to invite everyone in the neighboring parish where Elisabeth had been born and raised.

And the Chenowiths lived in the nearby house left to Norah by her great-aunt. Because they had vanished from her daily life, Susanna had allowed herself to forget how close they dwelled.

She squared her shoulders. If she remained out of sight, Franklin was sure to think that she still harbored affection for him. She did not love him any longer. Nor did she hate him any longer. She had forgiven him, and now she must forgive herself for wasting so many years of her life on recriminations.

Slowly she stood. She owed Drake an apology and an explanation, but first she must put her past to rest. Checking the glass, she saw her face was ashen and her eyes dim. She tried to smile, but it was a fearsome grimace. Somehow, she had to look natural. Unsure how, she left the room and walked to the ballroom.

Many of the guests, both of the *ton* and of the village, swirled and made intricate patterns in the center of the room. Other guests watched and talked and laughed.

Susanna scanned the room. Where was Drake? Had he left to find her, or had he left, disgusted that she had abandoned him in the middle of the ballroom?

Franklin and Norah stood a few feet away. Franklin looked as polished as ever, but she was startled to realize she preferred Drake's rough edges to Franklin's perfectly tailored clothing and black hair that lay sedately across his head as if not daring to be out of place.

Beside him, Norah had grown into the promise of her beauty. Her once-bright red hair had matured into a wondrous russet that flattered her porcelain skin. Her freckles had vanished, but her nose was still pert and her mouth looked ready to smile.

Susanna walked toward them, trying to keep her breathing slow. She clasped her hands behind her so neither Norah nor Franklin could see how they shook. With regret? With uncertainty of how to speak to the two people she had never guessed she would have trouble talking to?

When she was close enough for them to hear, she said, "Good evening."

Norah whirled and gasped, "Susanna!"

Franklin turned, but said nothing as he stared at her as if she had appeared out of midair.

"Susanna, it is so good to see you." Norah smiled and held out her arms as if she was about to hug her.

Susanna stepped back and saw Norah's face fall. Wanting to apologize, for her aim had not been to hurt her onetime friend as she had been hurt, she could not find the right words. Instead, she said, "I know Raymond will be pleased you came tonight."

They exchanged an uneasy glance, and she could not blame them. Her tone suggested they had never been anything but strangers.

"What about you, Susanna?" Norah said while her husband remained silent. "Are you pleased we came tonight?"

"I am glad to see you looking so well." She wanted to take the words back as soon as they left her lips. Why couldn't she say something from the heart instead of acting as if she had never met Norah before?

"Is there somewhere we can talk privately?" Norah

looked at her silent husband, then at Susanna. "Just the two of us. Please. I think we need to talk."

"Yes, it is long past time. Come with me." As she walked with Norah to the closest door, she looked back and saw Drake talking with Papa.

He glanced at her, a question in his eyes. Papa said something to him, and his brows rose. He took a step toward her, but Papa must have cautioned him, because Drake did not follow as she led Norah out of the ballroom.

Susanna said nothing while she walked to a room where she and Norah once spent hours talking and laughing together. They should not be interrupted there. The mingled sounds of music and voices were cut off when she closed the door.

"I always liked this room," Norah said as she gazed around with a nostalgic smile. She went to a large window that offered a view of the stars twinkling over the back garden. "I remember how we used to sit on the floor and listen to your mother tell us stories while she worked on her embroidery."

"After she gave up trying to teach us."

"I am surprised I don't have scars on my fingertips after all the times I poked myself with a needle. I still cringe at the idea of sewing. I am glad that my cousin Helen loves to sew, or my children…" She lowered her head.

"Why don't we sit?" Susanna clung to etiquette as a rudder to guide her through the unknown waters of what to say to a woman she once could have said anything to without hesitation.

Norah sat and waited while Susanna chose the chair across from a low table near her. "Until the invitation came for tonight's assembly, I had no idea why you declined any invitations I sent to you or why you did not ask me to call. Then I discovered that Franklin did not do as he had promised me."

"What did he promise?"

"Susanna, you need to remember that he loved both of us, and I know you loved both of us, too. I was closer to you than my own family." Tears glistened in her eyes. "Yet, I was aware that Franklin loved you in a very special way, which is why I was thrilled when he asked you to be his wife and you agreed."

"You wanted to talk about the wedding plans more than I did." She could not keep from grinning at the memory.

A fleeting smile fled across Norah's face. "You were happy, and I was happy for both of you."

"So why...?" She swallowed, unable to speak the unspeakable words to Norah.

"Why did I steal your betrothed? Is that what you are finding hard to ask?"

"Yes."

"The answer is simple. I was enceinte."

"Pregnant? You and Franklin—?"

"No! He is not the father of our oldest daughter, though he loves her as if she were his blood. Her real father was a man who took advantage of my yearning for someone to love me as Franklin loved you. What I did not know was that he was already married."

"Who is he?"

She shook her head. "I have never spoken his name, not even to Franklin, and that truth must die with me. My daughter's father has no idea that she is his child, and my daughter believes Franklin is her father. I want to keep it that way because it is best for my daughter.

You and Franklin are the only ones, other than me, who know the truth."

"Why didn't you tell me? I would have done anything to help you."

"I know, but when I realized I was in a delicate condition, I could not think of anything but how ashamed my family would be. I was scared. I had no one to turn to except my best friends. Yet how could I lay such a burden at your feet when you were in mourning for your mother and brother-in-law? That left Franklin, so I went to him. When he offered to marry me to save my reputation and my family's, I accepted. I assumed that he would explain to you, because I suffered greatly from morning sickness and was focused on hiding it from my family until we were wed."

"He never said a word." She reached across the table and across the years that they had been separated. Taking Norah's hand, she looked into her friend's eyes. "Norah, I wish you had told me. Even though I believed myself in love with Franklin, I would have stepped aside. No, I would have done more than that. I would have been there to help you in any way I could."

"I know you would. I knew it then, so that is why I was so hurt when you turned away from us." She blinked back tears. "Once you shut us out of your life, Franklin realized the time had come and gone when he could have been honest with you...and with me."

"That was the promise he made?"

"To tell you the truth, but he didn't want to hurt you, either. Time went by, and it became even more impossible."

Susanna stood and, not letting go of her friend's hand, sat beside her. "I am glad you decided to tell me."

She smiled. "Though I may punch Franklin because he was too scared to do as he promised."

"I will be happy to hold him still while you do." Norah laughed. "Susanna, I have missed you so much."

Hugging her friend, Susanna asked Norah about her children and told her about the little ones from the jolly boat. Soon they were talking as if they were young girls again, letting their laughter heal the wounds that had driven them apart. She could not wait to share the news of their reconciliation with her family and with Drake.

Drake!

She jumped to her feet. "Norah, I have to go!"

"Yes, your guests." Norah's eyes narrowed. "Or is there one special guest on your mind? Perhaps that handsome man you were dancing with? From your smile, I would say the answer is yes. Then let's go. I cannot wait to meet him."

"I cannot wait to introduce you to him," she said as her heart sang. *Thank You, Lord, for this joyous evening.*

It was sure to grow even more wonderful when she danced with Drake. She could barely wait.

Chapter Seventeen

Drake walked out into the back garden and drew in a deep breath of air that was clean of cloying perfumes. He would prefer to be dancing with Susanna, but she had not yet returned to the ballroom. When Lord Launceston explained that the woman with her was Norah Chenowith, Drake had to hold back his instinct to protect Susanna. The woman who had married Susanna's betrothed had injured her deeply already.

He waited in the ballroom as long as he could endure the subtle insults aimed at him by some of the earl's guests. It was silly to take umbrage from people who looked down at everyone in trade. He should let such comments slide off his back like water slipping through scuppers.

But he could not, so he came out to the back garden before he lost his temper.

"Captain?" came a whisper from the shadows.

"Benton?" Drake frowned as his first mate came toward him. "Why are you skulking out here?"

"I need to talk to you."

"You could have come to the door. The footmen would have let you in."

He grimaced. "Those high sticklers don't want my company, and I don't want theirs." Shaking his head, he said, "My ma was a kitchen maid in a fine house like this one. She was not allowed to look any of the family in the eye, and she had to curtsy when they walked by, even when it was one of the young ones and her knees were stiff and painful." He shook his head. "I have no use for toplofty people."

"Even the Trelawneys?"

Benton hesitated, then cleared his throat. "They seem like decent people, but we cannot forget who we are and who they are, Captain. When push comes to shove, they won't ever let us forget it."

Disliking the course of the conversation, which came too close to what he had been thinking about the earl's guests, Drake asked, "Why did you come here? Not to warn me to watch my back around the *ton*, I assume."

"Nay." He straightened and grinned. "*The Kestrel* is shipshape, Captain. All the holes are plugged. Even so, I want one final inspection. We have gone over every inch of her, but better to be safe than sorry."

Drake smiled. His first mate had gained wisdom in the years he had been working on *The Kestrel*. Drake would miss him when Benton had a ship of his own, but he did not want to hold his first mate back.

"Do that, Benton."

"We will be ready to sail on the morning tide."

Cold slashed Drake, washing away his excitement at hearing that his ship was repaired. Sailing? Away from Susanna? Away from the children? Somehow, he said, "Thank you, Benton."

"Will you want to inspect the holds, Captain?"

"When I return. I cannot be down in the holds in a lord's heir's fine clothing, can I?"

Benton snapped his fingers. "I almost forgot." He dodged back into the shadow and brought out a bag. "Here are clothes. I figured you would want to leave the other things here so we are not delayed leaving Porthlowen."

"Good thinking." He took the bag and thanked his first mate again before Benton returned to the ship.

Drake tossed the bag over his shoulder and went to the low wall that offered a view of the sea. His boots bounced against his back, a reminder he was no fine milord and should not be wearing dancing shoes. He was a working man with salt-stained boots.

Setting the bag on the ground by the stone wall, he sat and gazed down at the harbor. *The Kestrel* was rising along with the tide that swept around the curve of the cliffs. She floated proudly, straining at the ropes holding her to the pier. She was ready to ride the waves between here and their next destination. His beloved ship. His home. His refuge.

I will say of the Lord, He is my refuge and my fortress: my God; in Him will I trust.

The words burst from a very old memory, of a time when he had felt welcome with his parents' neighbors before they had made it clear he was not part of their family. Someone had been reading from the Bible. From Psalms, if he remembered correctly.

Had it been so simple all along? When he had felt most alone and most betrayed by love, God had been there, waiting for him to reach out and ask for a refuge from sorrow and pain. God had loved him, even when he believed himself unlovable.

As Susanna had.

He looked at the house. Light from the ballroom splashed onto the grass. He stared at the lights, crisscrossed by shadows, then down at himself in his borrowed finery. What was he doing amid the *ton*? He was the son of a sailor who had abandoned him. Despite that, he had come from nothing to being the master of his own ship. Those accomplishments meant nothing to the people twirling about to the music and gossiping.

But they meant a lot to Susanna.

Susanna... To live his life upon the sea, he would have to abandon his wife and any children as surely as his own parents had left him behind. He could not ask that of any woman, but most especially he could not ask that of Susanna. She had been deserted once already by someone she believed loved her, and she would be deserted by her snobbish neighbors if she, assuming she loved him, accepted his proposal. She would be marrying far below her. She might not understand what that meant, but he did. The people in that ballroom who had treated her with respect would snub her the next time they met. How could he consign someone he loved to that?

Pushing himself to his feet, he yanked off the borrowed coat. He heard a thread snap and took more care as he folded it before placing it on the wall. Unbuttoning the waistcoat, he did the same. He sat on the wall and pulled his boots out of the bag. He kicked off the shoes and drew on his familiar boots. They did not shine in the moonlight, but they were comfortable.

He stood, and the wind whipped his full sleeves as it would when he stood on *The Kestrel*'s deck and gave orders to his crew. Every wave offered another chance for an adventure; every horizon led to wondrous lands. That was his life. Not this one, where he would not be any more welcome than he had been with those neighbors in Plymouth.

It was past time for him to think of his obligation to his ship and his crew…and to his dream of a trading fleet sailing at his command.

Elisabeth smiled at Susanna, then looked past her. "Where is Drake? Isn't he joining us for supper?"

"I was about to ask if you had seen him."

"No, but it is impossible to see everyone in this crush." She gave Susanna a quick hug. "Thank you for your help in making our wedding day so memorable."

"I am glad that you are now truly my sister." Even as she smiled at Elisabeth, she was looking around the room.

"Go and find Drake!" Elisabeth chuckled. "We have a lifetime as sisters to talk."

Susanna nodded and stepped aside to let someone else speak with the bride. She had already made two circuits of the ballroom without seeing Drake. Papa had told her that Drake had excused himself shortly after Susanna went with Norah. Where was he? She even sent a maid to check the nursery to discover if he had gone to see the children. He had not, so where was he?

"Lady Susanna," asked Venton as she walked past him for the third time, "are you looking for Captain Nesbitt?"

"Yes. Have you seen him?"

"He left the ballroom about half an hour ago. He was headed toward the back garden. You might look for him there."

"Thank you, Venton." She gave her longtime friend a grin and a wave before she set off in what she hoped was finally the right direction.

The house seemed oddly silent and empty once Susanna returned to the family wing. The servants were tending to the guests in the ballroom and the large dining room.

A cool wind blew past the open French windows in the small parlor. Going to the doors, she looked out. She had to give her eyes a chance to adjust to the darkness before she noticed the pale glow of moonlight reflecting off a shirt by the low wall.

She bit her lower lip to silence her gasp as she watched the wind press the lawn back against Drake's brawny arms. She longed to have them open wide to welcome her into them.

He did not turn as she walked to where he stood. "Drake, we are about to go in to supper."

Pushing away from the wall, he faced her. The light from the house created deep shadows on his face's strong planes. "Susanna, I am sorry."

"Sorry?" She looked down at the neatly folded clothing. "You changed?"

"No, I have not changed, and that is why I am saying I am sorry."

"I don't understand. If you do not want to join us, that is fine. I know you are concerned about the progress of the repairs on *The Kestrel*."

"No longer."

"Why?"

"They are finished."

She pressed her hand over her faltering heart. "Finished?"

He nodded. "So there is no reason for *The Kestrel* not to sail on the morning tide."

His silhouette grew blurry as tears filled her eyes. "Are you sure there is no reason?"

"Susanna, you knew this day was coming. I am the captain of *The Kestrel*. My crew and my customers depend on me." His voice had no more emotion than if he spoke of how the sun would rise on the morrow.

"Will you at least say goodbye to Lulu and Moll and the other children?"

"The morning tide comes very early. There is no need to wake them when they will not understand why I am saying goodbye."

I don't understand why you are saying goodbye, either, she wanted to shout.

"They will miss you," she whispered.

"And I will miss them." He looked past her to his ship.

"They will not understand why you are abandoning them as their own families did. How can you do that to them when you know firsthand how they will feel?"

He flinched but kept staring at his ship. His beloved ship. The one he loved more than he loved the children. The ship he loved more than he loved her.

"They will find their ways, as I did."

"That is a cruel thing to say."

"I don't mean for it to be cruel, Susanna." He finally turned back to her. "I am a sailor. I have never pretended to be anything else." His voice hardened. "Except tonight, when I let myself be drawn into a masquerade. Maybe someday, when I am the owner of a grand fleet of ships that don't have to accept a pittance in exchange for transporting cargo, I will be accepted by the people in there as worthy of their company."

Her eyes widened. "Is this about Mr. Miller? I heard some of what he said, and you heard what Caroline said. Don't let yourself be chased away by an encroaching mushroom who is only pleasant to those he believes will help him with his climb into Society."

"It is not about Mr. Miller. I have met his like before,

and I will meet it again." For the first time, his voice broke from its cool tones as he said, "But I will never meet anyone like you again, Susanna."

She grasped his hands and entwined her fingers with his. "Don't go. Please, don't go."

"I must." He drew his hands away, and suddenly there was an uncrossable chasm between them. "I made myself a promise years ago that I would grasp the dream that everyone said would be impossible for a boy discarded by his own parents. When others laughed and called me a fool, I didn't care. I knew I would someday have my dream. I am partway there by being master of *The Kestrel*. I must not stop now."

Susanna bit her lip as she stepped past him and pretended to look out over the cove. She could see nothing as tears blinded her. Why had she been fooling herself with the idea of a future that included Captain Drake Nesbitt? *The Kestrel* was his world, and he had no wish to leave his life upon the sea. He had never lied to her, but her heart had. Just as it had before when she believed herself in love with Franklin. Now she had learned that the feelings she had for him paled in comparison with what she felt for Drake.

"You speak of success, Drake. What of love? Does that matter to you, or are you interested only in thumbing your nose at those who left you on your own?"

Chapter Eighteen

Drake wished Susanna would face him, but why would she when he had turned his back on her in every possible way? Was she right? Was his dream meant only to prove to those who had overlooked him that they had been fools?

He had so many questions, but he asked, "Do you love me, Susanna?"

"The children adore you," she answered, and he knew she would not answer his question. Because she loved him or because she did not? "I don't know how you can leave them without saying goodbye."

He put his hands on her shoulders, but she shrugged them off as he turned her toward him. Her eyes glistened with unshed tears, and he asked himself if he was doing the right thing. How could he stay when he knew no other life than the sea? Maybe once he had another ship or two… He could not ask her to wait for him, and what if she did not want to? Ruby had not wanted to wait, and he had been wrong to insist. Perhaps it was unfair even to ask Susanna if she would, because staying in her life could ruin it when the *ton* could not forgive her for spending it with a man in trade.

"We have been living a fantasy," he said quietly.

"What I feel is real," she insisted. "I thought you felt the same way."

"I do, but I should not." He shook his head, knowing he must tell her the truth. "You are an earl's daughter. I have never known my parents. The gap between us is too wide."

"You are being foolish."

"No, I am finally not being foolish. I am sorry, Susanna. I knew how this would end right from the beginning, and I should not have let it get this far. Any relationship between us has been doomed from the outset."

"How can you say that?"

"Because I know it to be the truth." He ran his fingers along her cheek, knowing it might be the last time he ever touched her. "I know because I made this exact same mistake before. I fell in love once with a woman named Ruby. Her father was a baronet, who would never have accepted me. For Ruby, I was just entertainment until she could find a man with enough status to please her father. She promised to wait for me when I went to sea, but she never intended to keep that promise."

"And you believe I would do the same?"

He shook his head. "No, but I cannot ask you to give up everything for the nothing I can offer you. Would you give up your family? The children?" When she opened her mouth, he put his finger to her lips, savoring this final moment. "No, Susanna, there is nothing you can say to change my mind. I care about you too much to ask you to make that sacrifice."

"So you will go, and that's it?" Her voice hardened on each word, and he knew he had wounded her far more than anyone else ever had.

"I will stop when we come back this way," he struggled to say.

"Before you leave again? Don't you realize that you will hurt them each time you do that?"

Again she spoke only of the children. Did she love him? Would she give him a reason to stay, even though his being in her life could ruin it, dragging her down from her prestigious place as an earl's daughter?

What was he thinking? It was better this way. Hearing her say that she loved him might make him throw aside caution and ruin her life. But, if it was better, why did it feel as if he had made the biggest mistake of his life?

"Then maybe I should not come back at all," he said.

"If you think that is best…" She gathered her gown in both hands and ran into the house.

His heart went with her. Having a part of him remain in Porthlowen was cold comfort, but it was all he had.

Susanna turned the page on the accounts book, then grimaced as she realized she had not given the ink on the previous leaf time to dry. More than an hour's work smudged and ruined. She would have to tear out the page and make the entries again.

Slamming the book closed, she shoved back her chair. It was useless. Her mind was filled with the horrible conversation she had had with Drake in the back garden last night.

She considered—again—going to see the children. She pushed the thought away. They were sure to ask about Cap and when they would see him. Breaking their little hearts was something she could not do when her own was shattered. She had no idea if anyone else in the house had noticed that *The Kestrel* was gone.

The door opened, and her sister walked in. Without a word, Caroline crossed the room and embraced Susanna. Weak tears squeezed into Susanna's eyes again, but she refused to let them fall.

Caroline stepped back and shook her head. "I am sorry, little sister."

"I am fine." She returned to the desk and reopened the accounts book to a page that was not ruined. "Did you need something? As you know as well as I do, it is important to take advantage of the time when the children are otherwise entertained to work."

Caroline pulled a chair closer to the desk and sat. She said nothing, and the silence thickened around them.

When Susanna could endure it no more, she looked up at her sister, who sat with her arms folded over her chest. Never before had she looked so much like their mother.

When she had been disappointed in Susanna.

"What is it?" she asked.

"You know quite well." Caroline's tone was cool. "You are making the biggest mistake of your life. How could you let Captain Nesbitt leave?"

"I did not *let* him leave. He went."

"But you did not follow."

"Would you have me run after him, shouting out my feelings?"

"Why not?"

Susanna pushed back her chair and stood, unable to meet her sister's stern gaze any longer. "That is absurd."

"Is it? You lost one man because you never told him how you felt."

"He fell in love with someone else." She must not reveal the truth she had learned last night because she had promised Norah never to speak of how Franklin had not sired her oldest. And she would keep that promise. For Norah. For Franklin. For the daughter who called them her parents. Hadn't she learned that love did not depend on blood? "It has worked out for the best because they now have a lovely family."

"But Franklin was in love with *you* first. He tried to show you in every possible way with kindnesses and attention. All you had to do was lower that blasted wall you have built around yourself, because you feel you have to take care of everything and everyone." She shook her head sadly. "Everyone but yourself. If you had given him any sign that you shared his feelings, he would have happily married you."

Oh, how she wished she could share the truth, but she would not. No matter what. Instead, she said, "Caroline, that is ancient history. Franklin and Norah are happily married and raising their family. I wish them only happiness. They were my best friends, and I hope someday I can say they are again."

"That is good to hear." Her sister came to her feet. "I don't know what brought about this change of heart, but I am glad you have accepted that the path God has for you did not include becoming Franklin's wife. However, I cannot say the same about Drake Nesbitt. I have never seen you so happy, little sister, as you have been since he came into your life."

She plucked at a thread on her apron. "But he is gone."

"And that is that?"

"What would you have me say?" she asked, her voice rising on each word. "That I wish he had stayed. Of course I do, but my dreams are not his. He wants to own a company of ships and build a successful trading venture." Bitterness crept into her words. "I should have known better after seeing what you went through when John was lost at sea. I doubt you would have made the same choices you did if you had known how it would end."

"Susanna, you are wrong. I would marry him all over again, even knowing how it would end and how soon. Each time John sailed, I placed him in God's hands. God was with John the day he died, just as He always was. Though I cannot begin to understand why God took him that day, I know John died doing what he loved doing. That thought has given me more comfort than you can imagine."

"Really?" She could not hold back her tears any longer.

Her sister stepped closer and pulled a handkerchief from her apron pocket. Dabbing at Susanna's tears, she said, "Yes. Having him happy made me happy. I missed him when he was away, but that made the times when he was here even more precious. I was so proud of how he turned down Papa's offer of a ship of his own. John believed he still had more to learn as first mate before he was ready to be a captain."

"I never heard that Papa was going to give John a ship of his own."

"Just as Papa had a house built for you and Franklin, he planned to do the same for us. He changed his wedding gift to the ship when he discovered how much John loved the sea." Caroline's loving smile had a taint of sadness. "Susanna, you don't know *everything* that happens at Cothaire."

"Probably not." She sank to sit on a chair's upholstered arm. "I am glad you found some comfort amidst your grief. I know John wanted you to be happy. That made him happiest."

"What would make me happiest," growled a male voice from near the door, "is for you to come with me."

Caroline screamed as she looked past Susanna.

Turning, Susanna forced her own shriek down her throat. A man in ragged clothes stood by the door. He held a pistol aimed at them. She instinctively stepped between her sister and the pistol. When Caroline cried out again in horror, Susanna stretched her hand back to clasp her sister's.

"Who are you?" Susanna asked in the steady tone she had heard Drake use in a tense situation.

"My name is not of importance. Come with me." He motioned with the gun.

Behind her, Caroline moaned, and Susanna knew her sister had heard what she did. The man spoke with an undeniable French accent.

She held Caroline's hand as they edged around the Frenchman. He kept his gun pointed at them. It jabbed into Susanna's back when they stepped through the doorway, and she felt Caroline flinch, as well.

Another man waited in the hallway. Saying nothing, he motioned for them to follow him. They did.

As they passed a rare window that gave a view of the harbor, Susanna drew in a sharp breath. In the middle of the harbor, beyond where *The Kestrel* had been moored for more than a month, another ship rocked on the waves. A French flag flew from the top of her tallest mast.

The gun poked her in the back again, and she started to turn to snarl at the Frenchman. A quick murmur from her sister halted her. She stiffened when both men laughed.

As they passed a staircase, Susanna did not look up. She must not want to give the Frenchmen a reason to search the upper floors of the house and find the children. Then she realized they probably already were ransacking the rooms, stealing everything they could carry away. Losing possessions would be a small price to pay if the children were safe.

A third ragged man stood by the door to Papa's smoking room. He opened the door and bowed them in with a mocking smile. She pretended not to notice as she went with Caroline into the darkened room.

The storm shutters were closed and a single lamp had been lit. Her composure crumbled when she saw more than a dozen strangers in the room along with her father. When Caroline gave a frightened cry and ran to him, Susanna did, too.

Papa stood up, even though she could see pain gouging lines into his face. He pulled them to him and put one arm around each of them.

"There is no need to terrorize this household," he said coldly. "Take our valuables and leave us and the village in peace."

"We are not here for your baubles," said the tall man who appeared to be in charge of the invaders. He would have been handsome if he did not wear a sneer on his gaunt face. "We are here for vengeance, because we grew tired of the hospitality of Dartmoor Prison."

Susanna clenched her hands at her sides. Were these men the same ones whose ship had attacked *The Kestrel*? She had not watched them march through the village on their way to prison.

"The rats ate better than we did," the man continued, "so we ended up eating the rats. That will not sustain a man, so when they asked for volunteers to help build the church, my surviving men and I were quick to raise our hands."

"They assigned you to work together?" Papa asked with a terse laugh. "If you think we would believe such a ludicrous tale—"

"Believe what you wish, *mon seigneur*."

"I believe you are lying, Captain Allard."

The French captain laughed. "You are right. We were not assigned together, but all it took were a few changes of clothing with men who had died. Your English guards never bothered to notice the difference. It took long weeks of digging the foundation and laying stones before my crew finally was gathered together on the same work team. Then we waited for the right opportunity."

The man by his side smiled icily. "Those guards will never turn their attention away again."

Pressing her hand to her stomach, Susanna tried to quell its roiling. She looked toward the door when she heard footsteps and the sound of a crying baby. When Miss Oliver entered with the children, she went to Caroline, who held her hands out for Joy.

Susanna motioned for the children to come to her, and the twins and Bertie rushed to grasp her skirts. She put her arms around their shoulders, herding them closer to her. She was glad Toby was safe at the parsonage. Or was he? Again her stomach cramped as she remembered Papa saying to leave the village alone. Raymond and Elisabeth and the little boy could be in the gravest danger. What of the Winwood sisters and others in the village?

"This is everyone," said one of the men who had brought the children into the room.

"The servants?"

"In the kitchen, under guard." He saluted the French captain, drawing her attention to him.

"Mr. Morel!" Her gasp was echoed by her sister.

The blacksmith's assistant gave her a smile so cold that her breath froze in her lungs. She tightened her hold on the children as she stared at the man who had betrayed them.

"Ah, I see you are familiar with Robert Morel." Captain Allard chuckled and said, using the French pronunciation, "Or, more correctly, *Lieutenant* Morel."

"What do you want?" Papa asked, and she knew he was growing impatient with the French captain playing with them, as if he were a cat and they were terrified mice.

"I told you. We want vengeance. Word came to us of a prosperous village in this hidden cove, and we were on our way here when we were waylaid by *The Kestrel*."

"But Mr.—Lieutenant Morel has been here for months!" exclaimed Susanna before she could halt herself.

"Who do you think informed us of Porthlowen? We have spies throughout England, obtaining information on possible targets." He gave Lieutenant Morel a satisfied grin. "He used his time here quite well." Looking back at Papa, he said, "I believe you recently suffered a fire in your stable, *mon seigneur*, and I heard about a cart filled with *les enfants* losing one of its wheels."

"It was simple to do," Lieutenant Morel bragged. "I heard how Lady Susanna intended to take the children to the mines. When everyone was busy cleaning up from the fire, I could easily slip away to rig the wheel to break. Too bad it broke too soon."

Susanna heard both her sister and Miss Oliver cry out in horror. She simply stared at the man who had been made welcome in Porthlowen. Behind his innocuous smile, he had hidden his atrocious plans. He looked away first, and she felt a brief moment of satisfaction until Lieutenant Morel pointed at her.

"Captain Allard, she is the one Nesbitt called on," he said.

The French captain eyed her as boldly as if she were for sale in the market. "I must say that Nesbitt has excellent taste in women. What is your name, woman?"

"Lady Susanna Trelawney," she answered with all the dignity she could put in her voice.

"Are those his brats?"

Before she could answer, Morel gave his captain a quick synopsis of how the children had come to Porthlowen. The captain guffawed and bent to crook a finger at Bertie.

The little boy shook his head before hiding his face in her gown.

"Come here, boy!" Captain Allard ordered. When Bertie did not move, he motioned to one of his men.

The man stepped forward to take Bertie. Susanna's hand striking the man's face echoed through the abruptly silent room.

"Touch him, and you will be sorry." When she spoke in the perfect French she had learned from her governess, everyone froze.

"The she-cat defends another's spawn," Captain Allard said in his native language. "How amusing!" He switched to English and gestured to Miss Oliver. "Nurse, take the boy."

Susanna bent and pried Bertie's fingers off her gown. "Go with Miss Oliver, Bertie." She gave him a gentle shove, and he ran to the nurse, who picked him up and turned so her body was between him and the French sailors.

"And one of the girls," ordered Captain Allard.

"Which one?" Susanna asked.

"You choose. It does not matter to me."

Unsure what he planned, she started to push both girls toward Miss Oliver. Perhaps the captain would see how terrified the children were and let them stay with the nurse.

It was a futile hope, she realized, when Captain Allard snapped an order, and one of his men grabbed Lulu away from the nurse and shoved her into Susanna's arms. Both twins howled in fear. She calmed Lulu while Miss Oliver tried to quiet Moll's shrieks.

"Your choice is made," the captain said. "Now I will make my choice. It is time for us to leave. Come, Lady Susanna, and bring the child."

"Come where?"

"You would be wise not to ask questions." His glare did not silence her, but the gun one of his men raised to train on her sister did.

Her father asked coldly, "Where are you taking my daughter and Lulu?"

"To give her one last look at her sweetheart before we sink him and his ship to the bottom of the sea." He took her arm and pulled her toward the door. "If you want to see Lady Susanna and the child alive again, do not follow us, and do not warn Nesbitt."

"*The Kestrel* is far from here," Papa said.

"Not far enough to avoid her end." He paused, then said, "I am not without a heart, *mon seigneur*. If you obey my orders to remain here and make no attempt to contact Nesbitt and his ship, Lady Susanna will be returned to you so she can share with you the tidings of *The Kestrel*'s demise."

"She will be returned in the same condition she is now." Papa did not make it a question.

The French captain put his hand over his heart in a wounded pose. "I am a gentleman, *mon seigneur*. Not like that cur, Nesbitt."

"Leave the child here," Susanna said, having no use for his posturing. "You don't need two hostages."

"Maybe if you give me enough time, I will decide on three."

Her face grew cold. She did not doubt he would have his men grab another child, simply to prove his power over them. "No," she whispered. "There is no need for that. Just promise that Lulu will be returned in the same condition she is now, as well."

"I give you my word."

She raised her chin and said, "Your word means nothing to us, Captain."

The Frenchman's face grew florid, and she hoped she had not pushed him too far. If she complied too quickly, he might make good on his promise to bring another child with them, so she had to walk a fine line between challenging him and submitting to his orders.

"My word may mean nothing to you," he growled, "but it means everything to me. I vowed to my men that I would free them from that prison and lead them to exact vengeance on Nesbitt. I have done the first, and soon I will have done the second. You will have a front-row seat to watch."

Without giving her a chance to say goodbye, he pushed her ahead of him out of the room. Lieutenant Morel gave a sharp whistle, and more Frenchmen appeared from every direction. He turned and locked the smoking room from the outside. He asked the sailors if the rest of the household was secured behind other locked doors and storm shutters so they could not escape quickly.

Satisfied none of his prisoners would escape, Captain Allard took Susanna out of the house and forced her into her father's closed carriage. The shades had been unrolled and lashed to the bottom of the windows. Holding Lulu close and trying to soothe the frightened child, she did not look at Captain Allard, who sat across from them. She prayed for their lives and for the lives of her family and her neighbors, as well as the safety of Drake and his crew. They were not expecting pursuit, and she knew as soon as he learned that she and Lulu were on the French ship, he would surrender. He might be unwilling to stay with them, but he cared about them.

The door was jerked open as soon as the carriage stopped. She stepped out and looked toward the church and the parsonage. She saw no movement there. Where were her brother and Elisabeth and little Toby? The village looked deserted, save for a line of men carrying heavy items from the smithy.

Cannonballs! They were bringing cannonballs to the French ship. Was Mr. Jenner a spy, too? She got her answer when she came around the side of the carriage and saw the blacksmith trussed in ropes nearly from head to foot. His eyes widened when his gaze alighted on her, and he struggled against his bonds. Realizing it was useless, he apologized with his eyes. She gave him a swift smile to acknowledge his apology. She wanted to remind him that he had done nothing wrong except for hiring a liar. Lieutenant Morel must have laughed hard when he convinced everyone that he was making cast-iron pots in those molds for the round shot.

Captain Allard led the way to a jolly boat moored to one of iron rings the fishermen used. Lieutenant Morel must have destroyed their boats, too, when he could not get aboard Drake's ship to do more damage. Su-

sanna thought of how she had urged Drake to invite the
blacksmith's apprentice aboard to help with repairing
the ship. Had she allowed Lieutenant Morel to damage
The Kestrel even more?

She pulled her elbow away from the French captain when he was about to assist her into the jolly boat.
Bending, she put Lulu on a seat in the center.

The little girl stiffened, then moaned. She did not answer when Susanna asked what was wrong. Lulu stared
about her, her eyes growing big with terror.

Suddenly Lulu shrieked, "No! No boat! No boat.
Way-dee Susu, no boat. Stay with Way-dee Susu. I be
good. Stay. No go! No boat!" She burst into hysterical tears and tried to scramble over the side and onto
the sand.

Susanna picked her up and cuddled her close, as-
tounded. The little girl's lisp had returned. Had her memory, too? It must have, if she was now scared of being
placed in a jolly boat. What a joyous moment this should
be! They should be praising God and celebrating. Instead, they stood in terror before their enemies, and Susanna was praying for the lives of those she loved.

"Shut her up!" ordered the captain.

"She is scared of the boat."

"I don't care! Just shut her up!"

Stepping into the boat, she sat and held Lulu close
to her. The child's hysterics eased to sobs that racked
her tiny body. Susanna wanted to cry, too, as the waves
buffeted the boat. She would not give the Frenchman
the satisfaction of seeing her weep. He would think
he had cowed her, not guessing how scared she was
of drowning. As she had in the carriage, she kept her
head down, alternately praying and comforting Lulu
while they were rowed out to the ship. She looked up

only once and saw the words *Le Corsaire* painted on the ship's bow.

The Pirate.

Captain Allard had named his new ship appropriately. She wondered how he had coordinated the ship's arrival in Porthlowen Harbor at the same time he and his men reached Cothaire. A shiver raced along her when she realized he might have been lurking nearby for days, watching them. No, if he had been close, he would not have let *The Kestrel* elude him.

She refused to give Lulu to one of the sailors as a rope ladder was dropped over the ship's side. Climbing with Lulu's arms wrapped around her neck, she heard grumbles behind her at her slow progress. She inched up the hull past an open port that revealed a row of cannons. She shuddered at the sight but, at the same time, hid a smile. Every minute she delayed them gave Drake and his ship more time to sail even farther from these French pirates.

The sailors on the main deck dragged her aboard roughly. When she glowered at them, they made rude remarks in French. She let them go on, until Captain Allard's head appeared over the rail. Then she lashed them in her best French and the low cant her governess had never expected she had learned. The men's mouths gaped, but they snapped to attention when Captain Allard dismissed them. His warning that he would speak with them later made them cower.

She was not fooled by Captain Allard's fake gentility. He was a pirate. Would he keep his promise to let her and Lulu return to Cothaire alive? She began to doubt that as Captain Allard ordered them imprisoned belowdecks.

He taunted her by saying, "I will not forget you,

Lady Susanna. As soon as *The Kestrel* is sighted, you will be brought up to watch my vengeance on Nesbitt."

Susanna did not reply. She kept her head high and tried to copy the expression Mama had worn when she was faced by something too base for her even to acknowledge.

Captain Allard endured it for less than a minute before his eyes shifted away. He muttered something unflattering about Englishwomen under his breath. When he looked back at her, she simply raised her eyebrows in a pose she had learned from Drake, and for a moment Captain Allard looked flustered.

"Capitaine!" came a shout from across the deck.

Susanna could not catch all the words because they were lost to the wind, but she heard enough. She did not try to conceal her smile this time when she listened as Captain Allard's crew yelled about a chain of debris across the channel between the cliffs. Turning, she looked at the shore. As she had suspected, all the fishing nets and the pieces of broken boats had vanished. While his crew had been looting the village, some of the fishermen must have gone out to the cliffs with what nets they still had. She suspected they had lashed the nets with pieces of iron and wood before stretching them across the water to trap the French ship in the cove.

Suddenly, she was grabbed and shoved toward a companionway. Holding Lulu close, she did not protest when they were taken down two decks and locked in a room that stank of gunpowder and rotten meat. Both must have been stored recently on its wide shelves. She tried opening the porthole to let in fresh air, but it refused to budge.

"Way-dee Susu, go home," Lulu cried as the door

slammed shut and a bar crashed into place. "Go see Moll and Bertie and Gil and Joy. Go home. Now!"

Dropping to her knees on the filthy deck, Susanna set Lulu in front of her. She folded her hands over the little girl's and began to pray that all of them would be safe in God's hand, knowing He was with them always.

No matter what.

Chapter Nineteen

It was useless.

Standing at the wheel of his beloved ship, gazing out over the waves that emerged from the spot where the sea met the sky, Drake was miserable. He could not enjoy the roll of the ship beneath his feet. He was oblivious to the wind in his face, luring him to a new adventure. Even the duet of the creaking timbers as *The Kestrel* climbed each roller and the flap of the sails did not make him smile. In fact, he did not hear it.

Since they had left Porthlowen before dawn, he had given orders to his crew automatically. His thoughts were not on *The Kestrel* or the search for her next cargo so he could pay off what he owed from the losses of the last one.

His thoughts—and his heart—were focused on Susanna. What a fool he had been to let her become such an important part of his life! Had he been an even greater fool to leave her? But he was not a part of her glittering world, where a man was judged solely by the circumstances of his birth. Her family had accepted him…as a guest. Would the earl have allowed a man who had been tossed aside as a child to marry his beloved younger daughter?

And the children… How could he have failed to bid them farewell? They had trusted him, and he abandoned them. Susanna was right. He, of all people, comprehended the bafflement and pain a child felt when learning the familiar world was not as he believed and that adults he thought he could depend on, in truth, did not care about him.

Would the children think of him as he had his parents and the people whose cramped house had been a poor home? He flinched, and his hands gripped the wheel until his knuckles cracked. Calling to a nearby crewman, he motioned for the man to take over steering the ship. He strode toward the bow.

Drake stared out over the bowsprit and the hawk figurehead beneath it. He had thought his path was clear. One ship, then another and another under his command. A life on the sea as both a captain and the owner of his trading company while he urged other captains to join him in setting fair prices for cargo. He even had a name for his company: Nesbitt's Shipping of Cornwall. Plain and to the point.

Now he could think only of what that dream was denying him.

Benton walked up to him. "Captain?"

"Report." Drake waited for Benton to give him an update on their location and a report on general conditions of the ship and the weather.

"I have to report that you have windmills in your head," his first mate said.

"What?"

"You heard me." Anger tinged Benton's voice. "For all the time we have worked together, Captain, you have had nothing but my respect and admiration. That changed when you had us sneak out of Porthlowen Harbor like thieves in the dark."

"I had my reasons."

"Stupid ones, no doubt."

Drake frowned. "That is quite enough, Mr. Benton!"

"Not until you hear what I have to say, Captain."

"You have nothing to say that I want to hear."

"Probably not, but you *need* to hear what I have to say." Not pausing to take a breath, his first mate hurried on. "I know you have been overly cautious since that Ruby woman cheated on you. Did you decide to leave Lady Susanna before she could leave you? Or is it that you thought she believed you were too lowborn for her?"

"She does not believe that. How can you say that after she welcomed those babies into her life as if they were to the manor born?"

"If she is not the one who thinks it, then you must."

"Leave off, Benton. I am warning you." His hands fisted at his sides.

Benton folded his arms in front of him and raised his chin in defiance. "Are you?"

"Speak one more word, and you will be sorry."

"If I am going to be sorry if I speak another word, then I am going to make it a good one. I never thought I would say this to you, but you are acting like a coward. Why couldn't you trust the woman who loves you, instead of fleeing?"

Drake grasped his first mate by the collar and saw Benton's shock. Other captains were heavy-handed and did not hesitate to use the whip to keep order on their ships, but not Drake. He recalled the shame and terror he had felt as a child when he was beaten publicly by the boys who had mocked him for being a charity boy who never knew his parents. That fear was not what he wanted on his ship.

His first mate was speaking the truth that Drake had tried to submerge beneath talk of duty and obligation in Cothaire's back garden. All of Drake's frustration was aimed at himself.

He released Benton. Turning on his heel, he walked to the closest companionway. He did not halt until he reached his private quarters. Going in, he shut the door. He intended to sit on his bed and regain his composure before he returned to the main deck. Instead, he fell to his knees.

"Is Benton right, Lord?" he prayed aloud, the first time he had ever done so outside of church. *"Have I lost my faith in others as I did in You? You know my heart, and You know Susanna's. Am I afraid to trust her? Help me learn to trust again. Help me trust You, so I can trust the woman I love."* Saying that he loved Susanna—aloud and without hesitation—sent strength through him. *"Help me trust myself and search my heart and my soul to find the courage to follow the path You have created for me, instead of running blindly away. I don't want to be like my parents, who took the easy way. I want to take the right way. I want to take it with Susanna, if that is Your will. Whatever Your will is, I will follow it."*

He bowed his head over his hands folded on the bed. A calm he had never experienced, not even when wind died on a flat sea, settled over him. From within his heart, a sense of belonging grew out to fill the void that had ached in him for so long. He had always been God's beloved child, even when he believed his heavenly Father was not watching over him. He had never

been alone, even during those darkest days of his childhood. He stayed on his knees, thanking God for never
forgetting him.

A knock sounded on his door, followed by a frantic
"Captain Nesbitt!"

Drake pushed himself to his feet and winced as his
knees protested. How long had he been on them? No
matter, because it had been time well spent. He had
been embraced by the love of God. To have that and
Susanna's love would be the sweetest dream come true,
far better than owning a hundred ships.

The knock came again, and Drake opened the door
to see Obadiah. The cook's eyes snapped with anger.

"Captain," he said the moment Drake stepped out of
his quarters. "'Tis happenin' agin. 'Tis the galley this
time. Supplies are gettin' soaked."

"We are taking on water again?"

"Aye, Captain."

Drake did not hesitate. He ran to the main deck and
sprinted across it. Shouting to his crew, he gave orders
to change course for the shore. They needed to get there
before *The Kestrel* sank with all hands.

The cove where *The Kestrel* anchored was wide-
open. Its sea cliffs did not resemble a pair of arms closing in an embrace like at Porthlowen. An inspection of
the ship turned up only a handful of holes on the upper
decks. The crew had not checked those areas because
there had been no leakage in the harbor's shallow waters.

Drake examined the holes and realized they looked
identical to the ones on the lower decks that had been
drilled by their unseen enemy. Setting the crew to fixing them, he and Benton went to the small village to

see if they could buy some sugar and flour to replace what had been ruined in galley stores.

He was astonished to hear his name called. Shading his eyes with his hand, he looked east and saw someone racing toward them. He recognized the lad from the stables at Cothaire. What was he doing so far from the earl's estate? Something must be horribly wrong.

Grabbing the lad before he could tumble off his feet, he sent Benton running to the village well to get some water. Drake waited until his first mate came back with a tin cup he had gotten somewhere. He offered it to the boy, who was gasping with exhaustion.

The boy tilted it back and drained it.

"More?" asked Drake.

He shook his head while he wiped his mouth with the back of his hand. "Baricoat sent me and another stable boy running to see if we could catch up with you at your next port of call. He told me to go west, while Jerry went east."

"What is wrong?"

"Frenchie sailors in Porthlowen. The ones you captured."

Drake's blood froze in his veins. "But they are in prison."

"They escaped. They have a ship in the harbor." The boy pressed his hands against his thighs as he struggled to catch his breath. He stood and went on, "They went to the earl's house, and when they came out, they had Lady Susanna and one of the little girls with them." He coughed again, but forced out, "Took them out to their ship."

Benton snarled an oath that Drake had never heard him use, then asked, "Your orders, Captain?"

He did not stop to consider the madness of his hast-

ily improvised plan as he outlined it to Benton. There
would have to be changes when they saw what they
truly faced in Porthlowen, but he had enough to get
them started.

As Benton ran across the sand to reboard *The Kestrel* and alert the crew to his orders, Drake looked at
the lad. "Tell me. What is the fastest route overland?"

"Your ship—"

"Never mind that for now. Tell me the fastest route.
Every second we lose may be the very one that costs
Lady Susanna her life."

Susanna heard running feet far overhead and muffled shouts. Had the French sailors finally cleared a
route out of the cove? The fishermen must have built
an intricate net from one cliff to the other. It had held
up *Le Corsaire*'s departure long enough for the tide to
fall and prevent the big ship from reaching the sea. *The
Kestrel* could handle the narrow channel with ease, but
the French ship required deeper water to keep the keel
from scraping.

But the tide was rising again.

"Go home?" asked Lulu, hopeful about the distant
sounds.

"I hope so." She sat on the deck. Picking up Lulu,
she set the child on her lap.

"Scared."

"Do you want to know what I do when I am scared?"

The little girl nodded eagerly.

"I ask God to put His arms around me and keep me
safe."

"God's arms?"

"Just like this." Susanna wrapped her arms around
Lulu and snuggled her against her breast. "When I re-

member that God will always hold me like this whenever I need it, I am not so scared."

"Scared."

"Just cuddle close and shut your eyes. Think of something pretty."

"Way-dee Susu pretty." She patted Susanna's cheek as she had so often.

Tears burned her eyes. In the past hours she had discovered that Lulu remembered a lot of what she had forgotten, though she had no memory of her fall and only jumbled images of the day the children arrived in Porthlowen.

The deck shifted under Susanna. Suddenly she slid sideways as a thump resonated through the whole ship. Had *Le Corsaire* struck something? A cliff?

More shouts and thuds came from the decks above them. She pushed herself up and put Lulu where she had been sitting. Another thump knocked her to the deck again. What was going on?

"Stay there!" she called to Lulu as she stood again, holding her scraped left elbow in her right hand. "Stay close to the wall."

The sound of running feet stopped. What was happening? Again, the deck moved. She had to grasp a shelf as the deck tilted. She looked out the porthole. Her heart sank when she saw the cliffs sliding past them. The ship was moving out of Porthlowen Harbor.

"No!" she cried before she was knocked off her feet.

Lulu giggled, clearly believing Susanna was playing a game as Susanna sat up and put her feet on the deck again. Beneath her, the deck was going both side to side and up and down at the same time. The capricious currents of the cove must be pulling it in different directions. She hoped Captain Allard was skilled. Otherwise, they would be dashed against the cliffs.

As Susanna waited, unsure what would happen next, Lulu grew restless. She wrapped her arms around Susanna's neck and whispered, "No scared. God's arms."

Susanna's tears fell as she thanked God for the blessing of this loving child in her life. She would protect Lulu for as long as she could, even though she had no idea how.

The door rattled, and she heard the bar being lifted. Standing, she pushed Lulu behind her. If whoever stood on the other side of the door wanted the child, he would have to fight Susanna to get to her.

She breathed a desperate prayer as the door opened.

"Surprise!" came a laughing shout.

Drake!

She ran across the deck, flinging herself into his arms. His lips found hers. Softening against him, she put everything she found impossible to say in the kiss. She had no idea how he could be on the ship. She did not care. He was alive, and she was in his arms.

"Cap!" shrieked Lulu with delight.

Susanna reluctantly stepped back to let the little girl hug Drake's leg. A score of questions exploded in her mind, but she was silent as she watched Drake kiss Lulu's soft cheek before he scooped her up.

He looked at Susanna. "Surprise!" He grinned. "Wait a moment. You don't like surprises, do you?"

"I love this one!" She threw caution to the wind, knowing they might have only seconds before the French sailors arrived belowdecks. "And I love you."

"Now, *that* is a surprise."

"That I love you?"

"That you would admit it." He brushed her tangled

hair back from her face. "Giving in to love means surrendering control of your heart."

"I know it's safe with you."

"It is," he said as solemnly as if he took a vow, then smiled again. "And you have my heart, which is firmly in your control because I don't ever want it back."

Susanna ached for more of his kisses but said, "We need to go."

"We are going. Out to sea now, but that will change as soon as I give the command."

"You?" She looked past him to familiar sailors swarming over the cannons, drawing them in and closing the wooden portholes to keep out water. "That is *your* crew."

"About half of them. The other half are aboard *The Kestrel*. With the help of the good folks in Porthlowen, they have already captured Captain Allard and the rest of his men whom we lured off the ship to fight hand to hand aboard my ship. Too bad Captain Allard forgot that one should never leave a ship with too few guards when the tide is high. It can easily be stolen by a small group of determined sailors. After we were alerted to the situation in the village and at Cothaire by one of your father's stable boys, I led half of my crew overland and hid in the village until *The Kestrel* made her appearance. Captain Allard unwisely was only watching seaward."

"Why are we sailing out to sea?"

"It will be easier to claim this ship as a prize if she is at sea." He laughed. "With God's help, this may become the second ship of Nesbitt's Shipping of Cornwall, though changing her name will be the first order of business. What do you think of *The Lady Susu*?"

Lulu clapped her hands and giggled, but Susanna's heart faltered again.

Drake loved her, and she loved him. That had not changed. Nothing else had, either. His life was on the sea, far from Cothaire. Hers was not, but her sister's words about her marriage resonated with her. Like Caroline, she must be willing to have the man she loved with her whenever possible. His infrequent visits would have to be enough to last her through the lonely times between.

Raising her eyes to his, she said, "That would be wonderful, Drake. Your dream is coming true."

"It is." He stroked her cheek with his thumb. "I know I am not worthy of you, Susanna—"

"That is nonsense. I told you that before. Will you believe me now? Do you think I care about your past? It is your present and future I want to share."

"You are the daughter of an earl."

"And you are the man I love." Taking Lulu from his arms and setting the little girl on the deck, she drew his mouth down to hers for a kiss. When his arms curved around her, she was sure that he understood what her words had struggled to say.

He laced his fingers through hers, and after she picked up Lulu, he led them up to the main deck. They walked to the bow. In one direction, she saw the open sea. In the other, the cliffs of Porthlowen with Cothaire sitting on the hill behind them.

He plucked Lulu out of her arms and whispered in the child's ear. The little girl giggled and squirmed to get down. He bent to make sure she was steady on her feet beside them, then dropped to one knee and took Susanna's hand. "Susanna, you have mended my heart and brought me back to God. You have banished the bitterness that filled my life and replaced it with love. If you will have me, sweetheart, I will gladly give up my other dreams on the sea and be yours forevermore. Say yes, and become my wife."

Her hand swept through his black hair as she lost herself in his dark brown eyes. No, she did not lose herself. She found herself, the woman she could become with his love.

"Yes, I will marry you. I will try to be the best wife any woman has been, whether you are in Porthlowen or far away at sea. But I will never again ask you to give up the sea. Your life on *The Kestrel* has made you the man I love." She touched the center of her chest. "Your heart beats here with mine, and I know how you love being captain of a fine ship. I was wrong to expect you to live my life. I want us to live *our* lives as husband and wife in whatever direction we go."

Coming to his feet, he did not look away as he called orders for his crew to turn the ship around and head back to Porthlowen Harbor. He lowered his voice and said, "Benton will be taking command of *The Kestrel*."

"When you take command of this ship?"

"No, I will hire a captain to sail *The Lady Susu*, if she is awarded to me by the Admiralty as a prize of war."

"What will you do?"

"Fulfill my dreams. I will find other captains who are interested in working together for the betterment of all of us. We should not let the customers pit us one against another so we make pennies on a voyage. I think of the miners on Warrick's land and how they bid against each other. If they stood firm, they would earn a better living for them and for their families. We merchant sailors can do the same."

Susanna smiled as she drew his arms back around her. "What a great plan!"

"I could use someone who is used to keeping accounts to help me get started. Do you know someone?" He looked down at Lulu. "Someone who has cute twin children to be a part of our family, at least for a while?"

Her joyous yes vanished beneath her lips as he kissed her again, making their sweetest dreams come true.

Epilogue

Susanna stood in the middle of the room and looked around. Furniture was scattered everywhere, and a rolled-up rug leaned against the marble hearth. She should decide where to put each chair and settee and table in the new house her father had started building when she first planned to wed. Did she want the gold curtains or the blue ones hung over the windows with the tempting view of the cove and the crashing waves?

Last night, a storm had risen out of the sea. The wind drove water ahead of it, raising the waves as high as the ones that battered unprotected shores. Now the thunder and lightning and driving rain were gone, and bright sunshine lured her to hurry down to the sand.

She heard two deep voices followed by the joyous giggles only little girls could make. She turned to greet Lulu and Moll, then scurried hastily out of the way as Venton came in, followed by a trio of footmen.

"Over there." He watched the men put the crates next to a pair of side tables, then waited for them to leave. He gave a terse nod in Susanna's direction before following them.

"Venton takes his new duties as butler very seriously,

doesn't he?" Drake walked in with the twins holding his hands. Love and happiness filled his gaze as it met hers.

"Very." She held out her arms, and the twins rushed to her. As she hugged them, she looked over their heads to the man behind them.

By this time tomorrow, she would be Drake's wife. She had counted down each day since—what the villagers called—the Battle of Porthlowen. With Captain Allard and his crew—including Lieutenant Morel—secured in prison, there had been no further destruction to Drake's ship or the village or Cothaire. The cannon from the privateer and cannonballs Lieutenant Morel had made at the smithy garnered enough money to repay Drake's customers for the cargo lost the first time his crew fought the French sailors.

Waiting for the banns to be read had been difficult, but gave Susanna time to begin to put together the home they would share. A home overlooking the cove and Cothaire on the opposite hillside. A home filled with the laughter of two little girls who would live with them until the puzzle of their origins was unraveled. A home where she and Drake could forget the past and embrace the future... as well as each other.

"Why are you grinning like a cat in catnip?" he asked as he walked toward her.

"I am happy. Why are you grinning?"

"I am happy, as well." He reached past the twins to wrap his arm around her waist. As the children skipped away to peer into an open crate, he added, "I have everything a man could want and more."

"More? What more could any man want than a house filled with unpacked boxes and rooms that still need to be painted?" When he laughed, she savored the joy within her.

"Read this."

Susanna took the page Drake held out to her. It was from the Admiralty, and the letter announced the decision of the disposition of the French ship. *Le Corsaire* and its contents were being awarded to Captain Drake Nesbitt.

"This came quickly," she said as she folded the sheet and handed it to him.

"Perhaps because the government is embarrassed at how easily the French sailors escaped from Dartmoor Prison." He gave her a wry grin. "Or it might be that your father's influence reached from here to the halls of Admiralty House."

"Either way, you deserve this reward."

He turned her to him. Leaning his forehead against hers, he asked, "Can I tell you a secret?"

"Of course." Her heart hammered as she curved her arms up his back.

"I will get the reward I truly want tomorrow when we exchange vows."

"You are a smooth-talking sailor, Captain Nesbitt."

"And you are a beautiful woman, Lady Susanna Nesbitt-to-be."

He tilted her lips below his, and she held her breath, waiting for his luscious kiss.

"Cap!" shouted Lulu.

"Cap!" shouted Moll. "Lady Susu, time to eat. Now!"

Drake shrugged with a lopsided grin. The twins would not give up until they had their luncheon. "Later."

"I will be waiting." As he was about to step away, she put her hand against his cheek and turned his eyes toward her again. "I will always be waiting for you, no matter if you sail to the ends of the earth. Don't ever doubt that."

"I don't. Not ever." When he claimed her lips, holding her against him, the children's giggles were the perfect music to match their hearts' song.

* * * * *

Dear Reader,

Thank you for picking up *Promise of a Family*, the first book in the Matchmaking Babies miniseries. How families are created in many different ways has always intrigued me. For many years, my husband and I were involved in adoptive family support groups. Two of our children are adopted, and we quickly learned that how a child comes into a family is far less important than how many blessings we all share with each other. Even though my children arrived by plane rather than a rickety rowboat, I really enjoyed writing about how hearts expand to welcome those who become an integral part of our family. I hope you enjoyed reading this book and will look for the next in the series, which will be out in October.

As always, feel free to contact me by stopping in at joannbrownbooks.com.

Wishing you many blessings,
Jo Ann Brown

REQUEST YOUR FREE BOOKS!

2 FREE INSPIRATIONAL NOVELS
PLUS 2 FREE MYSTERY GIFTS

Love Inspired HISTORICAL

YES! Please send me 2 FREE Love Inspired® Historical novels and my 2 FREE mystery gifts (gifts are worth about $10). After receiving them, if I don't wish to receive any more books, I can return the shipping statement marked "cancel." If I don't cancel, I will receive 4 brand-new novels every month and be billed just $4.99 per book in the U.S. or $5.49 per book in Canada. That's a saving of at least 17% off the cover price. It's quite a bargain! Shipping and handling is just 50¢ per book in the U.S. and 75¢ per book in Canada.* I understand that accepting the 2 free books and gifts places me under no obligation to buy anything. I can always return a shipment and cancel at any time. Even if I never buy another book, the two free books and gifts are mine to keep forever.

102/302 IDN GH6Z

Name	(PLEASE PRINT)	
Address		Apt. #
City	State/Prov.	Zip/Postal Code

Signature (if under 18, a parent or guardian must sign)

Mail to the **Reader Service:**
IN U.S.A.: P.O. Box 1867, Buffalo, NY 14240-1867
IN CANADA: P.O. Box 609, Fort Erie, Ontario L2A 5X3

Want to try two free books from another series?
Call 1-800-873-8635 or visit www.ReaderService.com.

* Terms and prices subject to change without notice. Prices do not include applicable taxes. Sales tax applicable in N.Y. Canadian residents will be charged applicable taxes. Offer not valid in Quebec. This offer is limited to one order per household. Not valid for current subscribers to Love Inspired Historical books. All orders subject to credit approval. Credit or debit balances in a customer's account(s) may be offset by any other outstanding balance owed by or to the customer. Please allow 4 to 6 weeks for delivery. Offer available while quantities last.

Your Privacy—The Reader Service is committed to protecting your privacy. Our Privacy Policy is available online at www.ReaderService.com or upon request from the Reader Service.

We make a portion of our mailing list available to reputable third parties that offer products we believe may interest you. If you prefer that we not exchange your name with third parties, or if you wish to clarify or modify your communication preferences, please visit us at www.ReaderService.com/consumerschoice or write to us at Reader Service Preference Service, P.O. Box 9062, Buffalo, NY 14240-9062. Include your complete name and address.

LIH15

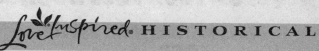
"Look at me, Meg," he said in that deep voice. "Who do
you see?"

"What?" She frowned, unsure of what he was doing
and wondering at the sorrow reflected in his eyes.

"Who do you see standing here?"

What did he want from her? she wondered in confusion.
"I see you," she said at last. "Ace Allen."

"If you never believe anything else about me, you can
believe that I would never deliberately harm a hair on
your head."

His statement was much the same as what he'd said the
day before in the woods. It seemed Ace was determined
that she knew he was no threat to her.

"Elton used to stand in the doorway like that a lot.
For just a moment when I looked up I saw him, not you.
I...I'm s-sorry."

"I'm not Elton, Meg."

His voice held an urgency she didn't understand. "I know that."

"Do you?" he persisted. "Look at me. Do I look like Elton?"

"No," she murmured. Elton hadn't been nearly as tall, and unlike Ace he'd been almost too good-looking to be masculine. She'd once heard him called pretty. No one would ever think of Ace Allen as pretty. Striking, surely. Magnificent, maybe. Pretty, never.

"No, and I don't act like him. Can you see that? Do you believe it?"

Still confused, but knowing somehow that her answer was of utmost importance, she whispered, "Yes."

He nodded, and the torment in his eyes faded. "You have nothing to be sorry for, Meg Thomerson. That's something else you can be certain of, so never think it again." With that, he turned and left her alone with her thoughts and a lot of questions.

Don't miss
WOLF CREEK WIDOW by Penny Richards,
available September 2015 wherever
Love Inspired® Historical books and ebooks are sold.

Love Inspired

Love the Love Inspired book you just read?

Your opinion matters.

Review this book on your favorite book site, review site, blog or your own social media properties and share your opinion with other readers!

Be sure to connect with us at:
Harlequin.com/Newsletters
Twitter.com/LoveInspiredBks
Facebook.com/LoveInspiredBooks